Memories of Us

Kennedy L. Mitchell

Published by Kennedy L. Mitchell, 2018.

enjoy! ♡ —

Kennedy

MEMORIES OF US

First edition. December 10, 2018.

Written by Kennedy L. Mitchell.

Prologue

WHAT THE FUCK HAPPENED.

A thick fog clouded my thoughts as I attempted to open my eyes. Their heavy weight made it feel like I'd been asleep for days. I tried to shift in the soft bed, but my legs and arms wouldn't cooperate.

Nothing was working as it should.

"You're okay son." Pappy's gruff voice cut through the fog easing a bit of my growing apprehension.

After several attempts my lids lifted. I took several slow blinks to clear away the remaining haze. Pappy sat in the chair next to my strange bed. The room was large, but not one I recognized.

White walls. White sheets. Monitors.

"Where the hell am I?" I gritted out as I pushed to sit up.

"A facility," he responded.

"What kind of facility?" I held my head between my hands and attempted to focus on the last thing I remembered.

Nothing. Not a single damn clue to what I was doing in this place or how I ended up here.

"A detox center inside a rehab facility."

"Why am I here?"

Pappy's gray brows rose high on his forehead. "You don't remember?"

"Fuck. What did I do this time?" It had to do with drugs or booze that much I was certain. I didn't remember details but being a coke head was something not easily wiped from my memories. "Is Caleb here too?"

Pappy's lips dipped in a slight frown. "No son just you."

Right. So whatever I did didn't involve Caleb. Good.

"You don't remember her?" Pappy asked leaning forward like he was asking the most critical question of his life. As he leaned forward, a few papers slipped from his lap and floated to the floor.

His question shot a bolt of fear to my core. Her? If I did anything to a woman while high that she didn't want, like my fathers living legacy, I'd never recover.

"No, I have no idea what you're talking about."

Like the weight of the world was removed from his slumped shoulders Pappy leaned back and gave a sigh of relief. "You didn't do anything wrong, Brenton. Don't worry about that; everything is fine. You're fine."

"Why am I here?" I bellowed. Frustration boiled the blood in my veins. Dumb ass memory needed to fucking start working.

Locking his green eyes with my own, he gave a small smile. "Fate, my dear boy. Fate brought you here."

Beneath the frustration, something else simmered. Something that told me that he was not only wrong about the fate shit but also holding back the truth.

Chapter 1

Brenton

THIRTEEN YEARS LATER...

"Yeah, I'll be there," I said through a deep exhale to the man on the other end of the line. "Thank you for calling and the condolences. I'll see you at the ranch for the funeral in three days."

With a deep West Texas drawl, the older man detailed the specifics of the service before ending the call with another "He was a good man" sentiment.

I slipped the phone back into my suit breast pocket as I moved toward the wet bar. The dark liquid of the various half-empty bottles called to me, begging me to pop one open for a quick swig. With a steady, focused hand, I reached past the whiskey's siren call to grab the near-hidden bottle of Perrier. It had been my mind trick during rehab and still was. With a little lime added and enough ice, it took the edge off the constant urge that simmered just below the surface for something stronger.

Bubbles rose to the rim of the crystal highball I had pulled from the cabinet above. Drink clutched in hand, I stepped out onto the penthouse balcony and leaned against the warm metal railing. Bright green lights glowed a few blocks over from downtown Dallas's Green Monster. The unobstructed view of the famous building was one reason Caleb and I chose this building, this exact loft, what seemed like a lifetime ago.

Back then, having a place large enough to host all our friends at one time, along with great proximity to the high-end clubs we frequented, was the priority. Some people might call those the good old days. Maybe for them, those who leached off us for so long, they were. For me, not even close. If I looked back now, from what little I remember of those years, I'd see a lonely, shallow shell of a boy who was on a fast track to nowhere.

But tonight there was no raging party, no Caleb begging me to join him for a wild night out. Tonight it was just me, the busy streets forty stories below my feet, and fizzy water. After the five-hour therapy session earlier, the quiet was exactly what I needed.

Ice snapped and shifted in the highball glass from the unbearable eighty-five-degree heat. As suffocating as it was, something was reassuring about the Texas summer heat that I'd in some ways missed the past few years. To a true Texan, it was merely a reminder of the constants in our lives. Your life could be shit, you could have no clue which way was up, but you could count on it being balls hot during a Texas summer.

After today, and the unexpected call just now, I needed that specific comfort.

Dead.

Gone without me there. Hell, I hadn't been back in years. Too busy was always the excuse, but looking back at the wasted opportunities to see the old man, was I really? Yes, this was the most extended leave I'd taken since joining the army, but would it have killed me to fly over and see him one weekend? I should've stayed after Caleb's funeral months ago instead of jumping on the jet moments after the final prayer.

I pressed the sweating glass against my forehead and rolled it back and forth in an attempt to settle the self-accusing direction of my thoughts. Pappy knew why I had to leave and never come back; surely he didn't hold it against me in the end. His death wasn't a big surprise—the man was ninety after all—but I guess I still thought there was more time before this moment. Maybe a future weekend when I could've flown out to see him, show him who I'd become since being the prick he knew: the idiot teen through my young adult years when I terrorized his ranch hands, stuffed enough powder up my nose to kill an elephant, and fucked any willing female.

Most importantly, I wanted an opportunity to show him I wasn't my father, or my brother for that matter. But now that chance was gone, and he'd never know that I wasn't the person I used to be.

Well, mostly. I'd grown from a spoiled prick to an arrogant jackass, if you believed the few girls I'd dated.

With a sigh, I downed the last few sips and tipped my gaze to the bright night sky. Against the lights of the city, not a single star blinked. Hell, with the pollution, even the moon was barely visible. At Pappy's ranch, the stars peppered the sky every night when I visited during those extended summer stays and holidays. Those stars and the vastness of the night sky were my favorite part of the family estate.

Long-forgotten memories flitted to the front of my mind, urging a small smile to curl the edge of my lips. That ranch, those nights, fueled my obsession with the sky, which drew me to the career I now love.

Damn, when was the last time I even thought of that place?

Most of the memories were hazy at best, diluted by those years filled with copious amounts of coke and booze consumption. There was too much I didn't remember, not only from those trips to the ranch but also from life here in Dallas before rehab. Even though it sucked, missing pieces of my life, it never nagged or worried me. What did keep me awake at night, kept my mind reeling, was the ever-present sensation that I'd forgotten something, maybe even a someone, that I shouldn't have—something or someone important. But how do you pinpoint the cause when nearly six years of your life were blurred?

Vibrations against my chest pulled my attention back to the present. I wiped the dampness from my hand to snag the phone once again. Brow furrowed, I stared at the bright screen that flashed with an unknown number. Considering it came minutes after the previous call about Pappy's death, there was no doubt who I'd hear on the other end of the line.

"Yeah." Turning on the heels of my thousand-dollar shoes, I strode back into the loft and straight for the wet bar. No doubt liquor would make this conversation easier, but no way would I let Dad be the reason I fell off my thirteen-year sobriety wagon.

"Did you hear?"

"Yeah." The gurgle of the clear fizzing liquid pouring into the glass echoed in the otherwise silent loft. A pang of guilt and loneliness hit at the reminder of my solitude.

No. Not going there now. Caleb made his own damn choices.

"Bastard finally kicked it. Damn. Have you heard when the lawyers will disburse the estate?" Dad asked. Steady bass and a loud giggle filled the background. Of course he was at the strip club minutes after his father died. And Dad wondered why Pappy never approved of who he became and how he dwindled his trust.

"No." Fuck, the conversation was already too long. The thick vein in my neck beat faster and faster with my rapid pulse. The dark granite of the bar was cool beneath my grip when I latched on to steady myself. Each breath grew shorter with the building anger and resentment. "What do you want?" I said through clenched teeth.

"Let's go out and celebrate, son. Tell your boss you need to head home for the funeral. Bring a few of your buddies with you. Damn, I should plan a damn parade. The mean bastard is finally gone."

Funny, the mean bastard in my life was still alive and well and wouldn't let me off the fucking phone.

No way could I tell him I was already in town. First, I didn't want to see him, and second, I couldn't tell my father the reasons behind the two weeks' leave I'd started three days before.

I couldn't tell anyone.

Two weeks to figure my shit out before reporting back to base. Two weeks to get my head back on straight so I could fly again. Safely.

I shook my head to bring my focus back to the conversation. "I'll be at the funeral." The large swallow of sparkling water burned down my throat, easing a bit of the growing tightness. "The man who called mentioned it would be at the ranch in three days. I assume you're going?"

"Damn, I miss your brother right now. He'd go out with me to celebrate this momentous occasion. When the hell did you get so damn boring?"

He cannot be serious.

Closing my eyes, I attempted to will my blood pressure to lower. Unfortunately, it didn't obey the direct command. He missed my brother, his son, who was dead because of the lifestyle he coaxed us both to need. No sign of remorse, just pissed he didn't have someone who would go party with him.

Sweat beaded along my temples and neck. I set the phone down on the bar and shrugged off my jacket. After hitting the speakerphone button, I snapped off my cufflinks and rolled up my right sleeve then left.

A loud, obnoxious giggle flooded the apartment. If I weren't so damn pissed at the whole fucked-up conversation, I'd roll my eyes at the typical scene playing out on the other end of the phone. My father, such a class act.

"Shhh," he chuckled into the phone. "Brenton, hey, I gotta run. I'll call the attorneys to see when the estate will be divided out. I could use that money to support the next club venture. Hopefully he didn't pour it all down the drain on those dumbass cows."

Right. Fucker. All he cared about was making the next dollar, which he then shoved up his nose or down some dancing girl's G-string.

When he hung on the line, a sense of dread settled deep in my gut. Staring at the phone, waiting for the next bomb to drop, I popped each knuckle. Twice.

"Oh and listen." I glared at the phone. "When you come into town, you might want to lie low. Not make a big deal that you're here, you know, but with this news, every gold digger in Dallas will be looking for a payday. Who knows what accusations will come out just for some damn hush money."

Hell, not again.

"What did you do?" I seethed. The glass trembled at my lips as I attempted not to chuck it across the room.

Being away from this place for so long, I'd forgotten who Dad was. *Who* I was. The son of a slimy, washed-up multimillionaire. Our family name forever tainted by the multiple assault accusations against him and the failing strip club empire he kept pouring money into.

"Nothing. It's nothing. Call you tomorrow when I know more."

Everything blurred as heat simmered beneath my skin, flowing through my veins and ticking up my temper with each rapid heartbeat. With a raging bellow, I flung the expensive glass across the room. The crystal splintered against the concrete wall, sending shards scattering along the floor.

My chest heaved as sweat dripped down my temples to my cheeks and neck. Fuck that bastard.

Sealing my eyes shut, I focused on the deep breathing exercises I'd learned to lower my stroke-level blood pressure.

The first "episode" happened moments after the call notifying me of Caleb's death. The second happened the day after the exhausting twenty-four-hour turnaround from Kentucky to Dallas to attend the funeral. I chalked those up to shock and exhaustion, but then it happened again. And again. And again.

Now here I was once again on the verge of blacking out. Darkness encroached from the corners of my eyes, soon to cut off my vision completely. My muscles trembled and weakened.

Slowly, carefully, I shuffled to the long leather couch and fell onto it. The cushions conformed around my back and thighs with a soft thump.

Deep breath in.

Deep breath out.

Shit, this couldn't happen again. It had to stop. I had to find the cause and the cure by the time I was due back to base. If I couldn't, there was no way in hell I could risk my brothers' lives for the sake of my pride. No, if I couldn't get my head back on straight, I'd file for medical discharge no matter how devastating it would be. And it would be. The army, flying, my brothers—it was all my family and life. They saved me, and I needed them as much as they needed me.

Chest puffed out in a deep inhale, I paused at a light knock at the door. Slowly I blew the air out through my nose and waited. Another knock came seconds later, a bit louder, persistent that time.

Who the hell knew I was home?

I pushed off the couch with a groan and gave myself a minute to steady. The first step was tentative, the next stronger until I was convinced the episode was over and I was strong enough to meet whoever was here with the strength and confidence of regular Brenton Graves.

It was bullshit that the word "episode" was even in my damn vocabulary nowadays. But really, what did I expect from Caleb's sudden death combined with years of hoarded anger, a high-stress job, and a fucked-up childhood? It's a wonder this didn't happen sooner, honestly.

Not bothering to look through the viewer to see who was there at such a late hour, I yanked the door open, ready for anything.

A tall blonde stood just over the threshold, hand raised ready to keep knocking at the now-nonexistent door.

"Sorry, I heard a crash and thought...." Her smile pulled wide, exposing brilliant white, straight teeth. "Hi, Bren."

Should I remember her? Hell, all those buried memories. Maybe she was the someone I'd been attempting to recall. But staring into her empty blue eyes triggered nothing, no flick of emotion or recognition.

I gripped the back of my neck and flexed my fingers to alleviate the tight tension building as I shot her a confused look.

"Right." She laughed. "It has been a while. It looks like you've kept the place though. Too many good memories to let it go?"

"Sure."

Her smile dropped, and she took a step closer, putting us toe-to-toe. A strong waft of expensive perfume saturated my nose and caught in my throat. "Sorry about your brother. Guess we all thought Caleb would grow out of it eventually. We still saw each other until... well, you know. It all happened so fast, and I'm just grateful I wasn't in the car with him that night." Tears welled at her lower lids, but still, I stood unaffected. "I miss him."

Nope. Not going there. Especially not with a damn stranger.

"Hey listen, I just rolled into town and—"

"Can I come in?"

I should've said no, but I'd love a way to blow off steam, and she was pretty enough. I didn't have to guess why she wanted to come in, where her mind was. Between being the wealthiest bachelor in Dallas and the military groupies back in Kentucky, it was always the same.

With a shrug, I opened the door wider and gestured inside the loft.

"Want a drink?" I asked over my shoulder as I headed to the wet bar to make another for myself.

"Vodka. Neat."

As I poured the drinks, she meandered around the loft, slowing to gaze out the floor-to-ceiling windows on the other side of the room. The click of her heels against the concrete floor drew my attention to her red stilettos. From the shoes, my gaze traveled farther north, up her long legs to lean hips and a nonexistent ass.

When did women buy into the lie that men wanted their women rail thin? What the hell were we supposed to hold on to in bed when there was nothing to grab? Where's the fun when your hand was larger than both ass cheeks?

Glancing over her shoulder, she caught my roaming eye and smiled. With each step closer, her sensual smirk grew. At my side, she flicked her bright blonde hair over her shoulder, drawing my gaze to the low dip of her dress.

"Like what you see?" The twinkle in her eye and soft laugh implied that she was used to men saying yes. After a short sip from her drink, her pink tongue swiped along her bright red lower lip to lap up the excess. "I've waited for you. Do you remember the amazing night we had together? Right here in this loft all those years ago?"

"No." No lies. It'd been a while since rehab, but pretty sure the last thing a recovering addict needed was to revert back to lying.

"Ah, well it's a bit of a blur for me too, but I remember having fun. Remember you being the best I ever had and waking up the next morning needing more of you." Her warm palm skimmed up the front of my dress shirt and curved around my neck to haul her body flush against mine.

"Listen...."

"Candice."

"Right. Listen, Candice, I don't—"

"The rumors are that all the money left in Caleb's trust shifted to you."

And there it was. Knew she was the type from the second the door opened. Just another socialite who was hunting her own sugar daddy. Little did she know her type wasn't mine. Not anymore.

Maybe it never was.

"Does that matter?" I retorted, then turned to look out the windows she was just admiring. I needed to get away from here. Maybe being at the ranch for a few days would be good, even if it would pull me away from the high-priced therapist I'd already contacted to help with my issue.

The sly smile and smirk she gave in return to my question said it all. "I've loved you since that night. Since all the nights we had together. I've missed you, wanted you to come home, and now you're here. It's fate. We're destined, don't you see that?"

I choked on the laugh threatening to erupt. This woman couldn't be serious.

"Listen, Candy—"

"Candice."

"Right. Listen, it's been a long day. You should—"

The hand around my neck slid lower and cupped me outside my suit pants. "Well then, Bren, maybe you should be the one doing the relaxing. Come on, baby, let me help you."

Taking the drink from my hand with her free one, she set it on the bar before guiding me to the couch. Standing toe-to-toe, she shoved her delicate hand against my chest, pushing me to the couch with a smile.

I'm no idiot. I knew where this was going. Also knew I should stop her since there was zero interest past this one night, but I wouldn't. Because I was Brenton Graves. And a Graves never said no. It was my heritage. All I needed to complete this family tradition was glassy eyes, lines of coke on the glass coffee table, and a raging party in the background.

Clinking of metal against metal pierced through the loft as Carley... Cathy... whatever her name was unclasped my belt. Soft brushes of her lips against the planes of my stomach relit my earlier temper.

"You need to leave Cassidy." I stood making her fall back to her ass. As I strode to the door, my raging hardon screamed I was an idiot for kicking a willing woman out of the loft.

"What?" she shrieked. "You can't be serious."

I swung the door open and gestured out toward the hall. "I am. Now Candy. Out."

"What the fuck is wrong with you?" she seethed as she stormed past and down the hall.

Only after the door slammed behind her did I respond. "I have no fucking clue."

It was the truth.

Between my blackouts and now the sudden disinterest in a woman on her knees, something was fucked up in my mind.

Wish I knew what and how to fix it.

Chapter 2

Rebeka

MY SKIN HEATED TO AN uncomfortable level through the back of my T-shirt where it touched the hot metal of the truck door, but I didn't pay it any attention. The only thing I focused on was Ryder's words.

"You're kidding me," I breathed into the phone pressed between my ear and shoulder, where sweat immediately made the screen slippery.

"Nope. The rumor mill says the whole family will be in town for it. Three days, Beka. Three. Did you hear that part?" Ryder asked. Sympathy and concern poured through each word. "What will it be, face him or hide?"

"I won't hide from him again," I grumbled. "I missed my chance to confront him at Caleb's—"

"Dr. Harding," called the man I'd completely forgotten was around.

"Shit. Have to run. I'll call you later." I ended the call, slipped the phone into the back pocket of my Wranglers, and forced a broad smile as I turned to face my client. With the hem of my Texas A&M T-shirt, I wiped the sweat from my upper lip as he jogged closer.

So over this day.

So over yesterday.

And the day before that.

Who was I kidding, I was just over this. Too bad I still had a shit ton of student loans to pay back before I could even think about choosing another career.

"Hey," the man exhaled loudly at my side. "Thanks for coming by and checking on Stella. I know it was a last-minute call, but I was worried about my girl. It's her first."

"And yours?" I asked with an arched brow. Newbies, so overprotective.

The young man pulled his Stetson down low over his brow and grumbled, "That obvious?"

With a comforting pat on his shoulder, I tossed my supply bag into the bed of the old Ford. "She'll be fine. Just let nature take its course. If she seems in pain or can't deliver on her own, then call me and I'll come back out. But from checking her just now, I'd say you're waiting for another two to three weeks."

His groan of frustration grated my already frayed nerves. The day started twelve hours ago, and in this heat, I had zero patience left.

Looking to the barn, he shrugged. "Women. Always running on your own schedule, am I right?"

The earlier smile fell from my lips and turned to a scowl. "I'd say it's more about the proper gestation period needed for a healthy colt. We want the babe in there to cook a little longer so he or she comes out healthy. Agree?"

Chastised, he hung his head and gave a slight nod.

Not waiting any longer to get out of there, I swung open the driver side door and hauled myself onto the bench seat. Immediately my already sweaty ass and thighs suctioned to my jeans as the heat from the fake leather seeped in. Hell, it was too hot for June. What did we do to deserve this early heat wave?

If it weren't a complete blasphemy for a Daughter of the Republic to curse the state of Texas, I'd be wishing the whole state would go to hell. Even though it felt like we were already there.

Add in that I chose not to fix the air conditioning this winter as I'd promised myself I would, and my shitty day just went from awful to... well, shitty.

At a four-way stop, I banged my forehead against the hard steering wheel. Why didn't I ever make things easy for myself?

Each bump along the unlit county road elicited a creative string of curse words. It was pitch black past the dim headlights due to the zero streetlights around, making every turn treacherous. I should have left over an hour ago, but that didn't happen. And they call women chatty. In the past year I'd been out of school, I'd met more lonely, isolated ranchers wanting to talk my ear off for hours than any woman in Midland.

That could be me though.

My unladylike talk and sailor's mouth didn't win any points with the self-important women my age around here. Which sucked because once you got past my somewhat gruff exterior, I was a girly girl. Beneath these dirty, horse-shit-covered boots and sweat-soaked socks, my toes were perfectly manicured and painted a deep purple to match my nails. I devoured blog after blog of beauty products and had a month's salary worth of face shit beneath the bathroom sink. I loved Hallmark Channel movies and enjoyed a good glass of white wine with an even better conversation. And of course, like any proper lady, I enjoyed a man who treated me like a lady in public but spanked my ass behind closed doors.

See, girly girl.

The glowing city lights of Midland shimmered in the distance, easing a bit of tension from my shoulders. It'd been home for over a few years now, but it still felt foreign turning toward it instead of heading the forty minutes west to my childhood home.

After graduating from Texas A&M, I took the first large animal vet job offered, and it just happened to be here. I didn't mind, because I loved West Texas. The sunsets on a clear day could still take my breath away, and the rough hands of a rancher or sunspots on an older woman's face were worn with pride instead of shame.

It was crazy that I ended up here, so close to home, considering I went seven hours away to College Station to put as much distance between me and the memories as possible. Away from the looks and stares of every person who thought they knew me and the real story. Even all these years later, if you listened to the gossips in town, you'd learn of the young, naïve country girl who foolishly fell for a man she'd never have a shot at keeping. They were correct about one piece. I did fall for him. Fell hard. Fifteen-year-old girls only fall one way—desperately, all-consuming, devastatingly in love.

Unfortunately for me, it was Brenton Graves who I fell for, the older bad boy who everyone assumed was a lost cause. But they didn't see the real him or know our full story. They weren't a part of the buildup to who we were together—friends to confidants to lovers to…. Everyone assumed they knew the details of our final night together, but they didn't; they only believed the lies they had heard. Only Ryder knew the play-by-play of that awful night, and I guess Brenton. Not that I'd know for sure, considering the last time I saw or spoke to him, I was screaming in pain while he lay unconscious in the driver seat.

Holding the wheel with my knee, I swiped both sweaty palms down my already damp jeans and cursed at the windshield.

Am I really considering going to the funeral for a shot at closure?

Haven't I moved on? I'm thirty years old, dammit.

Okay, a sad thirty-year-old who couldn't move on and maybe still thought about her first love, her first relationship, first lover nearly every other day.

"You're pathetic, Beka. Seriously pathetic. Grow a set and move on," I said to myself through the roaring, dust-filled wind pouring through the open windows as I sped down the smooth highway.

AFTER A LENGTHY, WELL-deserved shower, I fell face-first onto the bed with an exhausted groan. Like the rest of my body, the throbbing soles of my feet seemed to sigh. Being a veterinarian wasn't at all what I expected. Long hours, late nights, and very—and I mean *very*—little pay. The small practice that hired me after graduation decided to haze me into the group by giving me the unwanted cases and clients, which seemed to be most of them.

The chirp of an incoming message had me fake sobbing into the comforter. Damn me for leaving the stupid phone in the other room. The soles of my feet revolted, sending bolts of pain up my legs with each timid step. A new pair of boots were necessary, but those would have to go on the "want" list, not the "need" list. Both of which were growing.

Even though undergrad had been paid for by the asshat I was dreading to face in three days, graduate school was fucking expensive, leaving me with a healthy bill at the end. Add student loans to my other daily expenses, and I fell deeper into the red with each passing month. I could get by if I moved back home, but there was no way in hell that would happen.

And that wasn't an empty threat. I'd rather live on the streets than back with Daddy.

I fell onto a stool, catching myself before toppling over backward, and swiped the phone open.

Ryder: I think you should go. So does Kyle.
Ryder: You need closure, and this might be your last shot to get it.

My heart dropped to my stomach. Last shot?

Me: Why do you say that?

Me: And you talked to Kyle about what I should do?

Ryder: He is my fiancé and your other best friend, so yeah. Plus things are boring around here. This little development of Brenton coming back to town has everyone talking.

Ryder: And by everyone, I mean every eligible woman eager to get a glimpse of him.

Ryder: You know that ranch will go to Old Man Graves's bastard son. As soon as his name is on that deed, that place will be up for sale, which means no more Graves family ranch. No more chances of you running into him when visiting your dad.

Ryder: Think about it. It's been ten years. Get your last word in before it's too late.

Me: Thirteen years. But who's counting?

Ryder: You're killing me. Closure. It does wonders.

Ryder: And you need it, love.

Shit, she was right. Of course she was. It was only the topic of every late-night, drunken conversation since we were teens. Since the day she'd climbed into my hospital bed and held me while I sobbed on her shoulder.

Me: Enough about him. How are things?

Ryder: Things are good. Wedding plans are going well. Now back to him.

Me: What would I even say to him?

Ryder: What we've practiced every day since you left the hospital. Every night since we were kids. You got this. Kyle and I will be there too. You'll have backup.

Ryder: You can do it. But you have to be there to get the last word.

The phone fell to the cheap laminate counter with a thunk. I buried my face in my hands and groaned.

Fine. I'd go. I'd go looking smoking hot, give Brenton Graves a piece of my mind for what he did, and then walk away with closure and a sliver of my self-respect back.

Closure.

I stared at the kitchen cabinets and mentally flipped through my wardrobe. Now came the difficult decision. What in the hell did one wear to a funeral where they were attempting to make the ex-boyfriend jealous?

Hmm. Decisions, decisions.

A STEADY STREAM OF local ranchers and their wives weaved in and out of the main house, offering their condolences more to the staff than Old Man Graves' actual family. I scanned each person who passed with a held breath, and each time it wasn't Brenton, disappointment tripped my thundering heart.

He was there somewhere. During the funeral, I caught a quick glimpse of the back of his head, and a side profile when he hugged someone after the service, but that was it. Now standing in the kitchen with the ranch staff, there wasn't a clear line of sight into the formal living room where Brenton and his dad received the mourners.

"Was his dad smiling during the service?" I whispered to Kyle over my shoulder, my eyes glued to the swinging door in case Brenton magically appeared. "He's such an asswipe."

"I heard he's already reached out to potential buyers about the place. Old Man Graves isn't officially buried yet and that shitty excuse for a human is looking for the next paycheck."

"I don't get how Brenton would let that happen." I shifted back to let a caterer pass with a tray full of finger foods. "This place has been in their family for generations. Surely he'll do something to stop it."

"Why in the hell do you give that bastard more credit than he deserves?" At the anger in Kyle's harsh tone, I turned to face him. "Do you not remember what happened? How he deserted you? I sure fucking do."

I rolled my eyes and turned back to watch the door once again. "I remember. Kind of hard to forget something like that."

"You look smoking hot," Ryder said and wedged between Kyle and me. "Love that dress on you."

Looking down, I shoved my hands into the side pockets of the black A-line dress and smiled. "Thanks. It has pockets."

"But seriously, cowboy boots?"

Bumping her hip with mine, I smiled down at my tiny friend, who was shaking her head at my boots. "I like this look. And my other shoes weren't funeral appropriate."

"There's appropriate funeral footwear?" Kyle chimed in behind us.

"Yes," Ryder and I said in unison.

"Have you seen him yet?" Ryder asked, rising to her tiptoes to look over a group of tall cowboys gathering in front of us. "I only got a glimpse at the gravesite," she whispered as she leaned close. "But I heard two girls talking in the bathroom, and they both said he's still freakishly hot."

I cut my narrowed eyes down to hers.

"Sorry," she grumbled. "It's now or never. Let's go find him."

Gripping my hand in hers, she yanked me toward the door, but instead of going willingly, I dug my heels into the tile floor. A large hand smacked between my shoulder blades, propelling me forward with so much force that I almost stumbled into an older man. I glared back, ready to flick Kyle the bird, but found him smirking at his boots.

Damn those two.

But I loved them.

Fine. It was time to get this done. I'd have my say, let Brenton see what he left behind, and get my ass back to Midland where a half gallon of chocolate chip Blue Bell waited for me. And three bottles of wine. And a bag of Hershey Kisses.

In the expansive formal living area, a few neighbors mingled while sipping their coffee and munching on the provided food, which wasn't half bad. Ryder guided us through the crowd, weaving and shoving toward the target.

All too soon we were there, right in front of the man who starred in my dreams of murder as well as my lusty fantasies.

I couldn't move. Brenton's bright green eyes locked me in a trance just like they always had. By my side, Ryder spoke words I should've understood but didn't. All I could do was stare at the gorgeous man who stared right back.

A thick line formed between his pinched brows as he scanned my features, almost considering me. During that brief second, I took a chance to familiarize myself with this grown version of someone I used to know. His strong, chiseled jaw had filled out over the years, making him look more like a man than a boy. There was still a knot across the bridge of his nose where he broke it in a fight one summer with a ranch hand. The dark, silky, floppy hair I'd always loved running my fingers through was gone now, cut short in a trendy style.

My gaze fell to his full lips, which were moving. I cocked my head to the right and stared in an attempt to understand what he was saying.

The chatter of the people around us filtered back in, reminding me we weren't alone. "Huh?" I mumbled, finding my voice.

"It's you. I remember you," Brenton said in a low, deep tone, almost like he was uncertain of his words. "What are you doing here?"

"The hell?" Ryder snarled, drawing our attention. "Her dad, the ranch foreman? Ring any bells?" Her grip tightened, cutting off the circulation to my fingers. "Beka, don't you have something to say to this bastard?"

"Beka," he whispered, sounding like he was testing the name. Those green eyes found mine once again and widened in recognition. "No, not Beka. Beks."

My old nickname pouring from his lips, in his voice, snapped the trance. "Remember me?" Chest rising and falling at a rapid pace, I pursed my lips and drew in a deep breath through my nose. "You asshole! Good to know you remember the girl you screwed over, the girl you almost...." Building tears threatened to expose the devastation his words caused. "You know what? Fuck this, and fuck you."

Tears blurred my vision halfway through the room as I weaved toward the door. Behind me, he called my name, and Ryder yelled something in return. All eyes landed on me and followed the rest of the way out.

Great. Just want I needed, more attention to our drama. This was not the plan.

I didn't get my say, but at least this time I was the one doing the leaving.

Chapter 3

Rebeka

THE MOMENT I SHOVED open the heavy wooden front door, the midafternoon heat smacked my face and stole the breath from my lungs. The stomp of my boot heels vibrated down the stone porch steps as I continued my hasty retreat. At the bottom, I swiped away the traitorous tears rolling down my cheeks.

Remembered me? He couldn't be serious. Did that mean he'd forgotten me at some point?

Wish I'd been lucky enough to forget him these past few years.

I was almost to the makeshift parking lot the event company had sectioned off when someone yelled my name from the direction of the house. I paused to look back, only to turn and pick up the pace.

Hell.

Another glance over my shoulder showed Brenton gaining ground quickly, with Ryder hot on his heels and Kyle steps behind her.

The tips of my fingers grasped the truck door handle, but a set of large hands gripped my shoulders and swiveled me, pushing my back against the scorching metal. The brisk walk and proximity to him had my heart thundering against my ribs and my chest heaving with each labored breath.

"Where in the hell are you going? I told you to stop," he said, not even breathing hard after his chase.

"Home." I shifted to turn, but his grip only tightened. "Let go, B. You did it once before. I'm sure it'll be even easier the second time around."

"What the hell are you talking about?" he gritted out. "What did I do? Who did I leave?"

Mouth gaping, I relaxed a fraction, only to tense again when Kyle shoved Brenton so hard that the tight grip on my shoulders released.

"Get the fuck off her," Kyle yelled, taking a step toward Brenton with his fists raised.

"Listen, I'm just trying to—"

"What do you mean, 'What did I do'?" I asked, taking a step toward the two fuming men.

Brenton's green eyes cut to mine. "I—fuck! Get the hell off me." He shoved Kyle, sending him stumbling back several steps.

Attention back on me, Brenton moved closer, eyes searching mine. "It means I don't know what the fuck you're talking about. I don't understand why you're so pissed. Hell, I don't even know why I'm out here right now. All I know is—" He shot an annoyed look at Ryder and Kyle. "Can we have two seconds here?"

The two turned their scowling faces from Brenton to me.

Eyes narrowed, brows furrowed, I scanned Brenton's face, searching for... who the hell knew what I was looking for.

With a resigned sigh, I turned to my best friends. "It's fine. Give us a minute."

Ryder opened her mouth, but I stopped her with a raised hand. "You pushed me to find closure. I'll get it and come say bye before I leave." Still neither moved. "I'm serious, guys. I'm fine with him. But if you hear someone scream"—I glanced back to the stone-faced Brenton with a smirk before looking back to Ryder—"then you two have to promise you'll help hide the body."

Their features relaxed a fraction, and Kyle even huffed a small laugh. Hand in hand, they strolled back toward the main house. Ryder glanced back once to mouth something about shooting him.

"Friends of yours?" His even tone was saturated with sarcasm. He slid his dark blue suit jacket off and tossed it on top of the truck hood. "Damn this heat."

Well, at least we agreed on one thing.

"Come on." With a wave, I turned toward Daddy and Bradley's house. As the ranch foreman, Daddy had the largest house of all the live-in help, and it happened to be a short walk from where we stood. It might be awkward, but at least we'd be in the air conditioning while we caught up.

Hell. Caught up. With Brenton fucking Graves.

I'd dreamed of this moment. Fantasized about it. And now that it was here, I had zero ideas on what to say or do.

Neither of us spoke during the short walk, but I watched him take in the expansive property from the corner of my eye. "It's been a while," I said as we climbed the rickety wooden steps to the porch. "Does it look the same?"

The screen door screeched and the wooden door jarred open from the shoulder I shoved against it. Once inside, I toed off my boots, leaving them beside the door. The entire time, I felt his eyes on me, even as I tiptoed in socks to the worn leather armchair and relaxed into it.

"You grew up here?" he said, a mix between a question and a statement as he looked around the small, rustic room. After Mom died, Daddy didn't put much effort into decorating. Who was I kidding—he didn't put effort into anything except seeing how fast he could reach the bottom of a bottle. "I remember this place. Well, pieces of it. Why?"

I sank my teeth into my lower lip to keep a smile at bay. "Well, we didn't spend a lot of time in here. You don't remember?"

"No."

"You're not shitting me?"

"Shitting you? Why in the hell would I do that?" he said with a grimace. "Fuck, what did I do? Tell me. Now."

"I've been your game before, so why not now too, B?" I monitored his reaction, but only more remorse softened his twitching jaw and fiery gaze.

"Tell me." He fell to the worn couch opposite of me and leaned his head back, sealing his eyes shut. "You have to understand something. There are years of my life, whole years, that I don't remember. Maybe a few hazy memories here and there, like the ones with you that popped up, but nothing solid. When I saw you in the house, snapshots filtered through. Not real memories, if that makes sense."

"It doesn't. Listen, it was thirteen years go—"

"Please tell me. I fucked something up, but I don't know what. What did I do to you?"

Turning from his intense, imploring gaze, I stared over his shoulder out the window. "It doesn't matter. It was a long time ago. Wish I could forget as easily as you did." I looked back to him and shrugged. "Consider yourself closed." My palms slapped the leather armrests with a smack as I pushed to stand.

"What?"

"I needed closure, and even though it wasn't nearly as gratifying as I thought it would be, I got it. I can move on now."

Such a big fat lie, but he didn't need to know that.

He shoved off the couch and gripped my shoulders with his large, strong hands. That close, I had to tip my head back a bit to meet his gaze.

"What if I don't want to be closed just yet?"

"What?" I gasped and tried to step back, but his grip tightened, preventing me from going anywhere without his consent.

"What if I want to remember? Don't I get a say?"

The hint of desperation, the near-silent plea in his tone had me considering his request.

"Why?" I asked and lowered my gaze to the collar of his crisp, white dress shirt. "Why does it matter? You forgot about me, about this place, for years. Why not go back to forgetting?"

His hands slid across my shoulders, skimming up my neck to cup my cheeks between his callused palms. "I can't explain it now. It's... complicated. All I know is in the house, something happened when I saw you."

"What?"

"Peace. A settled, comforting peace. I need help, Beks, and I know I don't deserve it, but I'm asking anyway. Don't ask me why, but I think you're my only hope."

Wow, that was not what I expected from this conversation. Broken lamps, tears, lots of yelled names and accusations, but not that.

Help. He needed my help.

Staring into his bright green eyes, the honesty I found felt genuine. This man had done a lot of things, but lying to me was never one of them, and a piece of me wanted to believe that side of him hadn't changed over the years.

"Five days," he continued when I didn't respond. "The attorneys will be here in five days to settle Pappy's estate. I'll stay here until then, if you're willing to help." I opened my mouth, but he pressed both his thumbs against my lips. "I don't expect an answer right now. Come find me when you decide. I'll wait. But I hope you do."

He gave a long, considering look, searching my eyes before stepping back and turning for the door.

Long after he'd left, I still stood in the same spot, staring at the closed front door, dumbfounded at the unexpected turn of events.

I ADJUSTED IN THE HARD dining room table chair to ease the ache it'd caused from just the few minutes of sitting in it. From the seat, I kept a cautious eye on Daddy, who paced the length of the living room mumbling to himself. Too busy considering Brenton's request for help, I didn't go back to the main house after he left. Instead, I stayed here, texted Ryder that I was good and not to worry, and poured three fingers of the whiskey I found hidden in the back of the pantry.

"I don't like it," Daddy said.

For the last minute, he'd been mulling over the suggestion I offered of sticking around for a few days until we knew the ranch's, and his, fate. No way in hell would I tell him the other reason for me wanting to stay. He would flip the fuck out. Daddy hated Brenton back then, and no doubt hadn't adjusted his feelings toward the man these past few years. Because now, instead of being the older boy flirting with Daddy's young daughter, Brenton was the man I'd signed a legal agreement with to never seek him out or be involved with again.

Funny, Brenton didn't even mention that tidbit today. Guess that was another blip of history he'd conveniently forgotten.

I rolled the cold glass between my wrists to try and calm my racing pulse. The man wasn't even around and I was still affected by him.

After taking the last sip of whiskey, I slid the glass to the middle of the table and stood to stretch out my lower back. "It's only for a few days, and I can help out around here too."

"We don't need your help."

"Maybe we do." I glanced to Bradley, who sat on the couch playing on his phone. Dark brown eyes flicked up to meet mine. A bit of tension eased from my tight shoulders when I found his eyes bright, maybe slightly bloodshot but not glassy like they'd been for years. Getting my older brother addicted to their high-end drug was another reason Daddy hated Brenton and Caleb. Even though you couldn't blame the Graves boys too much considering Bradley used to be, and maybe still was, the guy you went to around here for anything illegal.

Ever since Caleb passed several months ago, I'd heard Bradley had cleaned up his act. Hopefully it stuck this time around.

Bradley shrugged and went back to staring at his phone. "Let her stay, Dad. After you fired those two boys last month, things have stacked up."

"What?" I turned back to Daddy, who attempted to look engrossed in the new Cavender's mailer.

"Lazy-ass kids is what happened."

Or they got tired of taking orders from your drunk ass perched in your leather recliner throne.

If I were a betting girl, I'd put money on that being the case rather than them being lazy.

"If you want to help around here, you could find yourself a husband like that friend Kyle of yours. Having another man around here couldn't hurt."

"A man," I deadpanned.

"More useful than someone like you."

Ouch. Good to know being born with girl bits still disappointed him.

"Maybe one day," I said back instead of all the pent-up hateful things I wanted to throw at him.

"Someday has come and gone, Rebeka. You spent all those years in school and now look where you are. No land, no husband, no family. Go out and get a good man, if you can find one at your age."

Sharp nails bit into my palms. Dammit, what was I thinking? No way in hell could I stay there. Not with him, not back to this.

The door slammed at my back, and I stomped to the porch swing before falling into it. A degree, a place of my own, strong, confident, and still not good enough for him.

Never had been.

And he wondered why I ran straight into Brenton's open arms all those years ago. What no one witnessed was the comforting, protective side B only showed me. The side that accepted me for me and listened night after night. There were never expectations, no judgments when we were together. Just us. Those late nights gazing at the stars, talking and laughing, we were free from our families. And maybe that was what I missed the most and had held on to for so long.

Even though I didn't will it, Daddy's words still stung. Deep down, I did want to belong to someone again. To have a partner in crime to share a life with besides Ryder.

Adjusting on the swing to look south, I scanned the main house and the few cars that still lined the driveway before focusing on their large ranch-style home. Loneliness gripped at my already aching heart. Who was I kidding? I didn't just miss the talks—I missed him. I'd missed him since the day he left. And today his touch and long looks ignited something long smothered inside me.

Thumb against my lips, I ghosted it back and forth as he had done. Just that simple touch, coupled with his hands against my cheeks, nearly did me in. How had I forgotten the sensation of my breath catching, the dip of my stomach like I was falling, the pounding of my heart against my chest so hard, so fast and loud that there was no way the rest of the world didn't hear it?

I was a fool to say yes to his request for help, but I wouldn't fool myself into thinking I could say no.

So there I had it. Five days with the man to help him... oh hell, he never mentioned what he needed me to do. I should've pressed him for details, but at the time my hormones and mind had swirled like an F5 tornado, making simple thoughts impossible.

The porch swing squeaked as I pushed it back and forth with the tips of my toes against the floor. Hopefully I could help him and get closure at the same time.

From inside the house, Daddy's and Bradley's cheers and the noises of the TV filtered through the thin glass panes.

Pulling my phone from my dress pocket, I swiped the screen and opened an old text string.

Me: I'm sticking around for a few days.

Ryder: At home. With your father. Is that such a good idea?

Ryder: What about work?

Me: Already took a few days off for this, so I'll tell them I need a few more.

Me: I'm going to help around here until we know the ranch's fate.

Me: Plus I just learned Daddy fired two people last month and hasn't replaced them.

Me: Which means there's a bunch not getting done. He definitely isn't doing shit, leaving it all to Bradley.

Ryder: Speaking of your brother...

Me: Oh no. What?

Ryder: I've heard through the rumor mill that some bad-news peeps are looking for him.

Ryder: Maybe the same who were looking for Caleb last year when Old Man Graves upped security.

Ryder: Keep an eye open if you're going be around there.

Me: Maybe you could send Kyle over to protect the house. Daddy would love that. You know, since I'm a girl and can't do anything right.

Ryder: Your dad is a sexist prick. I don't know who I'm more worried about you being around, him or Brenton.

Ryder: Which reminds me, how did the closure go?

Crickets chirped in the night as I stared at the last text. A hot wind blew a chunk of dark hair across my face, blocking the screen. I should tell her what was going on, but then she'd come over and talk me out of it, and that was precisely what I didn't want to happen. Because even though this was the worst idea ever, I wanted to see him again.

Me: Good. He says he was so messed up during that time that he doesn't remember anything.

Ryder: How convenient for him not to remember almost killing someone. I hope you gave him an earful.

Me: Yep.

Ryder: You okay? Need me to run by the liquor store?

Me: Nope, I'm good. It's too late to run by the apartment to get clothes, so I'll go in the morning.

Ryder: Okay, just stay away from your dad. And Brenton. And Brenton's slimy-ass dad. Shit, you sure this is a good idea? Want me to come over? I just got my LTC.

Me: That is terrifying. Why did you do that?

Ryder: You've seen the bar where I work. Shady as fuck. I needed protection.

Me: Do you even know how to shoot it?

Ryder: Stop being so judgy.

Me: That's a no.

Ryder: Hey, I had to qualify!

Me: Please tell me you bought something with a manual safety.

Ryder: You're no fun.

Ryder: It's heavy as hell though.

Me: Heavy? What kind of gun did you get?

Ryder: A .40 cal.

Me: Shit, Ryder! That's a hand cannon! No wonder it's heavy.

Ryder: Bigger the bullet, less you have to aim.

Me: It does. Not. Work. That. Way. I'm legit scared for the general public.

Ryder: Pew. Pew. Pew.

Me: You're ridiculous.

With a broad smile spread across my face, I shoved against the porch to set the swing in motion.

That girl. Hell.

I was still smiling as my gaze fell to the main house. It was too early to risk stopping by to give B the decision that I would help. Later, after dark, would be better.

Even though I was good with us talking again, there might be people who weren't. Which was why he needed to understand that I'd help him but, just like it used to be, no one could know.

Chapter 4

Brenton

EVERY CORNER OF THIS house elicited a new memory, some good, a few terrible. Growing up privileged wasn't as glorious as people thought it to be. The worst of those memories were exactly what I wanted to chase away tonight with the help of Pappy's extensive liquor trove instead of the clear fizzing liquid filling my glass. Thankfully the last of the locals paying their respects left a few minutes ago, leaving Dad and me alone.

Which was another reason my attention kept diverting back to the high-end bottles along the bar.

Shoulder pressed against the window frame, I stared out into the dark. Besides the few bright windows of Beks's father's house, nothing else was visible. Those few lights captivated my attention. With every breath after seeing her today, a new memory of her, of us, came flooding back.

Still nothing too specific, but snapshots of laughter and talking under the vast star-filled sky became more evident. And between the innocent memories, snippets of us skin to skin, my lips pressed against hers, my name breathless from her lips bubbled to the surface. Each time I tried to hold on to the memory, it slipped through my grasp and faded once again.

The therapist in Dallas had said the recent blackouts could be from repressed memories and emotions. Maybe it wasn't random memories I'd been avoiding, but ones that surrounded one specific person. Someone my mind had been fighting for years for me to remember.

Her.

Almost like she was the missing piece. Beks could be the cure.

The moment our eyes connected in the main room, the constant simmering tension and anger settled. A single look from her stilled everything. Each stolen touch freed me from some invisible bind that had held me back from truly living.

The past several years I thought I was happy, but now it felt more like contentment. The army gave me a family, a career, a diversion from the self-destructive path I had sprinted down. I'd never regret the decision. No doubt I was still alive because of the irrational, rushed choice made minutes after leaving rehab all those years ago.

Maybe she was the reason I made that decision. I had to survive for her.

But if she was that important, that impactful, then how in the hell did I forget her for so long? And the now burning question of what I did to her.

An unwelcome thought settled in my gut. What if I was like Dad? What if I forced—no, I'd never do that. No matter if I was drunk, high, or sober, I wasn't that type of person, no matter who my father was.

Turning from the window, I tipped the glass back and downed the last swallows of the drink. Dad watched with a smirk from where he sat on the couch.

"What?" After setting the empty glass on the side table, I leaned against the window once more and crossed my arms over my chest.

"Nice scene today. Glad we can still be a source of entertainment for these people."

The conniving glint in his eyes had me watching my words.

"Living up to our family name. Like you cared. You were high as a fucking kite all day."

"Hell yeah, I was. No way could I get through this day sober with all those damn people paying their respects like he was a celebrity around here."

Tension tightened the muscles down my spine and between my shoulder blades. "Pappy was a good man. Better than you."

"He had you fooled. He was a mean old bastard who enjoyed controlling everyone by dangling his damn money in their faces to get what he wanted."

As he spoke, the tension spread to my chest and up my neck before settling in the back of my head with a steady pulse. *Fuck, not here. Not in front of him.* I gripped the mantle and stared at the ornate clock in the center.

"That girl you were talking to, I remember her," he said. I flicked my gaze to him and found him smirking. "You had your fun with her, didn't you? Hell, the way she filled out, I wouldn't mind taking your leftovers. Imagine that long dark hair fisted—"

"Watch it," I gritted out. Darkness spread in the edges of my vision. I had to get out of there.

With a shove off the wall, I strode out of the room, leaving Dad watching from the couch. Needing fresh air, I turned left down the hall and stormed straight for the back patio.

Outside, the hot, dry air burned down to my lungs with each deep inhale. Stepping away from the house, my vision cleared and breathing eased to a regular cadence.

Crazy considering each step took me closer to her.

Beautiful her.

Fucking hot her.

Damn, that woman had curves that could tempt any man. Add in those sultry honey brown eyes and creamy tan skin and she was a walking pinup model.

I stopped at the edge of the patio and gripped the back of my neck. Beks better say yes. Damn, I hoped she said yes. If she wasn't the magical cure, it sure as hell could be fun while we figured it out.

Even with her nowhere in sight, my fingers itched to touch her again, as well as one other stiff body part. I was surprised she didn't say anything about the massive hard-on that was visible in my suit pants when I touched her. How could I not be turned on with her between my hands, under my control, loving it as much as me?

It was a small miracle I didn't give in to the need to kiss her.

But I would.

As soon as she said yes.

Chapter 5

Rebeka

DAMN, I SHOULD'VE BROUGHT a flashlight. The tiny light on the phone wasn't anything but a tease in the pitch black of the night. If I stepped on a rattler just to see B again, I'd take it as an omen to get my ass in the truck, drive back to Midland, and never think of the gorgeous man again.

With each cautious step toward the main house, my nervous energy ticked higher and higher. I was almost to the window of his room when a nearby bang sent me leaping a foot in the air with a quick yelp of surprise. Sounds of cursing and heeled shoes clicking along the flagstone diverted me from my original destination.

Prickly leaves scraped at my hand and arm as I moved a section of a tall bush aside. Through the hole, I watched Brenton collapse into a patio chair and lean forward to massage his temples. Even from there I could tell he was emotionally and physically exhausted. No doubt the day was difficult for him. Even if he couldn't remember me, or this place, surely he remembered his amazing grandfather and mourned the loss.

After a few minutes of gazing at his sexy profile from the shadows, I chastised myself. When did I become a creepy stalker? Without a glance back to where I was retreating, I took a step, eager to get away unseen. Dread shot through my veins, cutting off my breath at something soft and wiggly pinned beneath the heel of my boot. Terrified, I propelled myself forward, right into the bush. With a curse, I hastily disengaged myself from the branches and pokey leaves with a few swats, only to stumble back and land sprawled on the dusty ground.

Shit.

There was still a chance he didn't hear the commotion, though that hope was dashed when a dark, ominous shadow encroached. To my horror and absolute embarrassment, B stood over me, hands on his hips, smirking.

"What in the hell are you doing?" He squatted beside where I still sat in the dirt, too afraid to move in case the snake came back. "You okay?"

"I stepped on a snake, okay? Scared the shit out of me."

His dark brows pulled together. "Did it bite you?"

Rotating one ankle and then the other, I shook my head. "No stinging, and I didn't feel a bite, so I should be good."

Pulling out his phone, he shined the dim light along the ground. A deep, humorous chuckle eased my nerves and pissed me off in the same breath. He pulled the "snake" off the ground and held it up for me to see.

"This your snake?" For emphasis, he shook the black water hose. "Looks vicious. Wonder what kind it is."

"It felt like one, okay? And this time of year, snakes are awful. Hate those devils," I muttered.

"Now that our lives aren't in mortal danger, answer my first question. What are you doing out here?"

Using his knees as leverage, B pushed up and extend a firm hand down to me. With an eye roll he couldn't see, I took his hand, allowing him to pull me off the ground. "I was on my way to your old room when I heard you out here. I came by to tell you my decision on helping you."

"And?"

"And what?"

"What's your decision, Beks? Will you help me or not?"

I slid my hands into the pockets of the dress and rocked back on my heel. "I need to know what I'm getting into first. Then, if I decide to help, I have some ground rules."

Warmth spread along my palm and up my arm when his hand interlaced with mine. He led me to a long couch situated along the opposite side of the pool, somewhat hidden from the main house. Perfect. That way no one could stumble upon us unless they were looking for him.

For several minutes, we just sat in silence, listening to the gentle hum of the sparkling pool's jets and animated chirps of summer bugs.

"After Caleb died, I started having these episodes of blacking out. One second I'd be fine, and then the next I'd be sweating, couldn't control my blood pressure, and my vision would go dark." Looking away, he sighed and tightened his hold on my hand. "It's happened enough to drive me to take some time off work to get myself better. Before I got the call about Pappy, I was already in Dallas and had started seeing a therapist in hopes they could fix me. But then came the call, and now you. I can't explain it, but I think you can help me."

"But why me?" I asked, almost too afraid to hear his answer.

"The flashbacks, snapshots, are of us happy. Me happy."

"We were," I whispered. "But I still don't understand. You forgot about me, about this place, for so long. Why now? Why not go back to your fancy head doctor and move on?"

"I don't know. That's the truth. That's all I can offer you at this point. All I know is when you're around, everything feels right. My anger settles, and everything else fades in importance. Isn't that enough for now?"

Was it?

Looking up, I watched the stars before concentrating on him once more. "What would I need to do?"

"Be you, I think. Give it five days—four now—of us, of you helping me remember the pieces of my life that I can't. Then you'll go your way and I'll go mine. I have to get back to Kentucky."

"Girlfriend?" I questioned before I could think better of it.

"Army. I'm a helicopter pilot."

Wow. And bam, Brenton Graves somehow got hotter. Images of him in uniform flashed in my mind, shooting a spicy heat straight to my gut.

"Wow, we have a lot to catch up on," I said, somewhat out of breath. *Damn, Beka, pull it together.* "I'll help you, but I do have conditions."

"Conditions?"

"Yeah. Like it or not, I'm still pissed and need answers too. Maybe me helping you will help me too."

"Closure." He said it like the word was bitter in his mouth.

"Right. Which means we do this as friends."

"Friends as in...?"

"As in no sex."

"Not gonna happen. Hell, it's amazing that I haven't kissed you yet looking like you do."

I didn't try to hide my happy smile. "Looking irresistible was part of the plan to get back at you today."

"Does it make you feel better knowing you succeeded?" Brenton grumbled.

"Tons. And the no-sex thing is to protect me. You just made it clear that you're heading back to Kentucky. After you're gone, I'll go back to my practice—"

"Practice? You're a doctor now?"

"Vet. Focus, B. No sex, no touching, no instigating. I know you. I'm the one with the memory of us, and I don't think I could take having you to lose it all over again."

"Will you tell me what I did?"

"I'll help you remember, how's that? Do we have a deal?"

Looking up from the quiet pool, I found him stargazing. "How about this. I'll take it into consideration."

My smile grew. It was nice knowing Brenton wanted me like that again. I did too, badly, but I needed to play this smart. No giving up my heart again when he'd admitted to leaving. At least now I knew ahead of time instead of being blindsided.

"No touching," I insisted.

A minuscule nod was all I received in return.

Rolling my eyes, I moved to the next part of the negotiations. "And no one can know what we're doing. No one can see us together, see us talking or hanging out. We do everything on the down low."

Those furrowed brows came back in full force as he said, "I'm confused. You don't want people to see you with me?"

"I'm sure you are."

"What does that mean?" he said through clenched teeth.

"That you have no memories of how you left things, of who you hurt and left behind. Until you do, until you understand the stakes, we keep this between us."

"How in the hell will we do that?"

I shrugged and withdrew my fingers from his. "Do we have a deal?"

"Not yet." Faster than I could react, he gripped my hand and yanked me flush against his solid chest. Lips parted, heart hammering, I became lost in his green eyes as we lay nose-to-nose. "Just one taste." His soft lips brushed against mine.

Warmth bloomed at every point of contact between us, making the already hot night unbearable. One hand snaked into my dark, curly hair while the other stroked down my spine before grabbing a handful of ass cheek over my dress and pressing me harder against him.

My soft moan gave him access to deepen the kiss. Warning bells rang in my head, but my heart and everything below the waist urged me to ignore the what-ifs and live in the glorious moment. Because right then, in that moment, I was kissing him and he was kissing me.

In a controlled roll, he settled me beneath him, his heavy weight pressing my back into the soft cushions.

"Want to rethink the no touching, Beks?" he said against my lips before sucking down my neck. "I sure as hell wish you would. No way I'll be able to keep my hands off you. Not when you look like this, when you smell fucking delicious."

A soft content sigh passed my lips. Who was I kidding? He was right.

"Mr. Graves?"

At the familiar voice, my eyes popped open and focused in the direction of faint steps.

Shit.

Shoving against Brenton's shoulders, I leveraged him off just in time to crawl over the back of the wicker couch and fall to the pool's concrete decking.

A light chuckle sounded above. "You're ridiculous."

Staring out from beneath the couch, Brenton's dress shoes pressed to the ground facing our approaching unexpected visitor.

"Mr. Graves, there you are," said the head housekeeper. "Your father said you headed out this way."

"Something I can do for you, Mrs. Hathway?" There was no mistaking the lingering hint of humor in his tone.

Bastard.

If he knew the rumor mill started and stopped with her, he wouldn't find all this funny. The sweet, kind, judgy woman standing in front of him single-handedly ruined me. Okay, technically I did that to myself, but she was the one who spread the news around town. Wonder what Brenton would think of her if he knew that tidbit.

"Oh no. I was about to turn in and wanted to see if you needed anything else from the other staff or me."

Needed anything? Wow. How nice would it be to have someone check in on you? I'd love to raise my hand and ask for a bottle or two of wine, but considering I went to all the trouble to hide, I'd better not. This woman was public enemy number one when it came to who could not know about Brenton and me talking again.

So even though I'd forget the glass and drink straight from the bottle right now, I'd stay right there sweating on the ground until she left.

"No, ma'am. I'm fine, thank you for asking. But I guess you should know that I'll be staying for a few days. Until the attorneys come. I'm not sure of my father's plans, but please let the other staff know I'll be here."

The slight pause before her response spoke volumes. "Yes, sir, but may I ask you something?"

"Of course."

"Your decision to stay, does it have anything to do with that girl Rebeka Harding?"

Silently I groaned and tapped my forehead against the rough concrete. *Seriously, lady? Mind your own damn business and leave so I can crawl back under the sexy beast.*

"That woman, you mean. And no, it doesn't." No humor remained in his flat tone.

"Right, sorry, sir. None of my business, I guess."

"That's correct. Good night, Mrs. Hathway."

Damn.

Even as her shoes disappeared, I stayed on the ground. What the hell was I doing? It was a terrible idea. Kissing him, being close—I was playing with fire. He was the match and gasoline. Plus, once he remembered what he chose after the accident, what he had me sign, what would he do then?

"Coast is clear," B said, still on the other side of the couch.

The concrete bit into my palms as I pushed up to stand. "I changed my mind. This is a terrible idea." I didn't look up, focused on dusting the debris from my palms down my dress. "I'll go." Maneuvering around him, I took two steps before his hand wrapped around my wrist, tugging me to a halt.

"What?"

"This isn't a good idea. What happens when someone finds out, or when you remember everything? What happens when I can't do this?" I motioned between us with both hands and tossed them in the air, his tight grip releasing. "You don't know how it ended, B, and maybe that's a good thing. Even though I want to know why you did it, is it worth the repercussions?"

"No."

"What?"

"You're in this. I can handle whatever happens from here. I have to know. And as for you, I can't keep you from hating me or loving me, but I can give you the reassurance that my track record has been shit with women. Most end up hating me in the end. I'm an arrogant asshole."

"Good to know some things haven't changed," I said with a laugh. "But you can't kiss me like that again, no matter how bad you want to."

"Oh that." He shoved both hands into his pockets and turned toward the main house. "That was for you. Thought you'd like to know what you're missing out on."

"Arrogant bastard. You liked it too." Not wanting him to have the last dig, I stormed after him. "Admit it."

"Maybe." He shrugged without turning to face me, but from that angle, I still saw his cocky-ass smirk. "But I wasn't the one moaning like a porn star."

Anger like I hadn't felt in years surged forth. Gripping his shoulder, I yanked him to a stop. His smirk faltered as I jumped, wrapping my thighs around his trim waist and hooking my arms around his neck.

A low growl rumbled from his chest, vibrating against the apex of my thighs.

"Now who's moaning?" I whispered against his lips. "One thing you'll want to remember about me, I don't back down."

"Well, Beks, that'll be a problem because neither do I."

"And I get the last word."

"Not always."

"This will get interesting, then."

"What point are you trying to prove right now? From my perspective, you couldn't keep your hands off me, so you just attacked a man trying to walk away as you asked him to."

"That you want me too. This isn't a one-way street."

"Trying to prove it to me or you?" Slowly he lowered my feet to the ground. "Make up your mind. You want me to want you or not?"

Embarrassed because he was right, I shoved his chest and turned. Hell, I was the idiot female who couldn't fucking think straight when he was around. "I have to run home tomorrow to get some clothes for the week. All I have is this dress." For emphasis, I gripped the hem and pulled it out wide. His gaze zeroed in on the bit of upper thigh showing.

"Just buy new ones."

"Wow, you're... oblivious. Arrogant, oblivious, and cocky as hell. Can't wait to see what else has changed with you. I live forty minutes east. I'll be back by lunch, and then we can start whatever we're doing."

"I need clothes too. Wasn't planning on sticking around, so all I have is this suit." He spread his arms and gestured down his body. "And whatever is in the house from years ago. I'll come with you, and we can stop somewhere for me."

"Fine. Meet me at the truck at six. But remember, don't let—"

"Anyone see me. Yeah, I get it. Wish I could remember why you're this neurotic about no one finding out."

I paused my retreat and kept my back to him as I said, "Wish I couldn't."

Chapter 6

Rebeka

WITH EACH STEP, BRADLEY's old mesh shorts sank lower on my hips, forcing me to hitch them up to keep them from falling to the dirt and exposing my bare ass. With the soft material fisted in my grasp, I shuffled toward the truck, my attention on the mild morning sun peeking over the horizon and shining a glow across the flat land.

When I woke up at five, Bradley was already out starting chores, and Daddy was sound asleep in the recliner where he'd passed out the night before.

Most people were anti-mornings, but not me. The fresh air and coolish temperatures set the tone for the day. Plus, mornings offered that first glorious sip of steaming coffee. Most nights I'd fall asleep with visions of that first sip in my dreams.

But last night, my thoughts were not of coffee. I tossed and turned from varying dreams with Brenton as the star. Some were good, X-rated good, but others were quite terrible. The terrible ones had him leaving the moment he remembered why he'd forced us apart thirteen years ago and proceeded to re-count, in heartrending detail, why he decided to walk away.

"Whose clothes are those?"

I jerked my head in the direction of Brenton's voice. He leaned against the other side of the truck, glaring with narrowed eyes. Was that jealousy in his tone?

"Not mine." I knew I shouldn't egg him on, but where was the fun in that? "Problem?"

Annoyance flashed behind his green eyes, making them sparkle in the morning sun. If I didn't hate him, I'd swoon at the sight. But I did hate him. Yep. Hate. That was the warm tingling feeling simply hearing his voice invoked.

"No problem besides it's fifteen after and already fucking hot out here. I don't like waiting. Be on time when you suggest meeting up."

"Wow, someone's grouchy this morning." I gave him a wide smile and pulled open the driver door. "And hate to tell you, but the heat part is about to get worse before it gets better."

Brenton slid into the passenger side and slammed the door shut behind him. "Oh, and why's that?"

After situating my sunglasses, I shifted in the seat to tell him about the broken air conditioning, then cursed under my breath and looked back out the windshield to avert my eyes from his bare arms. "Nope. Out. Get out of my truck. Right now. Out."

"What the hell is your problem?" He tossed his hands into the air in exasperation but didn't make a move out the door.

"Nope. Out. We can't do this. Not with those." I gestured at his elaborately tattooed arms. "I can't." Shit, this was not happening.

Gorgeous. Military. Tattoos.

Did any woman have enough willpower to withstand that combo?

"What's your problem?"

Banging my forehead against the hard steering wheel, I kept my eyes sealed shut. "Can you put long sleeves on or something? A parka maybe?"

When I didn't get a response, I rolled my forehead along the hard plastic to sneak a peek at the sexiest man alive. His green eyes locked with mine after my long perusal up each arm, a cocky smirk pushing a faint dimple in his left cheek.

Shit. Dimples too.

Hell.

I might as well strip right here.

"Have a thing for tattoos, do you?"

After clearing my throat, I took a deep breath and twisted the key in the ignition. Keeping my eyes out the windshield and hands at ten and two, I started us down the drive. "Nope. They're quite offensive actually, so I'd appreciate it if you don't show them again. Ever."

"Right."

We didn't make it halfway down the long gravel drive before he was fiddling with the AC controls and adjusting the vents. Without making it visible, I cut my gaze back to his arms, watching the way his biceps flexed and moved beneath the ink. The pictures were elaborate and detailed with black and blue shading.

"Shit," he blurted and grabbed the door handle.

Oh hell. "Sorry," I yelled and focused on not overcorrecting the truck into the fence. "Guess I'm not awake yet."

Yep, that was it.

"What's wrong with your damn air conditioning?"

I tucked a rogue brown curl behind my ear with a grimace. "Uh, yeah that. It's broken."

"You're fucking with me."

"Unfortunately no."

"And what's that damn smell?"

"Cow shit, probably remnants of some animal placenta and..." I took an exaggerated whiff. "Old tacos mixed with Sea Breeze air freshener. Which is failing terribly at its one job."

While mumbling a stream of colorful curse words, he rolled down the window. "And I thought a helicopter filled with soldiers after a ten-day assignment was bad."

"Told you I always win."

"Is this something you want to win?"

"Winning is winning."

"How long has your AC been out?"

Right. The last thing I wanted was Brenton Graves to know how broke I was. "Not long."

"You just fucking lied to me."

Sweat beaded along my palms at the intensity in his statement. "What?"

"How long, Beks?"

"You can wait in the truck while I grab my stuff. Then we can run by Cavender's. Out this way, no one knows about our past drama, so we're okay going in together."

"Answer my question. Now. And don't lie to me again or I'll whip your ass."

On their own, my thighs clenched together in an attempt to relieve the rising throb his threat caused. "Last summer."

When he didn't respond, I glanced his direction. His attention was focused out the windshield, staring at the blank landscape as he white-knuckled the door handle.

"It's fine. Better for the environment." I shot him a wide smile, which he didn't notice. "Sorry, I'm sure you're not used to being uncomfortable. So fancy."

Still no response.

Whatever. One-handed, I popped the Stevie Nicks tape in and turned up the sound. Halfway through the first song, me singing along word for word, Brenton broke his random pouting session.

"What the hell is this music?"

"Um, Stevie Nicks," I said defensively.

"Who?"

"Stevie Nicks, lead singer of Fleetwood Mac who also went on to have an amazing solo career. You know, Stevie Nicks."

"She sounds like a dying cat."

"You sound like a dying cat."

"What?" he said through a loud chuckle.

Ignoring his comment, I twisted the volume knob to the right and went right back to singing along with the fantastic rock star.

An inner self-conscious piece cringed as I pulled into the parking spot in front of my building number and cut the engine. It wasn't the most beautiful place, a little old and run down, but it was cheap and safe. I'd never cared about the looks until that moment with him sitting beside me. Judging.

"I'd love a shower, and I need to pack. Do you mind waiting that long?"

I shoved his shoulder to gain his attention. Those green eyes cut over with annoyance behind them.

"There's a Starbucks up the road. Take the truck and meet me back here in an hour."

Not waiting for an answer, I tossed the keys in his lap and shoved open the door.

HE WAS DEAD.

I didn't give a shit how pretty he was or how much money he had, Brenton Graves was a dead man.

Two fucking hours—gone.

After pacing the sidewalk in the blazing hot sun for twenty minutes, effectively negating the shower I'd taken, I'd stormed back upstairs to wait in my somewhat less hot apartment. I peered through the thin metal blinds like a crazy neighbor, staring at the parking lot. What was worse, I was the idiot who never asked for his number, so I had zero way to get ahold of him.

For the hundredth time in the past thirty seconds, I spread open two of the blinds and peeked out.

"What the hell?" I muttered, leaping from my perch by the window. Overnight bag in hand, I stormed down the metal stairs, making a beeline for the smiling Brenton.

"Where in the hell have you been?" I seethed, dropping the bag at his feet, which his amused eyes tracked, to cross my arms over my chest. "You've been gone for over two hours. Did you get the shits or something?"

Behind his sunglasses, both dark brows shot up in surprise. "The shits? No. I skipped coffee to fix the truck's AC problem."

My hands fell to my sides and I sighed, now more frustrated with myself at jumping to conclusions. "You didn't have to do that, B. I was going to get it fixed when I had a chance. I've just been working a ton and need my truck so—"

He rested his callused hands on my shoulders. "Say thank you, Beks. I had the time."

Unable to resist, I matched his smile with one of my own. "Thank you. Really, thank you." Shifting my attention around the parking lot, I searched for my vehicle. "Now let's go get you some clothes. Where's the truck?"

"Behind me."

Eyes wide, I gaped at the brand-new F250 he leaned back on. "What. The fuck. Is that?"

"I didn't say *how* I fixed the air issue. Now remember, you said thank you."

"B, this is...."

"Amazing? Perfect?"

"The most arrogant gift. Ever."

He shrugged, hit a button on the key fob that started the engine, and tossed the keys into the air. Still staring at the beautiful vehicle in front of me, I snatched them before they hit the ground.

"You drive," he stated, grabbing the bag at his feet before walking to the passenger side.

My fingers brushed along the bright red paint as I inched toward the driver door. It was precisely the color I would've chosen out of all the options. Through the window, I smiled at the staring Brenton, rewarded with a broad smile of his own.

I shouldn't accept it. It was too much. Who gave someone a truck?

Brenton fucking Graves, that was who.

The heavy door swung open with ease. Giggling, I lifted myself inside and settled into the cold seat. My eyes shuttered closed at the air wafting against my ass and back while near-arctic air blasted my face.

"This is heaven," I mused, rubbing a hand over the soft leather steering wheel. "It's too much. I shouldn't accept it." Rolling the back of my head against the leather headrest, I slowly opened my eyes to meet his. "But I really, really want to."

"Then do. Consider it payment for helping me. And it was a bit selfish too. I was fucking hot."

"Fancy pants," I joked with a wink.

"I've been in rougher conditions in Afghanistan, but here, stateside, if I can help not being balls hot, I'll do whatever I can to be comfortable."

"Yeah, I needed to shower earlier. I had total sweaty ass from the hot drive out here."

"You're telling me you had swamp ass."

"Yeah, I guess, if that's the technical term."

"Wow, the shit you say, woman," he grumbled and looked out the window, almost like he was trying to hide his chuckle. "Come on, let's go get my clothes now."

"Where did you get those?" I asked as I carefully backed out using the back-up camera. Damn. Maybe with this I could parallel park.

"Found them in my closet. Guess I've gained some weight since the last time I was out at the ranch. These things are damn tight."

"You don't hear me complaining," I mumbled to the window.

At a stoplight, I fiddled with the stereo, programming my favorite stations.

"Do you have the awful dying cat singer albums on your phone?" I nodded while shooting him the evil eye, which made him chuckle. "I couldn't salvage your tape, but this truck has Bluetooth, so you can stream the songs directly from your phone."

That time I nodded with a wide grin instead of the death glare.

"You haven't stopped smiling," he said, drawing my attention to the fact.

"It's the nicest thing anyone has ever done for me. How could I not smile like an idiot?"

"Surprised previous boyfriends hadn't done it. That truck wasn't safe."

"First of all, no comment on the boyfriend part. Second, not everyone has enough cash sitting around to buy a truck for a friend."

"Friend," he mused with a lingering look at my chest.

"Eyes up here, B. And it's how we started originally." I shrugged and gripped the wheel tighter as the memories roared back to life.

His smile fell. "Did I never... was I good to you?"

I waited for a block or two to carefully choose my response. "We were kids, Brenton. But yeah, when you were sober, you were great."

"And when I wasn't?"

"You were gone. The Brenton I loved was hidden, stuffed inside this blank stare. You were never bad to me, but those times when you were high, it slayed me."

Silence fell as I backed into a parking spot. Leaving the truck running, I swiveled in the seat to reach across the large console and grabbed his forearm. His despondent stare shifted from the side window to where our skin connected.

"What happened? Tell me. I deserve to know."

My smile fell. "You're the one who forgot. You don't deserve shit."

Frustrated at the mix of emotions all this remembering conjured up, I stormed out of the truck and marched to the store door only to see the closed sign through the glass. I cursed at my watch. Another thirty minutes until they opened.

Turning to tell Brenton, I kept turning, not finding him directly behind me. I looked back to the truck and saw him still sitting in the passenger seat. When our eyes met, he smiled and gave an exaggerated point to his watch.

Bastard.

Defeated, I shuffled back to the truck and slid into my seat.

"How was your walk?"

"You're an asshole, you know that? How in the hell did I put up with you as long as I did?"

"Good point. How long was that again?"

I sighed and leaned the seat back to get comfortable. "Hell, two years? Three maybe." Out of the corner of my eye, I caught him staring.

"How old are you?"

I popped up and reached for the push start button. "You hungry? Whataburger is—"

He swatted my hand away and gripped my chin, making me face him. "Beks. Answer me."

"Or?" I said breathlessly.

"The same as I said before. I'll whip your ass."

Heat filled my cheeks. "You'd be wise to threaten a punishment I wouldn't enjoy."

The grip on my chin tightened a fraction, and his lips turned white as he pressed them together. Tension pulsed in the cab, the heat building between us.

"Thirty," I whispered. "I'm thirty."

That snapped him out of the lust-filled haze in his blazing green eyes. "Wait." Behind his eyes I saw that mind of his working out the math. This should be fun.

"Yep," I said with a small grimace.

"Fuck! What the hell was I thinking!"

"Now you see why everyone was... upset when they found out we were together. Especially my father."

"Please tell me my math is wrong that when we first got together... Please tell me I didn't sleep with a fifteen-year-old."

"You didn't."

"Thank fuck."

"We started hanging out when I was fifteen. I was seventeen when we first had sex."

"Not great—"

"Or legal."

"Better than fucking a fifteen-year-old when I was what, seventeen? Eighteen?"

"Eighteen."

While he processed the new-to-him information, I adjusted the seat and saved the settings. "I love the truck. I don't deserve it, and every rational thought is telling me not to accept it. But I want it." The whine at the end and the dramatic pouty lip were an attempt to ease our growing tension.

"It's yours, so stop fighting it. Once I get the title, I'll switch it over to your name and have it sent to you."

Right. Sent to me. Because he was leaving again, and this week with him was only a reprieve from life. Too soon I'd be shoved back into reality, without him.

Searching for a distraction from the sad thought, I focused on the clock. Still fifteen more minutes until the store opened.

"When did you join the army?" I asked, hoping to take the conversation off us.

"After rehab. I knew it was my only shot to stay clean. And I have. Stayed clean that is."

Leaning the back of my head against the hot window, I focused on the still empty parking lot. "You went to rehab." I bit my lower lip and smiled. "You always said you would go one day. I'm proud of you, Brenton." I looked at him through welled tears. "So proud of you. What made you finally go?"

"I don't know, really. Wish I could say it was my decision, but I woke up there. I always assumed Caleb or Dad—hell, maybe Pappy—put me in there. They kept me sedated for a while to ease the withdrawal symptoms."

"Brenton?" Unease fluttered in my gut and spread up my chest. "When did that happen?"

Not sensing my reluctance, he shrugged like his answer didn't matter. But it did. It could change everything.

"I don't know. Look, someone just opened the door. Let's do this."

Before I could stop him, he was out the door and rounding the hood. I was still staring at the passenger seat, processing it all, when the knock on my window startled me. Brenton stood on the other side of the door, motioning for me to hurry.

If he only knew what his revelation could mean, he wouldn't be as impatient.

Because if he didn't remember going into rehab, if the timeline matched up to our last night, then there was no way he drafted the agreement or made a choice as they said.

Which meant the man I'd spent the past thirteen years hating wasn't the one who broke my heart and left me in shambles.

Someone else did.

Chapter 7

Brenton

SEVENTEEN.

Hell. My greatest fear was true—I was my father. Getting out of Dallas all those years ago broke the addiction he'd groomed me to be dependent on, but genetics was genetics. I was a fool to think I'd ever be able to escape that family gene.

But the age thing wasn't the big secret she was holding back. Did that mean what Beks wouldn't tell me was worse than seducing a seventeen-year-old? I needed answers. Needed to know exactly what I did so I could beg for her forgiveness, which would hopefully fix my head shit. Remembering, getting better, going back to Kentucky—that was the plan, nothing else. I needed to keep my head on straight around her and not make this worse for her in the end. No matter what I did to her early on, I had the power, and the fucking willpower, to not get wrapped up in her vortex now.

Right. If I believed that, my blackouts weren't my only head issue.

For the second time in the past sixty seconds, I scanned the store looking for her distinctive curly dark hair. I squeezed my hands into tight fists at her talking and laughing with some guy. Her hands moved up and down as she told some story that had them both smiling.

Hell no.

She was mine.

On a mission to break that shit up, I weaved through the racks of jeans and pearl snap shirts, my determined gaze on her. Halfway across the small store, her attention flicked up, causing her smile to falter.

Tension built in my chest at him pulling out his phone and handing it to her.

"Hey, man," said the guy wearing a name tag, standing way too close to my Beks when I stopped beside her. "You need help with something?"

Not paying him any attention, I kept my gaze locked with hers. "The woman who was helping me needs you." I nodded behind me. When he didn't move, I shifted my hard glare to him. I was an ass for savoring the slight tremble in the guy's shoulders. "Go help."

Beks watched him retreat, a deep frown pulling at her pouty lips. "What the hell was that about?"

"I'm ready to go."

After glancing down, she looked back up with a quirked brow. "Without shoes?"

Shit. Forgot about that. I was in the middle of trying on boots when I saw that dipshit with her. "What were you two discussing? Do you know him?"

"He was in the process of asking me out, I think. Hell, who knows since you scared him off, being all territorial. Surprised you didn't whip out your man bits and pee on me."

Brows raised, I shot her a questioning look.

"Dogs, male animals, they mark their territory by peeing on things. Didn't you learn anything in biology?"

"You're the smart one. I didn't finish college, remember?"

"I only got to go because of you," she whispered.

The sales girl called my name, but my focus stayed on Beks.

"What does that mean?"

Her eyes turned down to the floor, her black-painted fingers tucking a bit of hair behind her ear. "It means you paid for it."

The hesitant tap on my right shoulder snapped my gaze to the person at my back with an annoyed growl.

"What?" I gritted out to the now-terrified salesgirl. Hell. I forgot how ter- rifying I could be when pissed. I'm no small guy, and add in the high level of intensity I put into everything, I was too overbearing for civilians—a civilian woman, no less. The boys on base weren't too intimidated, but by the way this girl's knees were knocking together, I was her worst nightmare come to life.

"Your boots, sir. They're—"

"I'll take those, every pair of jeans you have in the size I tried on earlier, ten pairs of socks in my boot size, ten pairs of extra-large boxers, ten pairs of boxer briefs, twenty of those dry-fit T-shirts in black, some shirts and a few of those Yeti hats."

Her blank stare fueled my annoyance.

"Do you need to write it down?"

"No... no, sir. I'll be—"

"We'll meet you up front."

The second the wide-eyed woman walked off, I turned back to Beks, who was still focused on the ground.

"What do you mean I paid for it?"

With a huff, she fell on to a display rocking chair and leaned back. "Brenton, do you really want to know? It's Pandora's box. Once you know one thing, you'll want to know the rest. Can't we leave it as the way things are now? I was happy then, you were happy, and we ended."

"What are you hiding?" Needing to train her focus back on me instead of the lock of hair she was intently studying, I dropped to a crouch and rested my forearms on her thighs. Her shoulders rose and fell in a noncommittal shrug. A dull ache settled deep in my chest at her slumped shoulders. "Hey, come on. It's okay. Nothing will change."

Unshed tears lined her lower lids when she finally looked up. "That's what you said before. Don't you get it, B? It didn't end well. You left me. I told you.... You knew, and you signed a very cut-and-dried document stating I could never reach out to you again, never find you, never mention we ever happened. I woke up in the hospital alone. Alone and scared. You turned your back on me when I needed you most. That's why I hate you."

She choked back a sob but couldn't stop the tears from escaping and falling down her cheeks.

"You paid me off. The money put me through undergrad. So every class, every book I bought, I thought of you and how to you I was a disposable fling. I loved you, you fucking bastard."

Her palms connected roughly with my shoulders. The hard concrete of the store floor did nothing to absorb the impact of my ass slamming against it. Still in shock at her assault, I stayed sitting on the floor as she shoved from the chair to stand over me.

Gone was the insecurity. Gone was the sadness.

Pissed-off Beks glared down with hurt and anger in her honey brown eyes.

The idea of her taking the money didn't sit well, especially since I had no fucking clue why she was paid off. She still wasn't telling the full truth about our story. And yeah, I was fucking pissed at myself for not remembering. I shouldn't take my anger and frustrations out on her, but like she and I had discussed the night before, I was an asshole and always got the final word.

"Sounds like you weren't too heartbroken over losing me like you've been making it out to be. What was I worth? Couple hundred grand? A million? Tell me, Rebeka, what price tag did you put on us?"

"Fuck you."

"Believe me, baby, I'm dying to, but you said no touching."

The fierce fire behind her eyes and the fisting of her hands had me shifting back an inch. She looked like she was about to fucking explode. Instead of resorting to violence, which was shocking based on her body language, she flipped me the bird with both hands and stormed toward the front of the store.

Damn, did I know how to pick them.

I shoved off the ground with a groan and dusted my shorts off as I scanned the store for her but came up empty.

Huh.

At the checkout counter, I rapped my black American Express on the wooden counter while the salesgirl took her sweet-ass time ringing everything up, Beks still nowhere in sight. A sinking feeling told me that wasn't a coincidence. When I pushed through the front doors, the two salespeople at my back, I was somewhat prepared for what I'd find and didn't overreact.

No idea why, since she stranded my ass in the truck I'd just bought her, I laughed at the empty parking space where the truck had been.

Chapter 8

Rebeka

HALFWAY TO THE APARTMENT, dread rolled my gut, making me queasy. What in the hell did I do? At a red light, I scanned the clean dash and took a deep, memory-making sniff of the new truck smell. No way would he let me keep this thing after leaving him like that.

Shit.

The quick consideration of turning around was dashed as my stubborn ruling side pushed the gas pedal down, urging me faster through the side streets, putting more and more distance between me and the asshole.

At the front door of my apartment, I dropped the truck keys the second it was locked behind me and turned for the kitchen. The half-empty bottle of white wine rattled against the pint glass in my trembling hand. Only after half the glass of cold, crisp goodness was in my belly could I take a deep, calming breath. I topped off the glass with the remaining wine, grabbed the emergency bag of last year's Halloween candy from the top of the fridge, and slid down the cabinets until my ass hit the cracked linoleum.

Vibrations against my ass sent my heart in overdrive, only to have it plunge when Ryder's name flashed on the screen instead of the person I wanted.

Ryder: Hey, just checking in. After yesterday and being around your dad, I wanted to make sure you weren't sitting on the kitchen floor drinking.

Ryder: You moved on from that asshole. Keep reminding yourself that. Nothing that happened was your fault.

Ryder: You deserve better than he could've ever given you anyway.

Ryder: Let's find Mr. Rebound. How about Dos Amigos my next night off? Kyle said he'd be DD.

Mr. Rebound. Even though it didn't sound appealing at the moment, I had no reason to say no.

Me: Count me in.

Ryder: All serious, you okay?

Me: Yes? No?

Me: I want to be. But how can I when he said he doesn't remember? How can I move on when I don't know if he's the one who sent me away or not?

Ryder: Either way, he didn't fight for you. That's what matters, doesn't it?

Ryder: Thirteen years, Beka. Thirteen. You owe it to yourself to move on.

Me: Yeah.

My thumbs paused over the bright screen at a pounding knock at the door. Instead of putting energy into standing, I crawled on all fours to the front door and pulled it open.

"Groveling?" Brenton said, humor lacing his words.

"Drinking."

"Ah."

Hot, dry air whooshed into the warm apartment as I shoved the door wider, allowing him to enter. Still on hands and knees, I crawled back toward my candy picnic. At the click of the bolt, I paused and shot a glance over my shoulder to find Brenton still at the door, blatantly staring at my ass.

Knowing exactly what I was doing, I gave it a little wiggle. His nostrils flared as his gaze shifted to mine. My breathing tripped and mouth went dry at the want pulsing off him.

"Careful, Beks." One more long look at my full, round ass and he marched past to the kitchen. "What do you have to drink?"

"Whiskey's in the pantry, vodka in the freezer, chilled white wine in the... wait, nope. All that is in my belly."

"It's been thirty minutes."

"I'm a pro, what can I say."

"Anything nonalcoholic?"

"Shit. Sorry. Um." I mentally inventoried the fridge's contents. "There's a gallon of tea in the fridge."

The solid cabinet door dug into my upper back as I sipped the crisp wine and eyed him while he moved about the kitchen. "How'd you know where to find me?" I asked around a mouthful of Mr. Goodbar.

"Asked your neighbors, who I have to say seemed shady as fuck. Did you have to pass a background check to get into this place?"

The thin foil of the miniature Hershey's bar crinkled between my fingers. "I guess? Who knows. All I knew was I could move in immediately, and it fit within my budget."

His knees cracked, and he let out a grunt as he sank to the floor beside me, tea glass in hand.

"Hi," I said, then took a sip of liquid courage. "Sorry for getting so pissed."

"And for leaving my ass."

"Well, technically you deserved that."

"The fuck?"

"Just agree and move on. Where's your stuff?" Leaning forward, I craned my neck around the small wall dividing the two rooms to the front door, searching for his bags.

He coughed and spat the sip he'd taken back into the glass in his hand. "What the hell is that?"

"Tea?"

"It's molasses."

"Oh yeah, it's a little sweet. I buy it from this place down the street. My one splurge. Where's your stuff?"

With a grimace, he took another tentative sip. "They're delivering it to the ranch."

I didn't stop my eyes from rolling toward the ceiling. "Right. Of course they are. Do you always get your way?"

Those green eyes slid to me. "Except when it comes to you."

"Do you like it? Being a pilot?"

Long, muscular legs stretched out before him, filling most of the small kitchen floor. "Yeah, I love it. I love serving my country and what the military gave me."

Warmth bloomed in my belly from the wine, strengthening my confidence and lowering inhibitions. Swiveling around, I leaned back, resting my head on his firm thigh. "What's that?"

"A family. A dependable family. One who pushes you to be better than you were yesterday."

"That must be nice." I focused on a dark smudge across the white fridge. "I'm guessing the blackouts you described are an issue for someone in your role."

An incredulous huff resounded through the small room. "You could say that. But I've never had an issue while flying. I came here to get help before that could ever happen. I won't risk my brothers' lives like that. If I can't get better, I'll file for a medical discharge, but that's the last resort. I want to go back. I *need* to go back."

The muscle beneath my head flexed when I shifted for a better angle to look up to him. "Why?"

His head was leaned back against the cabinet as he stared ahead. "With Caleb gone, I don't have anything good here. I can't tolerate five minutes around Dad, and I'm certain the feeling is mutual. In Kentucky I'm needed, wanted. Here... here I'm just reminded of how alone I am."

"You've never been alone," I whispered. "You know, I had a crush on you way before you ever noticed me." The sadness in his gaze disappeared when he looked down with a small smile. "Sometimes I'd follow you when you'd sneak out of the main house at night. I'd watch you watch the stars." Shutting my eyes, I focused on those memories. "One night I couldn't stop from going to you. Even though you were the boss's grandson, the prick everyone said you were, I walked out onto the dock and lay beside you."

The hard floor dug into my elbows as I leaned up to take a deep swallow of wine. "You were so angry, sad, upset—hell, everything. That day had been bad. Your dad was in town visiting, and as much as he and your grandfather tried to cover it up, I knew how your dad treated you and Caleb when no one was watching." Summoning some courage, I leaned back against his chest. The strong arm that snaked around my waist held me tighter against him, sending a wonderful sense of protection to sweep over me.

"How in the hell could you have known that?"

"I told you. I watched, and I listened. I saw things no one else did. And what I saw was something I related with. So I went out, lay beside you, and wrapped my hand around yours. Maybe it was a weak moment for you, but you didn't pull away. That night, we gazed into the night sky for hours, not saying a word to each other. When you got up to leave, you held your hand out to help me up, and it just happened. That moment... from that moment, we were us."

The neighbor's music blared through the thin walls, and the elephant man who lived above stomped like he was about to come through the ceiling. We just sat there, content, me in his arms on my dirty kitchen floor.

I smiled down at the empty glass in my hand. "Is this happening? You here?" Angling my face, I nuzzled his neck and took in a deep breath. "Sorry, I get snuggly with white wine. I'm not responsible for my actions after one glass."

The rumble of his words vibrated from his chest to mine. "And how many have you had?"

"One. For sure two," I breathed against his skin. "Okay, could be three. I guzzled a lot when I got home."

"Because you felt bad for leaving me?"

"Yeah... my bad."

"My. Bad. That's all you have to say? How about 'Sorry I left you, Brenton, and I'll gladly let you bend me over the counter to make up for it.'"

My half gasp, half giggle filled the kitchen, and I shoved his chest. Beneath my fingers, his chest shook as he chuckled at my reaction. Fine lines spread out from his eyes from a full, happy smile.

"The counter is too cold."

His green eyes twinkled with a challenge. "We could negotiate on the location, Beks. But until you amend the whole no-touching piece of our agreement, I'm hands off."

"I hate sober me right now," I grumbled, then grabbed his tea to take a swig. "Thanks." With the hem of my T-shirt, I wiped the remnants from my upper lip.

"Rebeka?" My full name and the restrained anger in the single word caught me off guard. Instead of looking at me, his eyes were zeroed in on my stomach. "What's that?"

Right. Mr. I Forgot What I Did To You.

"Not all my scars are emotional, B," I said, almost like a curse before pushing off his leg to stand. The room swayed at the quick movement, but strong hands gripped my shoulders, steadying me. I tried to shrug him off but couldn't loosen his grip.

"Answer me."

"No," I gritted out, then tilted my head back to meet his burning gaze. "Fuck you. You can't demand to know—"

"Fuck yes I can!"

"Not when you should already know, dammit. I wasn't as lucky." He dropped his hold and took a step back but kept his stare locked with mine. The cracking of his knuckles echoed in the kitchen. "And I know I'm a fucking bitch for being pissed at you for not knowing and to keep bringing this up, but you know what, I have that right. I have the right to...." As I stared into his eyes, a revelation pushed through. "I have the right to do whatever the fuck I want."

The force of my lips pushing against his knocked his head against the cabinet. I brushed my fingertips up the inked arms I'd been lusting after all day and gripped his shoulder, digging my nails into his tight muscles.

"Rebeka." My name on his lips pulled a throaty groan from my chest. "Rebeka."

"No, I don't want to think. I don't want to remember. I don't want to be mad anymore. Take me, right here, right now."

"Beks—"

Instead of letting him talk me out of my plan, I shifted against the very noticeable hard-on pressing between my thighs. The hiss that passed over his lips gave the opening I needed. Massaging his tongue with my own, I offered him everything I had in hopes of convincing him this needed to happen.

"Please, B," I begged against his lips. "I need this. I need you."

In response, his fingers brushed up the back of my spread thighs to grab a handful of ass, pushing me harder against him.

"Make me forget," I whispered, opening my eyes only to find his already open and staring down into mine.

"Make me remember," he whispered back.

Clutching the hem of my T-shirt between my fingers, I tugged it over my head and let it float to the floor. Callused hands skimmed across my scarred stomach. His thumbs brushed up and down causing a wonderful heat to spark each place he touched. Green eyes locked with mine his head dipped and slick lips pressed tender kisses along my ruined skin. My eye lids fluttered closed at the adoring way he treated the part of me I loathed the most.

Forehead pressed to my bellybutton his roaming hands paused just below my bra.

"Man up, Graves," I groaned. "I'm not drunk. I'm horny as hell, and I need you to fix the issue." Taking one step and then another, I leaned against the opposite cabinet. "We can go slow later if you want. I'll even whisper sweet nothings in—"

He covered the small area between us in one step. Hands around my waist, he hauled me up and set me not so gently on the counter.

"Holy hell, that's hot," I said against the skin of his neck. Angling back, I pointed to his shirt. "Off. Take it off."

"Damn, woman," he admonished, but still ripped it over his head, giving me a full view of his muscular shoulders, perfection pecs, and defined abs. White wine dripped from my lips. Yep, wine not drool. Wine.

"B."

"Beks."

"If you don't take care of this situation right now, I'll start without you."

"Bossy little thing, aren't you?" he murmured as his hand wrapped around my throat, tipping my chin up with his thumb. "If I wasn't so obsessed with winning, I might like to watch that show of your hand doing everything I told it to."

"Brenton," I begged. With a quick dip of my chin, I snagged his thumb between my lips and bit the soft pad.

Pressure released around my ribs, and the bra straps eased down my arms. Sharp nibbles traced along my collarbone, sinking lower and lower with each pass.

"You have fucking perfect tits," he mumbled against my skin, palming both breasts for emphasis. His teeth softly nipped at my peaked nipple, shooting a jolt through my body. I dug my short, dark nails into his scalp, holding him tighter against my chest.

After each bite, his lips and tongue sucked and licked to ease the pain, only to repeat the pattern all over again. The delicious mix of pain and pleasure had me squirming against the laminate in search for anything to relieve the building pressure between my thighs.

"Pants off, now," he commanded. At the slight hesitation, he pulled me off the counter and set my feet on the ground. Caging me between his strong arms, he said, "Now."

A shiver racked my shoulders as I stared into his hooded eyes. "And if I don't?"

Another chill raced down my spine at his intense stare. "Condom."

"Bedroom, side drawer."

Instead of bolting to the bedroom like every other male would've done, he widened his stance and crossed those inked arms over his broad, naked chest. "Came back with that answer pretty quick. Needed those recently, have you?"

"What?" I croaked. We were not having that conversation now. "Brenton," I whined.

"Answer first."

"Maybe once, twice. Hell, I don't know. Does it matter who I've slept with when they were all piss-poor fill-ins for you?"

Something I couldn't read flashed in his stare. With a curse, he stormed out of the kitchen, leaving me half naked, confused, and waiting.

And waiting.

One minute, then another passed without him returning. I snagged his T-shirt from the floor, slipped it over my head and tiptoed down the short hall to peek around the corner into the bedroom. He sat perched on the edge of the bed, staring at something clutched in his hands.

"You coming back?"

"I gave you this. I remember."

Inching around the doorframe, I eased into the bedroom and sat beside him on the bed. I pulled the stuffed pony he must have found in the drawer from his hands. "When you got accepted to SMU."

"I remember buying it, giving it to you after flying in from Dallas. You...." Turning, he leveled me with a hard, considering stare. "You were proud of me.

Believed me when I thought I could be more than what everyone expected of me. And I...."

"You promised you'd always come back for me."

The room's temperature dropped several degrees with the shift in his demeanor. Gently he pulled my forehead to his lips for a chaste kiss and took the stuffed pony from my hands. The mattress creaked as he stood and walked out the bedroom door, closing it behind him with a soft click without looking back.

Hot tears welled, but I held them in. Too many tears had been cried over that man. No more. But now the tears spawned from a new, different emotion.

For a man who had anything and everything he could ever want, I felt sorry for him.

Like a zombie, I brushed my teeth, stripped out of my jeans, and slid into the unmade bed. It was only early afternoon, but the roller-coaster emotions of the morning, plus the wine, pulled me into a deep sleep the second my head hit the pillow.

Chapter 9

Rebeka

A DELICIOUS SCENT CREPT into the bedroom and stirred me awake what felt like days later. A quick glimpse of the clock indicated it had only been a little over three hours since I lay down. Another waft of something yummy filtered through the room, urging me out of bed and toward the living room. I wasn't sure what to expect, but he came bearing food, so that was a positive sign. I eased into the living room where he lay on the couch, focused on the ceiling.

"Pizza's still hot," he said without looking over.

"Thanks, I'm starving." Not bothering with a plate, I grabbed a piece, flipped the cardboard lid closed, and took a bite. "Oh my goodness. Best pizza ever." After snagging a paper towel, I perched on a barstool and swiveled to watch him. It was only then that I realized he had on a shirt, which was crazy since I still wore the one he had on earlier, plus new shorts and tennis shoes. The man was decked out head to toe in Under Armour gear. "Did you go out?"

"Yep. I was hungry and decided to stop by Academy to get clothes that fit." His eyes shifted from the ceiling to me. "I left a note in case you woke up while I was gone."

"I would've gone with you."

"No, I needed to think." The deformed cushions of my old couch shifted and parted as he swung his legs over the side to sit up. Leaning forward, he clasped his hands between his spread thighs. "I remember. Everything."

A piece of hot cheese sucked down my windpipe. "Everything?" I asked between coughing fits. "You need to be more specific," I gasped.

"I stared at that damn horse."

"Pony."

He rolled his eyes and focused on his clasped hands. "I remember us. Remember our talks. And hell, Beks...." With a deep breath, he leaned back and closed his eyes. Our deep connection drew me from the stool to sit beside him. The muscles of his thigh bunched under the comforting hand I placed over it. "I remember what you told me about your dad."

With my free hand, I tucked a few strands of hair behind my ear and focused on his shoulder. "We didn't have very different childhoods. Yours was worse by far though. I never knew how you did it. Kept going back. Every summer, it took longer and longer for the real Brenton to break free."

"But I did."

"For me you did," I said with a smile.

"I need to know if remembering the past fixed me."

I shook my head and leaned back against the couch, putting our heads side by side. That close, his body heat seeped over, warming my chilled skin. "You were never broken. Did you turn the air conditioning down?"

"Yes, it was fucking hot in here."

"Dammit, Brenton, that shit is expensive."

"I told you I don't do uncomfortable if I can help it. I'll pay for the damn bill." He yanked me back to the couch when I tried to stand. "Sit down and piss me off."

"You're a selfish bastard for walking away from me half naked earlier."

Instead of pissing him off like I hoped, a smile pulled his lips up, popping that damn dimple. "Selfish bastard or gentleman. Could go either way."

"Fucking tease is what you are."

"Wow," he breathed. "You don't hold back, do you?"

"Guess that's another piece of me you haven't remembered yet. I'm pushy when I know what I want. I was the one who seduced you the first time we slept together. Before that I wasn't all innocent either, but that night I wanted more. You tried your best to hold back, you really did, but just like in the kitchen, I begged you. I wanted that connection between us."

I laced my fingers together and stretched them high above my head, arching my chest into the air.

"Except earlier had nothing to do with connection. It had everything to do with me being horny since our mind-blowing kiss last night, which became unbearable after seeing your tats this morning."

"Basically you were using me for my body."

I smiled and rolled my head to look at him. "You have a problem with that, flyboy?"

He barked a loud laugh and met my amused gaze. "The fuck? That's what they say to air force pilots."

My smile widened. "Oh well, I'm using it now. So, flyboy, you have a problem with me using your body?"

With a groan of frustration, he shoved off the couch and walked to the kitchen. "You want another slice?"

"Sure. Can you grab me a glass of tea too while you're in there? Oh, and another napkin. Mine is all greasy. Maybe I should use a plate."

His narrowed eyes locked with mine. "I offered to get you one slice, not the whole damn kitchen."

Even with his snarky comment, moments later he appeared from the kitchen, laid a plate on my lap with a large slice of pizza, a new napkin tucked on the side, and set a glass filled with my molasses tea on the side table. I allowed him to settle beside me before bringing up the question that had nagged at me since he'd deflected my earlier subtle one.

"Do you still want me to say something that will stress you out? Test this theory that remembering cured your head stuff?"

"Definitely. Piss me the fuck off. Which I know you can do."

Eyes on the greasy half-eaten slice of pizza, I said, "I feel like it was way too easy for you to walk away earlier." I picked a semi-warm pepperoni off the cheese and popped it in my open mouth. "And then when I woke up, I hoped you would be there beside me, ready to explain, but you weren't."

"It had nothing to do with me not wanting to spend hours kissing your naked body, believe me. But...." Summoning the courage to glance up through my lashes, I found his eyes closed. "After I saw that stupid pony you'd held on to for so long... I don't know, something shifted. The thought of being your relief lay didn't sit right. Not when we used to be so much more than that. And now I know. I know what we were. Who you are. I'll make up the past to you. Somehow I'll make up for lost time. I promise you that. What else? Tell me something terrible that I don't know. Tell me how we ended and why you hate me."

Really didn't want to bring that up, but he needed to know. Maybe saying it out loud would help me heal too.

"The scars you saw on my stomach earlier were from you."

A tremble started in his hands, which sent tea splashing down his wrist. Reaching across the couch, I grabbed the cup and set it on the carpet. His chest rose and fell at a rapid pace.

"Our last day together, we were in a car wreck. I won't tell you the circumstances or anything other than the basics right now. You need to remember the details surrounding that night on your own. My airbag burst, and the chemicals inside it attached to my tight shirt. Steam from the busted radiator or engine or something like that flooded the SUV. They said the heat caused a reaction with the chemicals." Reaching down, I raised the T-shirt. His eyes flicked over my mangled stomach before focusing on the wall across from the couch. "I had third-degree burns over 60 percent of my stomach and a little on my arms, but those aren't as noticeable anymore."

Chewing on my lower lip, I watched his chest heave faster and faster. The rough couch cushions brushed along my bare thighs as I adjusted to reach for him. I wrapped an arm around his broad shoulders and tried to pull him to me, but head in his hands, his posture remained stiff, unwilling to accept my comfort.

"You were knocked unconscious, or had just passed out—"

"Was I high? Did I cause the wreck?"

That was precisely why I didn't want him to push the topic too far. I didn't want to tell him, hurt him, but I had to. Maybe it would heal a piece of both of us. "Yes and no. If you hadn't been high, then maybe you wouldn't have lost control. But who knows."

"No wonder you resent me. I ruined your life. Hell, I almost took it."

The cup I pulled from the floor trembled in my hand. He had no idea the extent of my ruin from that night and what followed. But talking about it with him and seeing how distraught he was over the realization that he hurt me, the hate and resentment faded a fraction. There was still one question I needed an answer to for me to move on completely.

"B," I breathed. It was now or never. But he didn't respond. "B?" Instead of acknowledging me, his shoulders slumped forward and he crumbled to the side. "Brenton!"

The forgotten cup in my hand slipped to my lap, drenching me in tea. I raced to the kitchen, soaked a somewhat clean rag in cold water, and hurried back to the unconscious man on my couch.

Shit, he wasn't kidding about the blacking out episodes. It happened so fast that I didn't even know it was happening. How terrifying it must've been for him to have such little control over his own body.

"B," I whispered as I maneuvered him onto the couch, putting his head on the cushions and dangling his legs over the armrest. "Damn, you're massive. Come on, Brenton, wake up and help me move your fine ass." Still no response, but the rapid movement behind his closed lids sent a wave of relief, calming my tight nerves. "I don't blame you." I dabbed the cool cloth along his forehead. "I don't know if I ever really did. Everyone convinced me that you were the bad guy in it all. But were you? All they saw was the aftermath, the ugly side of who we were together, not the good. Not the two kids who gradually fell in love."

I took the faint moan that pushed past his soft, parted lips as a sign to keep going.

"What you remember me telling you about Daddy only got worse after the accident. The obvious disappointment and never living up to his standards when I did everything I could to make him proud. Getting that money and going to college saved me. I finished high school soon after the accident and bolted. I made friends who didn't know about my past, I dated, partied like every kid should when released from the clutches of their parents, but everywhere I went, you were there with me."

The rag slipped from my hand and fell to the floor with a soft thump. I traced the edges of his lips with the tips of my fingers, savoring each warm breath that brushed against them. With each pass, I inched my own lips closer and closer, needing to feel their softness against mine.

"Did you do it, Brenton? Did you choose your money over me? Or am I a fool of a woman, hoping for thirteen years that it was some misunderstanding, that someone talked you into it? I know you loved me and wouldn't have left us like that." I was so close that his breath warmed my cheek. My hands slid to hold his jaw, my lips hovering over his.

"I might hate you, Brenton," I whispered with my eyes closed, "but I love you more. I never stopped loving you, and maybe it's time I did. Then we can both move forward. I can move on."

Saying the words out loud sent a pang of heartache to clench my sad heart, but something else settled too. As difficult as it was, I pulled away from his paled face and picked up the cloth from the floor.

Minutes later, his green eyes fluttered open and fixed on me.

"I forgive you," I said with a teary smile. "For everything that happened. I'm sorry I held on to it for as long as I did, but I'm not anymore. I'm finally free from the constant anger and grief. Now that you remember, hopefully you can let go too."

He cupped my cheek and pulled my face to his chest. Tears spilled down my cheeks, leaving damp drops along his T-shirt. Needing to be closer, I wrapped my arms around his shoulders and squeezed until little air could fill my lungs.

Closure.

After thirteen years, I finally had it.

But which was worse: resenting him, or the loneliness that crept into the empty cavern in my heart left by the fading anger?

HOW IN THE HELL WOULD I explain the brand-new fantastic truck when we got back?

Daddy and Bradley would put me through rounds of interrogation the moment we pulled up. Who knew what they would say.

Not that I cared, of course. I was a grown woman, dammit.

Shit. And there was the issue of how to pull up in the new truck and get Brenton out unnoticed. He hadn't said a word since we left the apartment over half an hour ago. Who knew what was going on in that mind of his. Our earlier talk obviously gave him a lot to think over.

I flipped the blinker on to turn down our county road. Each tick of the signal in the silent cab increased my already rapid heart rate.

"I should just let him out here," I mumbled to myself. "Or give him the truck and I can walk." Nervous energy had me giggling at the thought. "I could die before I got there from heat exhaustion, but hey, it would solve my problem—"

"I'm sitting right here you know. Listening."

I slowed the truck to a stop and watched out the window as the dust from the road floated ahead of us in a big brown cloud. "I know, but this is my problem, not yours."

"What's the issue? Your dad? Brother?"

"Everyone," I said, still staring out the side window, pondering my options.

"I don't get it. Explain."

With a deep breath in, I shifted the truck into Park and swiveled in the brown leather seat to face him. "After the wreck, you had me sign something saying I wouldn't talk to you again, wouldn't seek you out, wouldn't sue the family. In return, you paid for my medical bills and a lump sum of $150,000."

"That's it?" He huffed a laugh and leaned against the door. "What a fucking cheap ass. I nearly kill you and offer up a hundred grand. No wonder you hate me."

"Yeah, completely about the money, jackass. Anyway, if I break the agreement, if people see us, then I'm scared I'll be forced to pay it back. And I can't." Reaching up, I tucked my unruly hair behind each ear. "I used it for school, all of it. Books, housing, classes, expenses. It ran out before I finished veterinary school, so I have a ton of student loans I'm still paying back. No way could I afford to pay that money back if I had to—"

"Fine."

"What?"

"Consider part of our new agreement that you'll help me, not caring who sees, and if it becomes an issue due to that old agreement, I'll pay what you owe."

"You already gave me the truck, which was too much anyway—"

"Why are you fighting me on this?" Brenton leaned forward to rest his elbow on the center console. "It's just money."

"Because I work for what I have. It's not much, but what I have is mine. Sometimes I feel... indebted to your family because of the money I took. It felt dirty."

Instead of responding, he leaned back in the seat, felt around the pocket of his shorts, and pulled out his phone. After pressing a few numbers, he held it to his left ear.

I opened my mouth to ask who he was calling but was hushed by a pointed look and a shake of his head.

"Landon. Graves. I need you to look into something for me. Thirteen years ago, I supposedly had the firm write up an agreement to keep a Rebeka Harding away from me. Locate it and email it to me. I want scans of the original documents, Landon. Make it happen."

The phone clattered into the cup holder between us. Mouth still gaping, I looked from the phone back to him.

"Now that's taken care of. I'll get to the bottom of it, but don't worry about the money or legal piece."

A weight I hadn't realized I'd been carrying around lifted. Gone. What felt like a great debt to his family washed away by a few words from Brenton.

Locked on those gorgeous, sparkling green eyes, I said, "But what if you remember why you created it in the first place?"

"Anything else I should know about that night?"

I forced my eyes not to show my deception and kept my breathing even. "No."

"Then we're good."

Unease at my lie roiled my stomach, making nausea bubble up my throat. It didn't matter. He wouldn't remember why we were in the car and where we were going. Right?

"Beks," he said with a frustrated sigh. "What else? Any other reason why you don't want people to see us together?"

My shoulders rose and fell in an exaggerated shrug as I concentrated on a seam along the leather seat.

"Good, because I'm holding you to helping me the next few days, and I don't give a fuck who sees us."

"Brenton—"

"And another thing. I accept what you said back in the apartment about you letting go of the anger and resentment. Fine, do what you need to do, but you're not moving on from me."

The confidence in his tone, the arrogance, willed my narrowed eyes up to meet his. "Is that so."

"You can let go of the Brenton you fell in love with years ago. I'll allow that."

"You'll allow it," I said through clenched teeth. "Who in the hell do you think you are?"

"The man who won't fuck up the only good thing in his life again. Once we get back, I'll change, then meet you in the barn. You're taking me on a personal reacquainting tour around the ranch this afternoon."

"Bastard. You're not even going to ask?"

An arrogant, cocky smile pulled at his full lips. Leaning back in his seat, he rubbed both hands down the soft leather. "Man, this is a nice truck, isn't it, Beks?" The pointed look he shot over left no room for questioning what he was alluding to.

I tightened my hands into fists, my nails biting into my palms. "Rotten bastard. You bought me this truck. I didn't ask for it."

"It's called leverage. If you want to win around me, better gain some. Quick."

Chapter 10

Brenton

I WASN'T ALWAYS AN asshole.

Fuck.

Maybe I was. The truck was a gift, not fucking leverage. But with her feisty mouth, she backed me into a corner, and I said what was needed to get out of it. If she didn't bend to my bossy ass, I'd leverage the damn truck that she couldn't stop smiling about to make her.

Damn, I was a dick.

Beks barely slowed the truck to a crawl in front of the main house before shoving me out the door. Which I had to admit was fucking hilarious. Only that woman would have the balls to pull that shit with me. That side of her was why I couldn't get enough, couldn't let her walk away, not yet. Not when the memories were coming back.

If all that made me a rotten bastard, as she called me, fine. I'm Brenton Graves, and I get what I want. And I wanted Rebeka Harding around more and more. And for some unknown reason, I needed her to love me again as she did years ago.

Okay yeah, that made me an asshole.

Guess I was finally living up to the family name.

But could someone fault a man for wanting one person on this earth to love him, to make him feel needed and wanted, like only a woman in love could? The surge of protectiveness and need to provide for her was foreign but welcomed. Hell, more than appreciated, it was fucking amazing. Never had a woman pulled that type of desire from me.

Using my teeth, I bit through the price tag on the shirt in my hands before slipping it on. Damn, the new clothes were comfortable. The jeans had room to move instead of the designer ones I had back in Dallas. Not that I wore jeans that much anymore. In Kentucky, it was all military-issued clothes around the base, and I could give two shits what I wore when I wasn't working.

The mattress molded beneath my ass as I bent over to pull the tall boot sock on.

What was it about her that I couldn't get enough of? The honesty, the crude mouth of hers, or the feeling of belonging and peace that settled in me every time she was around?

All I knew was I never wanted to feel the gut punch she'd landed this morning again. How could I forget nearly killing her? She said I was high, so it would make sense, but why was I in Odessa, and why was she in the car? There were still a lot of unknowns, and clearly she wasn't willing to help me remember. Who could blame her? No one would want to relive the moment they almost died and then were tossed aside by the man she loved and who she thought loved her.

One boot on, I stretched across the bed for the phone on the nightstand.

Damn, nothing from Landon.

I needed to see the document. Maybe reviewing the wording would help me remember why I signed it or confirm what I was almost sure of—that I didn't agree to or sign shit. The low dollar amount, the verbiage to stay away? That wouldn't have been me. Dad, fuck yes, but I hoped to hell I would've given the woman I loved more.

Which that was clear in my memories. I did love her. But was I *in love* with her was the question. And how did I feel about her now? We were kids, but there was no denying the strong pull we still had for each other. Hell, every time we were together, I was fighting an internal battle to keep my hands off her.

It didn't help that she was beautiful and somehow the sexiest woman without even trying. Her round, perky ass and curvy hips distracted me every time she moved. I'd had hot-as-sin models walk into my bedroom wearing see-through La Perla, yet somehow Beks earlier in granny panties and my too-large T-shirt had me harder than any of those women ever did.

After slipping the other boot on, I stood and balanced from one foot to the other, testing the comfort.

With all the uncertainty and hazy memories, there was one thing I knew for a fact.

I wouldn't let her slip away, not until I knew what this was between us and I had all the answers about that night.

And it might've made me an asshole, but I'd do whatever it took to keep her around until then.

Chapter 11

Rebeka

"YOU'RE TAKING ME ON a personal reacquainting tour," I mumbled and kicked a dried cow patty as hard as I could, sending it rolling a few feet to the right. "Asshole. Thinks he can boss me around. He's not the boss of me. I'm the boss of me."

The truth was I wasn't all that disappointed about the additional alone time with him. When we weren't talking about the past, when I wasn't being forced to remember, I had fun with him. A lot of fun. A few times the nasty nagging memories attempted to break through, but I pushed them away like I'd done for years now. And by the way his eyes would narrow when my mind drifted to what that wreck cost me, I knew he could see it, sense my mood shift.

Even if my loss was a direct result of his actions that night, I couldn't hold it against him. The man didn't remember a damn thing, so how was that fair to him? That's why I was moving on.

Moving on from the years of hurt, resentment, and, honestly, a little bit of self-loathing. And maybe I was letting go of the old Brenton. Based off what I'd seen the past twenty-four hours, young Brenton was long gone. Past Brenton was who left me lying in a hospital bed with nothing more than a few hurtful words from his father and a twenty-page legal document. The old Brenton chose his trust over us when ordered to make a choice.

This new and improved Brenton was stronger, sober, and intimidating as hell. Mix the new Brenton with the somewhat warm coals of feelings from the past and... well, I needed to keep my head on straight with him.

The guys I dated in school and the few after weren't like him—and not just compared to his ungodly good looks. It was his confidence, which drove me just as batshit crazy as it turned me on. The way he held a look longer than what was comfortable, or how he demanded things like the thought of someone not complying never crossed his mind.

Damn the demanding earlier.

A shiver shook my shoulders at the memory of his deep voice directing me to take off my pants before things went to shit.

There was also the way he moved and held himself, which told everyone in the vicinity he could hold his own.

All in all, Brenton Graves was perfect—besides being a royal asshole. Which actually made him hotter, as terrible as it was to admit.

I sighed and picked up a tumbling piece of trash from the grass.

We were good together back then, but with Brenton 2.0, we could be great. But he was going back to Kentucky, and I was staying here. He made that very clear.

End of story.

End of our story.

"Right," I muttered, then stormed through the wide-open doors of the barn, keeping my eyes to the ground. "Don't fall for him, you idiot woman. I bet he's terrible in bed or has some unknown STD that the doctors are still trying to cure. That's the real reason he wouldn't whip it out earlier. Gentleman, my ass."

"What did you just call me?" Bradley said from the other side of the stall he was cleaning.

With a curse, I stumbled back and pressed a hand over my racing heart. "Fuck, Bradley, you scared the hell out of me. Jackass. And I wasn't talking about you. I was talking to myself."

His gaze darted to the open barn doors and lingered. "What are you doing out here? Figured you went back to Midland considering Dad's hateful response to you sticking around."

I shrugged and leaned against the wall to peer over the side. A strong whiff of sawdust, horse manure, and urine filled my nose. "Nah, just had to run and get some clothes. I'm here for a few days." Brenton's comment on not caring who knew about our arrangement hummed in the back of my mind, but I said nothing. No need to bring it up until necessary.

Every few seconds, Bradley glanced back to the front door.

"You waiting for someone?" I asked.

"Nah, just wondering when you were leaving so I can get my shit done."

My brows pulled together as I watched him work. All these years of him using, I came to recognize the signs when something was up, and something was definitely up.

"Right," I muttered.

Again his gaze flicked up, but that time stayed. Craning my neck around to see what captured his attention I found Brenton marching through the doors, looking sexy as hell in his new ranch gear. Bradley probably wasn't taking in the stunning visual of pure masculinity, but I sure as hell was.

Damn. Wranglers looked good on him. And again with the visible tats. That man would be the death of my vibrator.

"What the hell is he doing here?" Bradley said loud enough for most of Texas to hear. "Want me to get rid of him?"

It had been a while since the overwhelming urge to hug Bradley had hit me, but his statement drove me around the stall door for just that. I wrapped my arms around him in a bear hug and squeezed. "Thanks, but he's the reason I'm out here. He wanted a tour of the ranch since it's been a while."

"Beka," he started, still focused on Brenton. "Is that a good idea? What that fucker put you through—"

"We're past it," Brenton said, now on the other side of the stall. "Good to see you, Bradley."

It took a few shakes, but Bradley finally broke out of my tight hold to grasp Brenton's extended hand. By Bradley's wide eyes, he was shocked at the gesture.

"No hard feelings, Mr. Graves—"

"Brenton."

"No hard feelings, Mr. Graves"—I hid my smirk behind an open hand at the look of annoyance Brenton gave my brother—"but you can shove it up your ass. I hope your dad does sell the place so we can get as far from your fucked-up family as possible."

My smirk fell as I stood motionless, shocked at Bradley. Without breaking eye contact with Brenton, Bradley threw down the shovel he was using, shouldered past Brenton, and stormed out.

"Beks." Brenton's cautious tone pulled my gaze from the doors to his green eyes. "It's fine. I deserved that. I might've treated you somewhat decent, but I do remember being a shithead to everyone else."

"It's how you broke your nose that summer," I quipped. "Your smart-ass mouth and cocky attitude got you in more fights than one around here."

"I admitted to being a shithead. Let's move on."

"But it's so fun helping you remember those parts."

He leaned against the stall and rolled his eyes. "That I remember just fine. It seems to just be you who has my memories hostage."

"Do you remember using Bradley as your drug connection when you and Caleb, and maybe your dad too, needed a fix?"

The way his features hardened told me he did.

"I have a lot of repair work to do with the people around here. Hopefully I can show them who I am without Dad's coke finger shoved up my nose. And the first person is you. Because honestly, you're the only one who matters."

"Me?" I squeaked.

"Yeah, you. I need you to see the man I am now instead of holding on to the memories of who I was and what I did. While we work on my fucked-up head, I'll prove I'm not that person anymore. By the time I leave, I'll make you see I'm the man you believed I could be."

"Why?" I said, near breathless. "You're leaving again. Why does it matter?"

"Because you do."

I swallowed back a lump of unshed tears and turned to pat the golden gelding in the next stall. Desperate to turn the heavy conversation, I shoved Brenton's shoulder and stepped out of the stall.

"Come on, fancy pants. Let's go on this 'tour' you ordered."

At my back, his low growl had the corners of my lips tilting up.

"These are fucking Wranglers. Stop it with the damn 'fancy pants.'"

"Wranglers with the tag still on 'em."

My deep, delighted laugh rattled through the open barn at his scowl before stopping to inspect his ass.

"There isn't... oh, you're going to get it."

I shot a wink over my shoulder. "Looking forward to it."

NEAR THE BACKSIDE OF the five-thousand-acre ranch, we spotted one of the longhorn herds grazing in the distance. We agreed a quick diversion was needed and pulled under a mesquite tree to watch the massive beasts for a while.

"Why vet school?" Brenton asked between long swigs from the Gatorade I'd packed us from the stocked fridge in the barn.

I shrugged and tossed my empty plastic bottle into the back bed. As I pulled my SIG from the dash, I said, "Guess I thought it would be the easiest transition, you know." Standing, I slid the holster on my hip and turned back to the cows. "I wouldn't know a thing about the corporate world, so business was out, and there wasn't anything else that drew my attention. I did well in my animal science classes, so I just went with it. That and...." I shoved off the John Deer Gator and looked back at him.

Attention fixed on me, he furrowed those dark brows. "And what?"

"I guess I wanted to prove to myself that I could do it. Maybe even try to make Daddy proud of me for something. What can I say, I'm a girl with daddy issues."

After a few steps, he fell into stride beside me. "I have a buddy in Kentucky who has 'daddy issues' radar. I swear that bastard can walk into any bar and pinpoint the girl who would go home with him that night."

"That's some superpower. You ever used him to find you a one-nighter?"

"Not answering that one."

"That's a yes. Watch for snakes," I said as I scoured the uneven ground. "Wish you would've brought a gun."

"I did," he said, like I'd somehow offended him.

I stopped mid-step and gripped the hem of his black dry-fit T-shirt. After an exaggerated look around his bare waist, I met his confused gaze. "And where is this mystery gun?"

"My boot."

"That's stupid."

He tossed his hands in the air. "And why the hell is that?"

"What will you do, tell the snake to hold on a second while you lift your pant leg, dip down into your boot, and pull the damn thing out? You'll have a hundred bites by the time you're ready to defend yourself."

Long, dark lashes fanned down to his cheeks with several considering blinks. "Touché." He reached down to draw up his pant leg and retrieve the gun.

Not letting the opportunity pass by, I cocked my head for a better angle of his ass while he readjusted his jeans around the boot.

"I thought I asked you to wear long sleeves," I mused, my eyes still trained on his firm, round backside. Damn, it truly was delicious. "You have an edible ass, you know that?"

Still bent over, he looked up with an arched brow. "Thanks? And I'd die of heat exhaustion out here in long sleeves. You trying to kill me?"

"Not before I use you for your body."

"Wow." He stood and tucked the gun into his waistband.

"What?"

"You're...."

"Honest?"

"Blunt."

"Same thing. Why not put it all out there?"

The herd didn't pay us any attention as we approached with caution. These beasts were beautiful—deadly massive, but beautiful—and you had to remind yourself of the dangerous part when you'd grown up around them your whole life. The soft nose of one of the older heifers nuzzled my hip, nearly toppling me over in a not-so-subtle request for me to pet her.

"What?" I asked after catching Brenton staring.

"I have something to ask you."

Resting my forehead against the coarse hair of the cow's neck, I sighed. "What?"

He massaged the back of his neck with a tight grip and eyes to the grass. "I have a few memories of women with me at my loft in Dallas. I don't remember when they are, as in time frame, but I do know it happened."

"Okay...."

"The thing is, I can't tell if it was during the time we were together or not. Was I that much of a shithead that I'd cheat on you?"

With a smirk, I peered over the tall cow's back. "No, B. I knew about the other women, but that was before we slept together. After that point, you said you didn't want to be with anyone else. But...."

"But what?"

I shrugged and continued to move through the cows with Brenton a few steps behind. "I never asked what you did when you weren't with me. When we took that step to sleeping together, I was seventeen and over six hours away. You were almost twenty-one, living a completely different lifestyle in college. I loved you, yes, but I wasn't under any pretenses of who you were in Dallas. Here you were mine, and there you were theirs."

"That's shitty."

"That was the fucked-up, complex shitshow we were."

Hands on his hips, he looked up with a pain-laced grimace. "I don't know if that makes me feel better or worse. How in the hell did you put up with my shit? Me saying I loved you but still sleeping around sounds like a pathetic excuse for a man."

"Boy. You were a boy. I was a girl who fell in love with you before you ever even noticed me. I was your dealer's little sister, the help. If it makes you feel better, you told me, a lot, that you didn't deserve a friend like me, someone who believed in you as wholeheartedly as I did."

"Fuck," he yelled as he dodged a massive horn.

"Don't yell at them," I admonished with a grin.

"He—" Bending below my line of sight, he stood a second later. "She, sorry, almost took off my head. They should pick on someone their own size, like a damn elephant."

"Well, maybe you should be more careful."

"How many do we have now in the entire herd?"

"Seven, eight hundred, I think? Not sure really, but it's grown over the past couple of years. Your grandfather stopped wanting to sell the babies." I shook my head and smiled at the cow in front of me. "He became softhearted toward the end."

"He was a good man," Brenton said so softly I almost didn't hear it over the quick burst of wind.

"He was."

"I noticed on the ride that most of the wells weren't active. Are they dry?"

"Nah, I don't think your place will ever be dry. They stop pumping when the price of oil drops below a certain dollar amount. When it jumps again, you'll see all of them moving."

Still smiling, I ran a hand down the cow's spine and moved deeper into the herd. Oil was how the Graves family made their fortune a generation or so back, and just like old oil money did, they kept getting richer and richer as the demand for it continued to rise. I didn't begrudge the family for it; this place was theirs, mineral rights and all. The story was Brenton's great-great-great-great-great-grandfather claimed it all those years ago when the land was still a part of Mexico.

A streak of something dark down the hind leg of a cow snagged my attention. Weaving between the massive beasts and their horns, I placed a comforting palm on the ribs of the injured female.

Careful to stay out of her kicking range, I inspected the wound. I angled my head side to side, the bright sunlight providing the perfect illumination to see four long, straight gashes down her hindquarters. The blood had turned dark and dry, signaling the wound was at least a day old. Only a few areas oozed clear fluid at that point.

From the looks of it, stitches weren't required, but she did need it cleaned and maybe a shot of antibiotics to ward off infection. Beside her, a baby calf considered me before dipping his head beneath her belly for a drink. My gaze stayed on the suckling calf. After as many births I'd helped with since graduation, you'd think I'd be over the mixed emotion. Which I was, I guess, with the birthing part, but watching the baby nurse, the natural beauty of a mom taking care of her offspring, opened an old, deep wound of my own.

"Everything okay?" Brenton asked from a few steps behind me.

I shook my head to dislodge my regretful thoughts. "She's hurt," I said over my shoulder. "From the looks of the claw marks, her gashes are from a big cat. I'd say a bobcat, but could be a cougar. I've heard reports of a few in the area. I bet she was protecting her little guy."

After a soft, loving pat down her side, I began searching for other injuries in the massive herd. A few looked like they'd battled with some barbed wire, but there was nothing like the gashes on the other, which solidified my initial thought of the momma protecting the only calf of the group. Through my inspection, I noted a few pregnant heifers, which meant new future prey for the unknown predator.

Someone had to stop the killer before those ladies gave birth.

Pausing in an ample open space, I wiped a layer of sweat from my forehead and lip with the hem of my shirt. Even with it being dry-fit, I'd sweated through the back. The heat index had to be over a hundred degrees even so late in the afternoon. I should've pushed back when Brenton suggested coming out, told him we'd do it tomorrow before the afternoon heat had a chance to turn the land into Hell's living room.

A loud, close rattle drew my attention to the ground.

And that was when I saw it—*them*—sending a bolt of pure fear straight to my core.

Chapter 12

Rebeka

FOUR LARGE DEVIL SPAWNS stared their evil beady eyes up from their perfect striking poses.

Shit. Shit. Shit.

Shit.

Two were well within striking distance while the others were far enough away that I didn't have to worry about them unless they were some snake gang and had planned an organized attack. Which I wouldn't put past them. They probably knew I was the girl who'd enjoyed using their family members as target practice growing up.

Close by, Brenton shouted, "What are you doing?"

"Trying not to hyperventilate and die. How about you?" His footsteps sounded closer and closer. "Stay where you are," I said, pure panic in my tone.

Breaking the staring contest with the closest rattlesnake, I glanced up to Brenton's confused face.

"Four rattlers. Two are close, too damn close. I think I peed my pants a little," I whined. I wasn't proud of it—the peeing of my pants or the whining—but I was scared. Terrified, really. Snakes were enemy number one in my book. Plus, I was running rogue these days without health insurance and couldn't afford a trip to the emergency room for antivenom.

"And you were just reaming my ass about watching where I walked."

"If I live through this, I will punch you in the balls for the jackass timing of that comment."

His chuckle inched up my nervous anger.

"This isn't fucking funny. I'm going to die a slow miserable death, and you're fucking laughing."

His loud laugh reached my ears as he walked into the small clearing. At my back, Brenton wrapped his hands around my waist. I tensed at the contact, which made the snakes rise higher.

"It's okay, Beks. You're fine."

"Shoot. Them."

"I'd prefer not to get trampled to death. I didn't survive multiple deployments to die out here."

Dammit, he was right. But still, they were snakes, live ones that needed to be vanquished.

At first I fought his slight pull urging me back, but then I gave in to the comfort of his protective grip and calm, soothing orders.

"Easy. Slow steps, okay? Right foot. Good. Left foot. Now pause." There was no way he couldn't feel the way my entire body trembled in fear. "Beks, come on. You're fine. I'm here, and I won't let anything bad happen to you, okay?" Two more steps back. "If the snake does get to you, I'll suck the venom out." Another step back and my shoulders dropped from their high perch by my ears. "Is it bad to hope they bite you in the pussy so I can have a reason to suck on that for a while?"

And just like that the fear drained, sending my blood pumping fast and hot for an entirely different reason.

"You don't need a snake bite for that, B. All you have to do is ask." His hands still on my waist, we ducked and weaved as one between the longhorns. "But before you ask, let me shower. I wasn't kidding about me peeing my pants."

Fine lines burst from the corners of his eyes with his broad smile. "Deal."

Over the next hour, we drove through the remainder of the beautiful property, checking out a few areas even I hadn't seen since I was a kid. A few times he'd point to something and ask about a memory, wondering if it was true, which would launch me into a story about us. It was perfect with the brilliant sunset off the horizon that painted bright colors across the open sky. But then again, it was always perfect when it was only us two. It wasn't until other people got involved that everything went to shit all those years ago.

A dark SUV pulled away from the barn as we grew close. With my brows raised at the unfamiliar car, I shot a quick, concerned glance to Brenton. He merely shrugged and went back to watching the sunset. Even though he thought nothing of the incident, a slight uneasy feeling developed in my gut.

The sensation worsened as we eased into the barn and parked in the spot reserved for the Gator. I shut off the engine and paused. Not sensing the same thing, Brenton slid off the bench seat and stretched out his stiff back, turning when I didn't follow. He gripped the roof to lean into the cab, momentarily distracting me with his inked, flexing biceps and spread muscled chest.

"You coming?"

"Yeah. Hey, I want to get that damn cat before the other calves are born. I might go out tonight to see if I can get it myself. Wanna come with since we didn't work on your head stuff today at all?"

"Sounds like a party. We staying out all night?"

"Depends on the kitty, I guess. I'll pack enough food and drinks in case it turns into a long hunt. I'll double-check the weather too; I noticed a few thunderheads a ways west." After a glance at my watch, I looked back at him expectantly. "Let's head out after dinner. Two hours from now?"

He nodded but didn't make to move.

"What's wrong with you?" he asked with a single arched dark brow. "Something's off."

"Something's off in general. I don't know—"

My name said in a deep, painful moan cut me off. Both our heads whipped in the direction of the sound. In sync, we withdrew our guns and walked toward the other end of the barn with near-silent steps.

Another agony-laced groan tugged at my gnawing gut. I licked my dry lips and glanced to Brenton, whose intense focus was on the closed tack room door.

My sweaty, unsteady hand gripped the metal handle as I again regarded Brenton, hoping for direction. In response, he raised his gun, stepped forward with a confidence I didn't have at the moment, and nodded.

After a deep, steadying breath in, I jerked the door wide open. Brenton moved through first, gun at the ready.

"Bradley?" he said once inside.

My held breath whooshed from my lungs. I holstered the pistol as I stepped around Brenton and fell to my knees beside my barely recognizable brother.

"Bradley?" I whispered, raising a hand to touch his bloody and bruised face, but pausing inches from his cheek. "I need a clean rag," I demanded to the looming presence at my back. "No, wait. We need to get him out of here."

I shoved off the stained concrete floor in search of a cart of some kind, only to have Brenton shoulder around me. In one smooth motion, he squatted beside the still-moaning Bradley, slid his arms beneath his shoulders, and set him up to adjust his grip. Snapping out of my daze, I bent down to help him pull Bradley up to a somewhat standing position, but my brother collapsed in our grasp. I tucked my shoulder under one armpit before he could fall face-first to the ground while Brenton did the same on the other side.

Each short step we dragged him sent Bradley's limp head lolling from side to side.

"Any idea what happened?" Brenton asked almost halfway to the house. By the way he kept leading our trio and his steady, even breaths as he talked, Brenton wasn't as taxed by hauling a grown-ass man as I was.

"Guess," I started, out of breath, "something to do with that SUV and... stop. I need to stop."

"No need. You're slowing me down more than helping anyway." He didn't conceal his taunting smile as he wrapped an arm around Bradley's waist in replacement of the help I was offering. "Knowing how to haul a grown man fully loaded down with gear out of harm's way is military 101. We perfect it in boot camp."

Right. New Brenton was a soldier.

A sexy soldier.

Summoning the little energy I had left, I jogged to the truck as I asked over my shoulder, "You did remember to get my gear out of the old truck before you sold it, right?"

The incredulous glare he shot back had me running faster. By the time I had the bag filled with various bandages and supplies, Brenton was climbing the front porch, hauling Bradley up stair by stair.

My stomach dropped at the squeak of the screen door opening and the sight of the man standing in the doorway.

Great, just what we needed.

"Rebeka, what the hell did you do?"

"What did *she* do?" Brenton grunted, stopping a foot in front of Daddy. By his flushed cheeks and sway, he'd already had too much tonight. "You think your daughter is capable of beating your son to shit?"

"Mr. Graves," Daddy grumbled in greeting. "This is none of your concern. Sorry my daughter dragged you into another family drama. Leave the boy here and we'll take care of it."

It, not him.

It.

I held my breath, waiting for Brenton's response.

"I'm right where I need to be." With that, he shoved past Daddy into the house.

"Second room on the right," I said at his back. A vice grip around my bicep held me just over the threshold.

"What happened?" Daddy seethed inches from my face in a spray of beer and saliva.

"I don't know. I wasn't there. Now let go of me."

His grip tightened instead. "Your little incident with that boy almost ruined my job here before. Don't fuck it up again." Instead of releasing my arm, he gave me a hard shove, forcing me to stumble a few steps.

I shouldn't care what he thought or said. Shouldn't give a rat's ass about his words or his tone or his annoyed look. But he was my dad. How could I not?

Tears welled as I shuffled back to Bradley's bedroom. Before stepping inside, I stood outside the door to shake out my trembling hands and take a deep breath to face Brenton.

His intense, narrowed green eyes greeted me the second I entered and tracked my every movement toward the bed where he'd laid Bradley.

"Beks." The restrained anger in that one word wrenched my wounded heart.

"It's fine," I whispered.

"It's not fucking fine."

"Not now. I need a few wet rags to get the blood off. It looks like his cheek split, but that's all I can see at this point." Behind me, he lingered close a few seconds before squeezing my shoulder and disappearing out of the room. "What happened to you?" I whispered to my unconscious brother.

A minute later, cool droplets of water coursed down my back. Without turning, I reached for the rag, which Brenton gently sat in my waiting palm. Each swipe of the clean cloth across Bradley's face revealed a different cut or bruise. Across his right cheekbone was the deepest gash; everything else was superficial, but it would take several days before he'd be able to see from his right eye or move without terrible pain.

Not daring to stitch him up without numbing medicine, I placed several Steri-Strips along the gash to close it as tight as possible. Brenton stayed silent as he played nurse, taking the dirty rags and returning with clean ones. Not once did Daddy come in to check on the progress.

Finished with doctoring his face, I prodded along his collarbone, checking for breaks before moving down to his ribs. A few places I poked drew a gasp or moan.

"A few cracked ribs, but nothing is broken that I can tell."

The brooding man in the corner gave no response.

"I don't know what's going on. Ryder mentioned some people were looking for him, but I didn't think—"

"Didn't think I needed to know that? Hell, Rebeka. Those men were here. They were near you. What if you hadn't been out with me? What if you'd been in that barn when...?" Not finishing, he turned to glare out the window.

"I'm sorry."

"You're sorry." His sarcastic tone reopened the wound Daddy had left.

"I'm a disappointment. I get it. Don't have to remind me."

He was at the window one second, then had me in his arms, pressed against his hard chest the next. Not caring about how I smelled or the blood still on my hands, I wrapped my arms around his waist and held him even tighter than he held me.

"That's not what I'm saying, Beks. You've never disappointed me. I'm pissed those men were on my property and I didn't do anything about it. Now you're in danger and...." His chest ballooned out with a deep breath. "I'll hire a security firm tomorrow. No one gets on this property without approval. I can't do much after I'm gone, but I can at least do this to protect you."

Right. For a minute there, safe in his arms, I'd forgotten.

Releasing my hold, I stepped back and tucked a lock of hair behind my ear.

"What that fuck?" said a loud, angry voice from the doorway.

Our wide eyes focused on Kyle scowling from the doorway.

"The hell are you doing here?" I stepped farther out of Brenton's hold, which he noted with a directed scowl.

I rolled my eyes to the ceiling. Enough of these men today.

"Me? What the hell is *he* doing here?"

The two men moved toward each other.

Instead of watching the pissing contest that was about to commence, I stepped between them with both arms outstretched. "Stop it, Kyle. He helped me get Bradley in here and while I fixed him up. Now answer me, what the hell are you doing here? Where's Ryder?"

Still glaring at Brenton, Kyle inclined his head out the door. "Your dad called me. Said you needed help, and I was close by."

I tossed both arms in the air and cursed, startling both men.

"Why in the hell did he call you?" Brenton asked while keeping a cautious eye on me.

"Because Daddy wants me to marry someone like Kyle. Hell, maybe even Kyle himself." Kyle gave a nervous laugh while Brenton stayed stone-faced. "I've passed my time of finding a good husband, and I'm nothing without one of those. So there you have it. I have a fucking degree from Texas A&M, and I'm nothing without a set of balls by my side guiding me through life."

"Ah, Beka—"

I cut Kyle off with a raised hand. "I'm over this." Cutting my eyes to Brenton, I nodded in the direction of the barn. "Be ready in thirty minutes if you still want to come with me tonight. If not, I'll see you when I see you."

Chapter 13

Brenton

DAMN, THAT WOMAN WAS stronger than most men I knew.

On their own, my gaze fell to Beks's ass as she stormed out of the room, shoving past the Kyle guy. I needed to figure out what was going on with her dad. The fucker would find his ass out on the street if he touched her like that again. Can't believe Pappy kept a bastard like him around.

After she was out of sight, I glanced up only to find the asshat staring me down.

"What?"

"Stay away from her," he said with a hint of anger. "You did enough damage the last time around. I'm not going to sit back and watch you do it again."

"What's going on between us is our business. Stay the fuck out of it. Now, what do you know about the guys who did this?" I asked with a nod to the unconscious man on the bed.

For the first time since he walked in, Kyle's eyes dropped. Watching the carpet, he shifted on his boots. "I don't know if I should tell you, but hell, you might be able to solve the problem. Through my sources, I've heard Bradley here owes his suppliers some money. And rumors are some of what he owes is left over from your brother."

A knot built in my gut and tension crept up my spine. "How much?" I gritted out. Shit, I could not pass out. Focusing on the wall behind the idiot, I took a deep, calming breath in.

"I'm not sure on the exact amount."

Deep breath out.

"Ballpark it," I said through clenched teeth, making it sound more like a hiss.

"Over ten grand. Hey, man, you okay?"

Fuck.

The edges of my vision darkened, and I leaned against the wall to use it for support. "Fine. Didn't drink enough water today, I guess. Fucking hot out there."

"That's a Texas summer for you."

"I'll cover what he owes, but I need to know who they are." Thinking back to Beks and how those men could've been there when she was made the tension worse. "I'll make the payment and make it clear that if they step one foot on my property again, I'll shoot first."

"And ask questions later."

"No. Bury their asses where the cows will shit on their graves."

A small smile pulled at the guy's lips. "Damn. I might like you after all, Graves. But you do know that girl out there is stubborn as hell and won't let Bradley take your money."

No shit. Thinking through the different ways to present the option to Beks lessened the darkening fog. Wow, just thinking about her cleared everything, which meant whatever was going on with my head was tied to her, but more than just our past because I'd remembered that part. Well, most of it. There were still pieces I didn't know.

I glanced at my watch and cursed. If I was going to make her new time frame, I had to hustle.

"I'll make it work. Listen, watch him and don't let that bastard of a father in here." At the door, I gripped the frame and turned to look over my shoulder. "She won't tell me everything about what happened. Can you fill in any of the gaps?"

Kyle looked past my shoulder into the empty hall. "All I know is for some fucked-up reason she's still hung up on you. What happened that night is y'all's story, not mine. She'll tell you when she's ready." He paused to look me straight in the eye. "When she is, you better be ready to hate yourself as much as we all do."

Chapter 14

Rebeka

BRENTON MUST HAVE SENSED my foul mood, as not a word was spoken while we packed up the supplies and coolers in the Gator before heading out a little over thirty minutes ago. The last of the sun's rays had dipped beneath the horizon, cloaking the property in the unending darkness. Dark clouds sprinkled the sky, but a few patches of stars still shone through.

Sliding a hand off the wheel, I cradled my growling stomach. Skipping dinner in exchange for the time to take a shower was not the brightest idea I'd ever had. But a tiny piece of me hoped Brenton would make good on his promise from earlier, so a shower was the priority over food just in case. Having his gorgeous face between my thighs would make this never-ending day a lot less awful.

To the east, flashes of light sparked across the sky, amplified by the billowing thunderheads. The weather channel reported the storms would stay east of us by a few counties, so we would be okay—if they were right for once.

"Is it as pretty up there as it seems it would be?" I asked, breaking our comfortable silence and nodding to the sky. "Not sure how it would be possible."

He sighed and leaned back to perch his new boot on the dash. "Hard to believe, but yeah, it is. At sunset, it's almost like you can reach out and run your fingers through the colors pouring through the clouds."

"Do you like it? The flying?"

"I like the control and sense of accomplishment it provides, plus the pride in serving my country. Every deployment, every successful mission... I can't describe the feeling. It just feels fucking fantastic, like nothing can touch me. It's how I used to feel at the height of a high."

My grip tightened on the steering wheel to maneuver the deep hog ruts in the makeshift road. "So you traded one high for another."

"I guess, but this one isn't illegal or harmful."

I lifted a shoulder in noncommittal agreement. "Maybe. Depends on what you have to keep doing to get to that high. How many more times will you reenlist? What will happen if you can't?"

His lack of response told me he'd never thought of it that way.

"You mentioned you like control," I mused.

"I don't like control. I need it."

"Why?"

"Because I remember what it's like to have none, and I won't let that happen again."

"I can see that. Wonder if maybe Caleb's death left you feeling helpless because you couldn't stop it, couldn't control the outcome. Not only that, but you weren't there when it happened, which made you feel even more impotent."

"Choose a different damn word."

The Gator bounced down the temporary road, shifting us side to side. Our thighs brushed, sending a jolt of warmth to spread. Damn, I was so on edge that if he just kissed me, I might explode.

"Fine," I said with a grin. "That could be it, but there's only one way to find out, and I have an idea."

He groaned and let his head fall back against the hard seat. "I don't know if I can take any more revelations from you today."

My growing smile fell.

If he only knew.

"Hey." Reaching over, he grabbed my upper thigh and gave it a tight squeeze. "I didn't mean that. You can tell me anything. I'm dramatic."

"Can I get that on record?" I chuckled. "Fancy pants and dramatic. You've been in Dallas too long."

Instead of pulling his hand away, he inched it higher and slid his fingers inward to tuck them between my pressed thighs.

Hell.

"How can we test this theory of yours?"

The tip of my ponytail swiped across my shoulders as I shook my head and pointed ahead. "We're almost there. Let's set up, eat something before I gnaw my arm off, and then we can test my theory."

I parked the Gator at the edge of the herd we'd been with earlier and slid out to get the gun set up.

"That's one sweet weapon," Brenton said in awe as he took the AR from my hands. "Is that a night vision scope?"

With a nod, I gently pulled it from his grasp and went back to situating the muzzle on the end of the barrel. "And a silencer. Wild hogs have become a problem on the property the past few years, and this gun, plus the gadgets, help Bradley take down several a night instead of one or two. It's the only way to attempt to control their growing population."

The hard plastic of the tailgate dug into my ass as I situated myself to reach into my cooler.

"I can feel it," Brenton said beside me.

As I dug through the contents of my hastily packed cooler, I said, "What's that?"

"The peace being out here offers." He flicked on a flashlight, momentarily blinding me. "If you're hungry, I had Mrs. Hathway pack extra food. I assumed you weren't in the mood to eat earlier after patching up your beat-to-hell brother."

I eyed the contents of my cooler again. An old package of Pop-Tarts, a half-opened bag of chips, peanut butter crackers, and five packages of Little Debbie Zebra Cakes stared back at me. His light moved to my face, and I shielded it from my eyes with a raised hand. "Yeah, that'd be great. I didn't pack as much as I thought I did."

As he pulled out the two sandwiches and waters, I kicked my legs back and forth beneath the tailgate and smiled in the dark. His warm hand lingered on my lap when he set the food down.

At the first bite into the homemade club sandwich, a moan escaped around the somehow still crispy bread.

"Did you moan about a sandwich?"

Between ravenous bites, I said, "It's like a fucking orgasm of flavors in my mouth. Damn, I wish I was rich."

His loud laugh echoed through the sparse trees and caught on the breeze. "An orgasm of flavors." He chuckled and took another bite of his sandwich.

I flipped the flashlight off and looked up to the cloudy sky. "Huh."

"What?" he asked around a mouthful of food.

"The clouds seem to be getting closer than I expected. Are you ready for my enlightening thought on your condition now?"

"We're hunting a cat. Shouldn't we, I don't know, stay quiet?"

"Fine," I grumbled as I polished off the sandwich and tossed the trash into my cooler. Using my palms as leverage, I scooted back into the bed to lean against the cab. AR resting on my lap, I became transfixed on the surrounding darkness, looking up every so often to the few visible stars.

"I wonder if the stars are up there talking about us."

"Huh?"

"The stars. Some of them are old enough to remember us doing this as kids. I wonder if they're up there jumping up and down that we're back enjoying the peace they offer for free, or if they're turning their back and pouting because we've been away for so long, taking their eternal beauty for granted."

Another gust of wind whipped around us, shifting my hair to the side and sending a chill down my bare arms.

"I think," he said after settling beside me, "they're proud they can still burn bright for people like us. Kids who grew up needing their light and have come back to appreciate them, maybe even thank them."

As we sat there gazing, more clouds rolled in, covering what few stars were left for us to watch.

"Between your dad and mine, we used those stars, didn't we?" I breathed.

We both paused at a loud snap nearby. Gun pressed against my shoulder, I situated the night vision scope against my eye and swept the area, searching for the source.

"Huh." I set the gun down across my lap and leaned forward for the flashlight. Shining it toward the herd, I showed Brenton what I'd seen and found odd.

The entire herd was lazily moving as a group toward the direction of the main barn.

That was when I felt it. A low pulse settled in the back of my skull at the quick barometer shift just as the wind shifted with a strong gust.

"Fuck," I shouted and jumped from the Gator to dismantle the gun accessories. "We need to get out of here. The damn weather guys got it wrong. Again."

Another gust of mighty wind blew, sending Brenton jumping from the bed to help. With the gun safely packed away and everything covered in the back, I slammed the tailgate shut.

The first drop of rain hit my forearm as I climbed into the passenger side of the Gator.

"I don't think we have time to get back to the barn," I yelled over the rumble of thunder and now howling wind. A bolt of lightning several miles away zipped down, lighting up the sky. "We need to find cover away from the river in case of a flash flood."

"Where?" Brenton shouted back as he turned the key.

"There's a little shelter for this kind of thing." Glancing down at the compass on my watch, I pointed west. "That way."

It only took a few minutes to get there, but by the time we made it to the basic structure, the lightning had grown close and filled the sky with quick, jagged bolts. Sheets of rain pounded against the thin tin roof above us seconds after we pulled in. With the earlier snake scare still fresh in my memory, I spotlighted every inch of the dusty floor—twice—before stepping out.

Brenton stood along the front of the shelter with his shoulder pressed against a support beam, watching the downpour. A cool mist blew in, leaving a damp sheen along my exposed arms and face. Even with the warm temperature, a shiver shook my shoulders at the contrast between the two.

Another spark of lightning illuminated the sky, followed by a resounding crack of thunder.

"You learn to have a healthy respect for storms like this as a pilot. They can pop up anytime, or sometimes you even have to fly directly into one to complete a mission." He sighed and cracked his knuckles. "I miss it. Miss them, my brothers. But...." The next flash of lightning showed Brenton's attention fixed on me instead of the storm. "This, us, will be a challenge to walk away from. Maybe me not remembering was my mind's way of protecting myself from the greatness of what I had to leave behind to outrun my addictions. But which was the greater cost? Losing the addictions, or losing you?"

The thud of the tailgate falling was eliminated by the pounding rain all around us. Situating myself on the edge, I kicked my boots under me and focused out into the darkness. "You chose the route that cost less monetarily. But think about this—you also wouldn't be here right now if you hadn't walked away. You can't make amends dead. And that's what would've happened. Just look at your brother. Look at what almost happened to mine."

"About that." The Gator jostled under his massive weight as he sat to my right. "I'm paying off the money Bradley owes, and you're not going to say two shits about it. It was Caleb's debt, and I won't allow your brother, or you, to pay for it."

"Fine," I grumbled. "Figured that was coming, so I'd already mentally prepared myself for it."

His shoulder nudged mine. "Something tells me you like orders more than you let on."

A broad smile he couldn't see broke across my cheeks. "You have no idea, but hopefully, one day, you will. Now that we aren't hunting and we have some time on our hands, I'll tell you the revelation I had on your head stuff earlier. This will be hard to hear for someone like you, so prepare yourself."

The bed shifted beneath us as he wiggled around. Light from the next flick of lightning revealed him on his back, a hand tucked behind his head.

"Ready as I'll ever be. Hope this works."

My fingers skimmed across the rugged plastic in search of his. I sealed my eyes shut when my fingertips touched the soft skin of his forearm. Up and down I brushed along the solid muscle, savoring each inch. Reaching his fingers, I laced his with mine and set our connected hands on his strong thigh.

"Here it goes. You actually have zero control over the things you think you do." His fingers tightened around mine, cutting off the circulation. "I know that's hard to hear, but for a control freak like you, you're under this false sense of security that you can control outcomes, control other people's actions. You have to let go of the weight you're carrying from Caleb's death. It wasn't your fault, Brenton. Caleb made his own choices, just like you did. Just like I did. The only control in this world we truly have is in what we say, how we make others feel, our thoughts and actions. Outside of that, no one has control. No one. Not even rich, arrogant men like you. Stop fighting it. Accept it and try to move on."

The near-deafening beat of the rain around us filled the small space.

"I could've done more," he choked out. "Hell, I have more money than most countries and still.... Maybe if I wouldn't have left—"

"Stop. You think you had control over the outcome, over your brother's actions? You didn't. It was all Caleb's choice. You loved him and didn't give up on him. That's all you could do." Ass growing achy, I stood and maneuvered my hips between his spread knees. "You know how, before takeoff, the flight attendant says, 'Put your oxygen mask on before assisting others—'"

"Do they say that?"

"Seriously? You've never listened?"

"I've never flown commercial. It's either been private or military for me."

"Wow. Skip fancy pants. You just moved yourself up to Sir Fancy Pants. Anyway, yes, they do say that. At least they did the one time I flew. And that's what you did when you left. You put your mask on first. You can't save someone if you're suffocating too. And not only that, B. You can give someone the mask, but you can't make them breathe."

"I'm just so fucking angry. Angry at myself, at Dad—hell, at the world. I don't know how to let it go. Every time I think about my past—"

Gripping his thighs, I squeezed them hard to get him to stop talking. "Brenton, your past does not define you. My past sure as hell doesn't define me. It molded us, yes, but it's not who we are now. For me, being the brunt of Daddy's frustrations and the cause of everything wrong in the world isn't who I am, but it made me stronger, I think."

Damn, this was confusing. When did it become my therapy session too?

"Beks," he said, barely louder than the pounding rain.

I shifted closer to his lips, my heart hammering against my chest at our proximity and position. "Yeah?"

"Don't take this the wrong way, but I don't think I'll ever recover from this."

Chapter 15

Rebeka

A BOOMING POP OF THUNDER had the small shelter shuddering. I jumped out of reflex and turned to gaze into the pitch-black night to avoid the emotions his words invoked.

"Sorry," I said, shifting to lean my ass against the tailgate. "Thought it would help."

Wide hands slid up the back of my arms, creating goose bumps in their wake. A small gasp escaped past my lips at his warm breath against the sensitive skin of my neck.

"Not that. This, being with you. How do I walk away from someone as amazing as you?"

My next word was out before I could think better of it. "Don't."

"I have to." A gasp pushed past my parted lips at the brush of his against the shell of my ear. "I don't want to hurt you again."

"I'm a big girl now, B. I can handle myself, and this time I know you're leaving. Last time it was a shock, and I resented you because I expected more."

"Is this you giving me permission?" he whispered into my hair with a deep inhale.

The utter darkness enveloping us hid any lingering anxieties I had. In that shed, I could have the fantasy nights I'd dreamed about the past several years. Would I regret it? Probably, but then again, I'd regret not having this moment with him just as much.

"This is me begging you."

There was no holding back my throaty groan of pleasure at his teeth nipping my earlobe.

"There's still so much I want to know."

His roaming hands skimmed down my waist. Unabashed desire flooded my veins at the sensation of burning heat that soaked through from his chest to my back. Eyes shuttering closed, I relished in each inch of skin he touched.

"We still have time," I breathed. No way could we stop now to chat.

The soft tip of his tongue lazily skimmed down the length of my neck, pausing at my collarbone before sucking the delicate flesh between his lips. My hands tightened around his thighs to steady my trembling legs.

His deep, commanding voice ordered, "Turn around."

A quick, irrational thought floated through of disobeying to see what happened, but instead I willingly complied, eager to keep the passion between us rising.

All around us, the strong summer storm raged, shaking the shed with the mighty wind and rain. But here with him, between his thighs, being cherished by his tongue and hands, I felt safe. Protected.

I faced him in the dark, the need to touch him bringing my hands up his chiseled chest and down his strong arms, savoring the taut muscles beneath my palms.

Brenton's demanding hands massaged up the back of my thighs to grasp my ass. My entire body trembled at his deep groan of ecstasy when he had a handful of each cheek. Callused skin scraped my overly sensitive flesh as he dipped under my T-shirt. Too dark to see his beautiful face, my eyes shuttered closed to savor the intimate caress of his hands on my body.

The soft cotton of my T-shirt tugged over my head, followed by my sports bra. Mist from the wind and rain coated my bare back. With the coolness behind me and his heat at my front, the overwhelming sensation of the opposites had me swaying between his thighs.

Blindly I searched for the hem of his shirt; it only took a single tug for him to release his hands from my body to help finish pulling it over his head. Two hands encased my face, stroking my cheekbones with the pads of his thumbs before pulling me forward, sealing our lips against the others.

Hot and desperate, we latched onto one another. Every ounce of passion and lust boiled over, heating the small shed. His tongue danced with mine, teasing and flicking along the roof of my mouth. Each glide gave a tasty hint to what it could do elsewhere.

Damn, the man knew how to kiss.

A sigh pushed from my mouth to his, and I felt the corners of his lips pull up in a smile.

Loosening his hold on my cheeks, Brenton skimmed his fingertips down to my bare chest. He palmed each breast, torturing thumbs flicking over both peaked nipples and forcing a gasp of surprise as I pulled back an inch. Again those lips stretched to a small smile. On repeat, he flicked harder and smoothed over the small hurt with the soft pads of his thumbs.

The relentless throb between my legs turned demanding. In search of anything to relieve the pressure, I inched deeper between his spread thighs. Like he could sense what I needed, he tugged behind each of my knees, urging me up to straddle his lap on the tailgate.

Fuck yes.

The moment I settled over him, spreading my knees as wide as I could to press down against his stiff jeans, Brenton's passionate, desperate kiss resumed. Not holding back, I skimmed my fingertips up and down his arms, then dove into his short dark hair. With a tight grip on the longer section, I gave it a slight tug.

"Fuck, Beks," Brenton growled against my lips. With a hard shove off the Gator's bed, he stood with me wrapped around his waist to flip our position. His firm, gentle hands guided me back until I lay flat against the bed liner.

First my right and then left boot fell to the dirt with a thump. My heart and breathing stilled at his fingers pulling around the button of my jeans before turning his attention to the zipper. Using my back as leverage, I arched up to make it easy for him to pull off my jeans and underwear.

"Damn, I wish I could see you," he muttered against the inside of my thigh as he kissed his way up to the apex. I savored the blindness the darkness offered; he couldn't see the scars I was still self-conscious of when naked in front of a man. The rough bed liner scraped at my back as I squirmed in need. "I want to see every beautiful inch of your amazing body. I want to bite every perfect damn inch."

"Yes," I encouraged.

"I'll mark you as mine and mine only. Feet on the tailgate, baby, and don't move."

I complied, resting socked heels on the edge of the metal and widening my knees. The first swipe of his tongue liberated all the pent-up tension from the day's events. When he sucked that tiny part of me between his lips, everything but us was swallowed up by the darkness. Desperate for more, I scooted farther down the tailgate, pushing myself into his mouth.

"That move I'll allow." He laughed and gripped my hips tight enough to leave bruises along the skin.

I groaned as one finger slid inside, then moaned louder than the thunder when a second followed while his tongue and lips worked me just above. His free hand pinched a pebbled nipple just as he sucked hard. A tornadic release barreled out, forcing a garbled version of his name through my lips. My back arched off the bed, but he held my hips tight, continuing to work his magic through it all.

Seconds, maybe minutes later, when I could focus back on reality, the rain was only a slight trickle outside the shed.

Wow.

When was the last time I'd had a soul-crushing orgasm like that without the assistance of a toy?

As I continued taking in deep, calming breaths, his slick lips skimmed up my stomach to linger over mine.

"This is something I'll always remember. You, your sounds, taste, and smells, the storm. Everything combined makes it a dream I never want to wake from."

His scruff-covered cheek scraped along my palms. "Me either." I drew him close for a kiss so gentle, so loving, as happy tears dampened my lashes.

Dammit, what was I doing? I was setting myself up to fall over again by getting more wrapped up in him than he was with me. I was a fool, but hell, it could be fun while it lasted.

Damn the consequences of enjoying this limited time with him. I was already in too deep to try and back out now. He was leaving, and I was staying. That was that. Maybe he'd learn the truth about that night. Perhaps he wouldn't. None of it mattered at that moment. What did matter was his sculpted bare chest pressed against mine and our lips sealed together, savoring our perfect moment like two people desperately in love.

Three more days.

I could protect my heart from new Brenton for three more days.

He could use my body—and holy hell, I hoped he would—but my heart was mine. And I'd do whatever it took to protect it from him.

THE SUN SHINED IN FULL force through the cheap blinds and thin curtains, burning into my exhausted eyes when I turned in the bed. Instead of popping up for the first cup of dark bliss, I flung the light blanket back over my head and rolled over with a groan of annoyance.

Tired.

Way too tired to even think of leaving the bed.

It was around three in the morning when we made it back to the barn. Then we had to unload, plus a quick shower, which put me rolling into bed around four.

Our night together couldn't have played out any better than it did. After the storm moved on, we drove through the thick mud back to our original spot to continue the predator hunt, but the kitty never showed. Maybe it was due to the crazy storm, but I'd bet it was our loud laughing, and of course, my exaggerated hand motions when I was involved in a story, and the constant back-and-forth conversations.

Well, in-between the hot and heavy make-out sessions, we did all that.

Brenton's lips were irresistible, a perfect fit to mine. And damn that man could kiss—demanding yet still somehow soft, combining to form some cosmic union of all things perfect in this world.

Being out on the land with his lips against my body was like a teleport back in time to all those years ago when we did the same thing, laughing, talking, kissing.

A shout from somewhere in the house dragged reality back in. After swinging both legs off the bed, I stretched both arms up high to work the stiff muscles out of my lower back. On silent, bare feet, I tiptoed across the worn carpet to the closed door and pressed an ear against it.

Daddy. No surprise. That man was always upset about something Bradley or I did.

Awake and mobile, the basic need for hot coffee turned dire. With a wide openmouthed yawn, I stepped out into the hallway, pausing the beeline I was on toward the kitchen when I was outside Bradley's room. The scene was all too familiar, with Daddy ranting about shit not getting done, but it was still a lot to take in considering Bradley's injured state.

Daddy turned those light brown eyes to me, narrowed in obvious annoyance. "What do you want?"

Instead of responding, I shifted my full attention to Bradley, who shot me a sympathetic look with his one good eye. "On my way to get coffee and heard you," I said.

"Get me some," Daddy commanded back with a dismissive wave.

"You have two legs. Get it yourself."

Eyes a bit wild, he faced me straight on and balled his hands into tight fists. "What in the hell did you say to me, girl?"

Somehow the terror he used to invoke in my soul as a little girl seeped right back in. But instead of cowering, I repeated, "Get it yourself." Only a slight tremble in my voice gave away my nerves of standing up to this man.

With each step closer, the heels of his boots thumped against the thinly carpeted floor, sounding ominous in the otherwise quiet house. "You always were useless, weren't you. You and that pathetic brother. Sorry excuse for kids after what all I did for you two."

"Right, because a kick in the ass and constant degrading is exactly what every kid needs."

"You lie. Always have been a damn liar. You lied to Mr. Graves about your mother, then conned his grandson into getting you pregnant, which turned the entire Graves family against me. I knew it from the beginning. Just like your mother. Nothing but a useless whore."

With each vicious word, he moved closer until he was in my face. I pressed a trembling hand against his thin chest and shoved him back a step. "Wow, it's a little early for all this, don't you think? Let's wait until after my morning coffee to start with the oh-so-typical rant of who ruined your life and when." Summoning a bit more courage, I glanced over Daddy's shoulder to Bradley propped up on the bed. "You need anything?"

At the quick shake of his head, I cast a final dismissive glare at Daddy and compelled my feet to move. Turning my back to him as I walked away was way more difficult than I expected, but I did it. Somehow, someway, the time with Brenton had strengthened the crumbling confidence Daddy was hell-bent to obliterate.

On the front porch swing, knees tucked against my chest and a steaming cup of coffee in hand, my tense shoulders finally relaxed, lowering inch by inch away from their permanent residence by my ears.

The fresh coffee scalded the tip of my tongue at the first hasty sip. Fine. With a longing look, I placed it on the swing beside me and pulled out my phone.

Six missed texts from the night before.

Shit.

Ryder: What the hell is going on? Kyle just got home and said Bradley got his ass kicked and Brenton was THERE, helping you?

Ryder: You told me you were done with him. Beka, please tell me you're done with him.

Ryder: Please tell me you're not doing what I think you're doing right now.

Ryder: I'm disowning you until you respond.

Ryder: Okay, that was a lie. I need to know what's going on and that you're okay.

Ryder: Call me, you hooker!

The last text made a smile pull at the corners of my lips.

Me: I'll do a tell-all, but I need donuts. Lots and lots of donuts.

Ryder: Oh hey. Good to know you're alive. It's not like I was WORRIED or anything.

Ryder: Thanks for returning my texts last night... oh wait. You didn't. Get your own damn donuts.

Ryder: Tell me one thing. Were you with him?

Me: Yes.

Ryder: You're a hot mess. See you in fifteen.

Chapter 16

Brenton

THE SLOW, CONSTANT throb of my blue-as-shit balls had me adjusting on the leather couch to find a position that would take pressure off the tender boys. Hand wrapped around my swollen nuts, I shifted them back and forth, which only made it worse.

Fuck the gentleman shit. I should've taken her up on returning the favor. What the hell was I thinking anyway? I always got mine first, and there I was offering up another round for her to have some fun before even thinking about my relief. That woman was fucking with my head, and not in the way I needed.

Or maybe she was.

Hell, this was complicated.

I didn't do complicated. Order, process, routine—those offered the control I needed. With control, I could keep the constant want for a stiff drink or line of coke for an easy escape at bay. Control offered the safety net I needed to keep from plunging back into a free fall to addiction.

For the hundredth time that morning, I watched out the large window.

Who in the hell was over there?

An older truck had pulled up half an hour before, but I didn't see who got out. And it was driving me fucking crazy. I should've paid attention to the type of truck that dipshit Kyle guy drove last night when I left to change.

Unfamiliar jealousy swirled in my chest at the mental image of him being with my Beks. Alone. Her dad thought he was the perfect match for her, so maybe he called the guy back under the ruse of checking on Bradley.

Someone scurried into the living room, but still I kept my attention on the small house and unknown truck. Knowing Dad had left yesterday for Dallas kept me from tensing at the presence of someone in the room.

"Would you like some lunch, Mr. Graves?" said a soft female voice by my right shoulder.

"Yes, that would be great. The same that was made for dinner last night, and make extra again, please."

"For her?" she asked, drawing my attention.

The girl couldn't have been more than twenty. Freckles lined her cheekbones, accentuated by her fiery red hair. Under my scrutinizing gaze, she shifted her focus to the floor.

"Uh, sorry," she stammered and took a step back. "None of my business."

"Wait." If Beks wouldn't give me the information, maybe this girl could. She was too young to remember what happened thirteen years ago, but I bet there was still gossip around this place. "What do you know about her?"

The girl's hazel eyes looked past me to the house I'd been monitoring all morning.

"Not much, sir. Sorry, I shouldn't—"

"Stop, please. What do you know?"

A bit of fear lit in her eyes as she retreated another step.

Hell.

Frustrated, I leaned forward and rested my head in my hands.

"All I know, sir, is in a town like this, what you two did...." Her pause made me sit up straight and swivel on the couch to give her my full attention. "She's always been kind to me, so I won't repeat what they called her, both to her face and behind her back, but she didn't deserve it. We all make mistakes. The whole town turned against her when she needed them the most. If I were her, I wouldn't have ever come back."

At that, she vanished around the corner, leaving me more confused than ever.

CACKLING LAUGHTER MIXED with the rhythmic squeak of metal against metal filled my ears before the two lounging on the porch swing came into view. A wave of relief barreled through at the sight. Not the guy, but it was the feisty tiny woman who gave me hell at the funeral.

This could be interesting.

Hopefully Beks had already lessened the woman's disdain toward me by explaining I wasn't the man I used to be.

Noticing my approach, Beks paused midconversation, her wild hands up in the air, and smiled. Her friend followed her line of sight and glared with more unease than hatred. It was a start.

"I brought you lunch." The tightly wrapped sandwich floated in the air toward Beks and landed beside her on the swing. Not wanting to be within clawing distance of her friend, I collapsed into the porch chair opposite the swing. After a pointed look to the empty donut box at their feet, I leaned back and smirked at the two. "But it looks like I'm a little late. I'm Brenton, by the way."

"I know who you are." Beks rolled her beautiful eyes and shoved her friend's shoulder. "I'm Ryder, the best friend. And just so we're on the same page, Brenton, I don't like you, and I think you'll fuck my friend over again. If you have any respect for her, you'll walk away now and never come back."

Holding her hard stare, I smiled my best arrogant asshole smile. "Good for me that your friend doesn't feel the same way."

"She should."

"Says you."

"Um, guys, I'm sitting right here. Listening," Beks cut in with a laugh.

The muscles of my jaw twitched as the two whispered back and forth during their long goodbye hug. Before Ryder stepped off the porch, she looked back and said, "See you tonight. We'll come by and get you."

Ryder's old Ford was halfway down the drive when I glanced at Beks with both brows raised.

She held up both hands in surrender. "Ryder is a little overprotective," she said with a shrug. "Thanks for the sandwich. Even though I ate my weight in donuts, I'm somehow hungry again."

The first bite prompted the same dick-hardening moan as last night.

"So good. Thank you again. Did you bring any chips, by chance?"

I didn't shield my wide smile at her hopeful tone. "Sorry, no chips. Simply orgasmic seasoned sandwiches."

With a huff, Beks uncurled from the swing and marched past me into the house, only to return seconds later with a bag of Cheetos. I watched in disgust as she settled back onto the swing and stuffed the sandwich full of the cheesy chip.

"Stop staring at me like I asked you to eat my ass," she said with a smirk. "When you're on the road as much as I am, driving between various clients, you learn how to make the most of your mealtime. Stuffing your sandwich full of chips is one of them, and it's good."

"How's your brother doing?" No way would I comment on her ass-eating statement. Not with her father and brother within earshot. If she or any of them knew what I wanted to do to that ass, they'd shoot me before I could convince her how great it would be.

Fuck.

My dick throbbed against the zipper of my jeans, desperate to pop out and play. I needed to stop thinking about her ass and staring at her amazing tits. Why didn't she have a bra on anyway? I knew how perfect her breasts were, and there she was taunting me with her perky nipples poking right through the Texas A&M T-shirt.

The tips of my fingers and tongue tingled with anticipation, eager to feel her again.

A wadded napkin smacked the side of my face. Knowing full well I was caught staring, a cocky grin spread up my cheeks as I pulled my gaze to meet hers.

"Don't ask a question if you won't bother listening to the answer," she said with an eye roll.

"Then don't taunt me with your perfect nipples poking out, stealing my attention."

Beks huffed a laugh around another bite of sandwich and chips. "You're the one who walked over here unannounced. Or did you forget that tidbit."

Right. To avoid acknowledging the accuracy of her words, I took a healthy bite of sandwich instead of responding.

"Bradley is fine. Not great, but fine. Now that we're on the subject, how do you plan on finding the men he owes the money to?" The slight dip of her tone told of her worry, which made my damn day—it meant she did still care about me. I'd begun to think she wasn't kidding about using me only for my body.

Did that make me an asshole? Yeah, probably. But I wanted her to care because I did, even though there was no future between us. Her home was here and mine in Kentucky, plus being gone six months to a year at a time on deployments. The army wife life wasn't the life she needed. Beks deserved better than that. Hell, better than me.

I pushed out of the chair with a stifled groan and collapsed beside her on the swing.

"I'll talk to your brother, or maybe Kyle can help me. I'll get it taken care of, and believe me, I've been around worse people, so don't worry."

She peered up through dark lashes with those sultry, honey brown eyes. "Okay, no worrying. Listen, this morning I want to find and patch up that injured heifer we found yesterday, and I overheard Daddy talking about some things that need to be done that I'd like to do. Wanna play ranch hand with me for the day?"

One boot on the ground, I crossed the other over my knee. "Do you ever slow down?"

"That's life in the country, Sir Fancy Pants. There's always something that needs to be done, so no. No one around here does."

I fixated on her hypnotizing eyes, in awe of the woman she was. Beks had no idea how sexy that drive and work ethic made her. When all I'd been around were Dallas socialites looking for an easy life and military groupies who only wanted someone to provide a stable life, Beks was refreshing.

But it was also unacceptable for someone like her. Someone who deserved to be cherished and spoiled rotten.

"Has anyone ever treated you the way you deserve?" I asked as I slid my hand into hers to intertwine her long fingers with mine. "Spoiled you?"

Her incredulous snort in response made me chuckle.

"Besides some rich, arrogant bastard buying me a brand-new truck? No, B, and that's okay. I don't need any of that stuff to be happy."

"What do you need to be happy?" I asked, truly interested.

Beks's thoughtful, deep sigh made uncomfortable pressure build in my chest. Anything she said, I'd give her. Hell, I could give her the entire world on a platter if she just asked. But knowing what little I did about this woman, money wouldn't be a part of the happiness equation.

"Honestly, that's a good question. One that I'm not entirely sure on the answer." She shifted against the wooden slats of the swing to lean against the armrest and tucked her toes under my ass. Dammit, just that simple touch had my finally semi-soft dick stiff again. I needed a long cold shower. Now. "I thought after getting my degree, I'd be happy. Thought after I got into a groove at the practice, I'd be happy. Then I thought after getting closure on our past, I'd finally be happy."

"But you're not."

Beks's gaze focused over my shoulder as she tucked a lock of unruly dark brown hair behind her ear. "I'm not unhappy, just... not *happy*. Being out here though, minus the unpleasant interactions with Daddy, a bit of the happiness I'd lost somewhere along the way has resurfaced. Maybe it's remembering the fond memories of us instead of the bad, or working a piece of land I have pride in." Honey brown eyes locked with mine. "Or maybe it's you. Being with you the past couple of days reminded me of what true happiness is, of what it feels like to have a permanent smile stuck on my face. I don't know. Maybe before your grandfather's funeral, I was simply content."

My gaze didn't falter from hers when I responded, "I know what you mean."

"Do you though? You have everything you could ever want. How in the hell could you not be happy?"

I scanned down to her plump pink lips, to her perky perfect breasts, to her delicious center that pushed against the seam of her pajama pants, begging me to lick it. Like Pavlov's dog, my tongue slid along my lower lip, impatient for another chance to taste her.

"Money only emphasizes who you already are instead of changing it. You watched my fucked-up family life, saw the life Caleb and I lived. If you're a mean old bastard who's unhappy with life, money makes it easier to spread that misery. And I have to think—not that I'd know, of course—that if you're happy, truly happy, the money part isn't the foundation. It's just a plus, because that isn't what makes you happy."

"Do you want to be happy?" she asked in a soft voice.

"Yes," I said, still focused on her crotch. "But it might be too late for me." Breaking my entranced stare, I flicked my eyes up to her amused smirk. "But it's not for you. Tomorrow we're getting you out of here. Tomorrow we're doing something just for you."

Shock registered on her face as she held out her hands. "No way. You've already done too much with the truck and offering to help—"

"Tomorrow." Unable to fight the insistent urge any longer, I leaned forward to seal my mouth over hers. "I need to make some calls," I said against her lips.

"You go change and meet me in the barn. I'm helping you with that chores list today."

Without another word, I sucked her bottom lip between mine and shoved off the swing. Halfway to the barn, I glanced back to make sure she was obeying, but instead of finding an empty porch, I saw Beks still in the swing with a broad, happy smile spread across her beautiful face.

Chapter 17

Rebeka

THE HEM OF THE DENIM skirt grazed along the backs of my upper thighs as I smoothed it down with both hands. With a scowl, I glared at my reflection. Last time I wore this skirt, it was looser—damn donuts—but it was the best and only option I had. Paired with a loose white V-neck T-shirt and brown wedges, I was ready for a fun night out on the town.

Which I was. Especially since Brenton was coming too. Somehow while repairing a small section of mangled fence, I'd mentioned the fun plans for tonight with Ryder and Kyle. It must've been the effects of heat exhaustion to mention it, and for Brenton to ask if he could join us.

Okay, he didn't ask. Brenton Graves doesn't ask—he tells.

The mental image of Sir Fancy Pants in Dos Amigos mixing and mingling with all the roughnecks and ranch hands made me internally cringe every time I pictured it.

I shot a worried look to Ryder, who was focused on freshening up her bright red lipstick. Her eyes rolled to the ceiling and stayed there.

"Listen, don't worry about me. I'll be nice to the guy, promise. But don't let him being there prevent you from hitting on other guys." Right, like possessive Brenton would let that happen. I already felt bad for any guy who breathed too close to me. "Because those other guys aren't leaving and could be more than just a fun four-day fling."

Ouch. But she was right, even though what Brenton and I felt for each other was deeper than a fling.

I cringed at her brutal honesty and turned back to the mirror. "I know."

"Do you?" she said with an annoyed tone that was rare for her to use toward me.

"No."

"That's what I thought. Does he know that?"

Looking at her sitting on the edge of the bed through the reflection, I gave a noncommittal shrug. "I told him I know he's leaving, and at least this time it wouldn't be a shock. I begged for what happened last night between us. Begged him. Don't make him out to be the bad guy. Before, yes, when he chose his inheritance over the baby and me, he was the bad guy. But now I'm older, he's older, and we're two adults who know what's on the table."

The bed squeaked when she pushed off the mattress. Tiny arms wrapped around my waist, and her warm cheek pressed against my bare bicep. "I don't want to see you get hurt again is all."

"I missed it."

In our reflection, her eyes flicked up to mine. "Missed what?"

"Being someone's. I love being in his arms, protected and cherished. It might be a short-lived thing, but it's amazing feeling this way again. I feel wanted, desired every time we're together. I never want it to end."

My vision blurred as I stared unseeing at our reflection.

Was I an idiot for playing with the same fire that burned me before?

The sun had already set, the heat from the day less brutal, when we stepped through the front door out onto the porch. I paused to watch Brenton and Kyle in an in-depth discussion. Both the men's brows were furrowed, scowls of concentration on their faces. Brenton's eyes flicked over to where I stood just outside the door. Warmth bloomed in my stomach, twisting and turning at his unabashed perusal up my bare legs.

"We're driving separate," he announced to the other two, keeping his heated gaze locked with mine. Each stomp of his boots made my heart skip, inching up the anticipation of what naughty things he had in mind. A callused hand wrapped around mine as he passed to tug me along with him.

The passionate heat between us blazed hotter the moment the doors to the truck slammed closed. Instead of pulling me to him like I expected, Brenton pressed the Start button and kept his attention out the windshield.

"You look nice," I said to the window as I stared out into the darkness. It was a complete understatement. He looked like he belonged on the cover of a sexy cowboy calendar. The way his dark denim Wranglers hugged his ass was almost sinful, and the crisp, white, pearl snap shirt somehow brightened his already striking green eyes.

The corners of my lips dipped when he didn't respond or return the compliment. I cut my eyes to the driver side and found him gripping the wheel so tight his knuckles were white.

Whatever. I looked cute and wouldn't let him dampen the fun night ahead.

The second the thought crossed my mind, Brenton whipped the truck down an old county road and slammed on the brakes. He snapped off the headlights, dousing the entire area in darkness; only the faint glow from the navigation screen and controls on the dash highlighted the inside of the cab.

"If you don't want your panties ripped off your fine ass, I suggest you take them off. Now."

My shocked gasp sounded over the arctic air conditioning blowing through the cab. Through the soft glow of the lights, he kept his eyes locked on mine while his hands blindly worked on his belt.

"I won't ask again, Rebeka."

Not a single muscle responded. All I could do was watch his hand wrapped around his massive cock, squeezing so hard it looked painful. Wetness pooled between my legs at the sight. In a dense lust fog, my fingers fumbled with the seat belt latch, eager to get closer to him. The center console pushed into my ribs as I leaned over to the driver side.

Demanding fingers dove into the depths of my hair at the first lick of my tongue from base to tip.

"Fuck," he breathed. Those fingers tightened against my scalp at my soft hum of agreement.

My ass was in the air as Brenton shoved the thick denim to bunch at my waist. The sting of elastic stretched to its max against my skin lasted a few seconds before it snapped under the pressure. I groaned around him and shifted my angle to take him deeper with each dip of my head.

Fuck, that was hot. Never had my underwear ripped off my body before. Never had someone need me with that much intensity.

The first smack across my bare ass caught me by surprise, but the second I leaned into, silently asking for more. His hot palm skimmed down between both cheeks and dove between my legs to slide two fingers inside.

One hand still in my hair, he held me close as he shifted his hips off the seat.

"Fuck, yes. Damn your perfect mouth," he groaned as he thrust faster. Each tilt of his hips was more demanding than the previous. In rhythm with his thrusts, his fingers pushed into me. We urged the other for more, desperate for release.

A quick twist of his fingers pressed my sensitive spot, shooting me over the edge. My moans and gasps triggered his own with a loud curse.

Fog covered the windows and our heavy pants echoed in the cab as we came down from the high. "You'll be impossible to let go, Beks," he said into my hair after pulling me against his heaving chest.

As much as I didn't want it to, his words sparked a ray of hope in my heart. Maybe this time he wouldn't leave after all.

AS WE MADE OUR WAY through the parking lot of Dos Amigos, the stiff denim skirt brushed against my sensitive ass cheeks, still stinging from Brenton's rough slap. Music blared from inside the doors as a local band played on a small stage. With Brenton's hand pressing against my lower back, we weaved through the crowd toward the bar.

A clearly frustrated Ryder stepped in front of us, blocking our path before she gripped my arm, yanking me toward the bathroom.

I glanced back at Brenton, who also looked confused, and shrugged. Whatever she wanted to talk about was urgent. Maybe she and Kyle got into a fight on the way over and needed a quick venting session.

Once inside the bathroom, Ryder leaned a hip against the sink and gave a knowing glare. "You reek of sex. Did you fuck him in the truck?"

All the other murmurs in the small space paused, and ten sets of eyes turned to me.

I tucked a piece of hair behind my ear. "Not technically." Shit, she was mad.

"Girl," Ryder admonished. Pulling her disapproving gaze from me, she focused on the chipped mirror to touch up her lipstick. "You better know what you're doing. Because from my perspective, you're an idiot woman who's letting that hottie out there play you like a fiddle. Again."

"And so what if I am?" I tossed my hands in the air before running them through my hair in frustration. "What does it matter if I like being around him again, or like the way he makes me feel? I'm just as confused as you, believe me. I'm still in love with the man who left me, but Ryder, that wasn't him. He's a good man, and an even better one now. What he did was terrible, and I should hate him, but guess what? I've hated him for years and it hasn't gotten me anywhere. And you know what else? It feels damn good to be wanted by someone again, to have that connection. So yeah, maybe I'm getting carried away, but I'm thirty fucking years old, not seventeen."

"Don't be mad at me for saying out loud what you already know," she deadpanned.

"What, that he's a good man who made a mistake?" I gritted out.

"That he's a Graves, and the moment you're not useful anymore, he will toss you aside. Again."

"He might not! Tonight he said—"

"Oh, you should believe what a guy says after you let him fuck your mouth."

"Stop it," I yelled and turned for the door. "You don't get it. And I might not understand it either, but I'm not going to let that stop me from trying to be happy. Even if it's just for a few days."

The door slammed against the wall when I shoved through it and stepped into the growing crowd. Glancing around for Brenton, I came up empty.

Where in the hell is he?

Damn, I need a drink.

A few cute cowboys tugged at my arm to detour my pursuit, but I shrugged each one off. At the bar, I hopped onto an open barstool, not giving two shits where Kyle and Brenton—or Ryder, for that matter—were.

The somewhat cute bartender with tattoos up his arms and neck leaned against the bar and asked what I wanted. Three days ago, I would've swooned over this guy, but now all I could do was appreciate the inked artwork.

After ordering two shots of tequila, I watched him pour out three. With a wink, he clinked one against the shot glass in my hand and tipped it back. With a tight smile, I followed suit, then again with the second one.

I raised my hand to order another when a massive, rough, old hand grasped mine and eased it back to the bar.

"Slow down there, sweetheart," said the older cowboy perched on the stool to my right. "Going to the bottom of the bottle isn't the solution to whatever you're fightin'. I would know."

I glanced at the plastic water cup in his hand while I wiped the remaining cheap tequila from my lips. The alcohol swirled in my near-empty stomach.

"The bottom of the bottle seems like a nice place to hide though." The rounded edge of the bar pressed into my ribs as I leaned over to flag down the bartender for another round. Out of the corner of my eye, I caught the man's gray brows rise in surprise. "The boy I was in love with as a kid is back in my life after royally fucking me over. But here's the kicker—he doesn't remember doing it. And now I'm here wondering if what happened was his doing or someone else's, and on top of that, the man he is now is amazing. Military, gorgeous, tattoos...." I sighed and downed the shot the bartender placed in front of me. "I'm playing with fire, I know I am, but hell, I've been cold for so long, the heat is welcomed."

"You think he'll mess you over again. That's why you're drinking."

"My best friend and I just got in a fight about it."

"Ah, she disapproves?"

"Yeah. She pretty much said I'm an idiot, and this time when he fucks me over, it'll be like taking it in the ass with no lube."

Our entire side of the bar turned their attention to the old man after he spewed water across it. Wide-eyed, he turned on the stool to face me straight on, tipped his Stetson, and smiled.

"Is that an invitation?"

I choked on the fourth shot. "What?"

His soft chuckle and smile soothed over the anxiety his question had triggered. "I'm just playin' with you, sweetheart. Besides, my drinking days are over, and no way in hell would I go into a fight with your man sober."

My man. Right. Brenton wasn't my anything.

Wait.

"How do you...?" I followed his pointed finger across the bar to find a pair of striking green eyes already staring back. "Oh." While I watched, a pretty blonde walked up and attempted to talk to Brenton, but he ignored the woman to keep his sole attention on me.

"He's been there since you saddled up next to me. And since I'm the sober one of us two, I'll tell you something. That man hasn't taken his eyes off you. I think you should be more worried about the idiot who tries to get near you instead of worrying about that boy breaking your heart." His wise eyes flicked across the bar. "Because I don't see any leaving in those eyes."

"How—"

A thick, hairy arm stretched between my new best friend and me. Instead of pulling back after grabbing the beer from the bartender, the obtrusive man stayed angled between us.

"Well aren't you the prettiest thing in here tonight," he said with a slight slur.

The old cowboy gave a high-pitched whistle. "Boy, I'd watch it."

The brute shoved off the bar to tower over him. "Oh really, you think you have a shot? Your balls are too shriveled for someone like her, old man. Let me show her how young cowboys ride."

Oh hell no.

I swiveled on the stool, the room spinning as I turned, to face the jackass. "Hey, lay off my friend here. I bet his shriveled balls are still bigger than yours, fuck face. Go practice your bolstering elsewhere."

"My what?" he said, obviously confused.

"Showing off, you idiot."

"Girl, you dissed my balls and suggested I'm ignorant—"

"Not suggesting. I said it. To your face."

Instead of deterring him like I hoped, his smile only widened. "Come on, you owe me a dance after all that sass."

I rolled my eyes and shook my head before turning to the old cowboy whose wide-eyed stare tracked a course down the side of the bar.

Too busy trying to locate Brenton again, I didn't notice the man's closeness until his tight grip wrapped around my forearm. "I asked nicely. Now come on, dance with me."

I snorted. "That was a damn command, not you asking."

Stale beer breath wafted up my nose when he leaned in too close and said, "Bet a tough woman like you likes being ordered around."

A tingling sensation of being watched had me glancing over my shoulder. Brenton stood two feet away, his glare promising a slow death locked on the man touching me.

"I only take orders from him," I said with a nod in Brenton's direction. "Not sure why I'm warning a douchebag like you, but leave, now, before he rips your ass apart for touching me."

The burly man looked in the direction I nodded and smirked at the stone-faced Brenton. "That pretty boy? Ah hell, baby, ditch that city boy and let me show you a good time."

The stupid shots of tequila had me snorting again before I turned back around to the bar in obvious dismissal.

The old cowboy smirked down at his water cup. "A lady like you shouldn't defend a man's balls. I think you castrated me."

"I'm no lady," I said, then raised my hand for another shot, only for it to be smacked down to the bar. "Hey," I shouted, glancing over my shoulder with a scowl, knowing exactly who I'd find being so damn bossy.

Brenton's fiery green eyes pulled me back an inch in surprise. "No more shots. I don't know what you're trying to do or what happened between you and Ryder, but you're not getting blackout drunk on my watch." His heated stare shifted down to the short skirt that was now barely covering my girly parts. He leaned down to brush his lips against the shell of my ear. "And don't forget you're not wearing any underwear." With an exaggerated inhale, he closed his eyes and groaned. "Fuck, I can smell you. Let's go home and—"

Just as I closed my eyes, ready to get lost in his words, his lips pulled away. With an exaggerated pout, I swiveled back around.

My mouth gaped at the scene unfolding just feet away. The brute had wrangled up a couple of friends. Two big friends. All three men surrounded a relaxed and smirking Brenton.

"Let him fight," said the old cowboy who'd also turned around to watch the show. "He's itching for it." At his tilted nod, I focused on Brenton's fisted hands. "It's a guy thing, sweetheart. Defending our women and all."

A small frown dipped the corners of my lips. "He just likes to fight, always has. I'm not his anything."

The old man tipped his head back with a loud bark of a laugh. "Women. Let me guess. He hasn't told you, hasn't explained how he feels about you."

I tucked a lock of dark hair behind my ears and looked to the sticky floor. "Well, yeah. I mean no...."

"Listen, I'll fill you in on us guys. We don't fight for just anyone. We only fight for the ones we love. And whether he's said it or not—hell, he might not even know it, but that man loves you."

The four—or was it five?—shots were playing with my hearing. That or the old man was lying about the water and it was actually pure vodka in his cup. I not so casually leaned to take a quick sniff. Nope, not vodka, just water like he said.

Huh.

So did that mean what he said could be true?

Did Brenton Graves love me?

Warmth spread up my belly into my chest, and the noises of the bar turned hollow. I needed to leave before I turned into a drunk fool.

I stretched up high, using the barstool as leverage to scour the dance hall for Ryder, but came up empty.

Oblivious to the chaos behind me, I shoved off the bar to stand and stepped back while looking at my phone.

The old man's eyes went wide and he lunged for me.

Unfortunately he was too late to stop me from stepping right into the middle of a bar fight.

Chapter 18

Rebeka

SOMEWHERE, RYDER SHOUTED my name.

I twisted toward her voice just as something solid slammed against my right cheek. The room spun at the force, and I stumbled back, arms outstretched in search of the bar or stool to steady me.

Stars still blurred my vision when an arm snaked around my waist and hauled me against a solid body. Somewhere in the distance, a rage-filled bellow vibrated in my ears.

"You're okay, sweetheart," my old man friend whispered. Rough hands scraped down my arms and his hold tightened, securing me to his side. "Holy shit," he murmured in awe, more to himself than to me.

At the astonishment in his tone, I blinked several times to push away the haze clouding my sight and attempted to focus on the chaotic scene in front of us. But none of it made sense. The three men from earlier lay groaning while flat on the floor, Brenton standing in the middle with his bloodied hands on his knees.

"What's going on?" I said, blinking again to clear the tears building in my right eye.

The old man started to respond but stopped as a crying Ryder pulled me into her arms.

"What's going on?" I asked again, still a little stunned. Hell, why did I take so many shots?

"You're okay. I'm here," she whispered. "Those fucking bastards hit you, and that dumbass started it all."

Her grip around my waist dropped as she turned to face the devastated-looking Brenton. The sadness lurking behind his eyes shredded my heart. Even though I wasn't quite sure what happened, there was no way he could've prevented it.

A loud smack echoed around the quieted area when Ryder's hand connected with Brenton's cheek. He didn't flinch. Didn't drop my stare. The next hit was directed to his face, but that time it was a punch.

The third hit nailed his balls.

Brenton's grunt of pain set my feet in motion toward them. Cutting me off, Kyle hauled Ryder away from Brenton, who was hunched over with his hands cradling his crotch.

Ryder thrashed and pulled at Kyle's arms, shouting at him to release her.

"Ryder, stop," I slurred, my jaw stiff. "Don't hurt the part of him I like."

At that, she dropped her fight. Chest still heaving, she said, "He started the whole thing."

I looked around to the men on the floor. "More like he finished it. See that guy—"

"Why can't you see it now, Beka? He's no good for you. Every time you're around him, you end up hurt in some way. Walk away. Get the hell away from the bastard before he gets you killed."

I turned from Brenton's stare and glared at my best friend. "Stop."

Her eyes widened. "You gotta be fucking kidding me." A disappointed look flashed across her features as she shook her head. "I won't sit back and watch him hurt you all over again. He'll break you and never look back. Call me when you come to your damn senses."

Tears welled as I watched her shove out of Kyle's arms and storm off.

The shouts and band playing flooded back as a hand gripped mine. "Sweetheart, you gotta get your boy out of here. The cops are on their way."

In a daze, I took the three steps to Brenton and gripped his forearm. Instead of resisting like I expected, he flipped my hold to grasp my elbow and guided us through the staring crowd. Eyes focused on the sticky floor, I concentrated on putting one foot in front of the other, hoping to not trip over my feet or someone else's. The last thing we needed was Brenton getting into another fight because someone accidentally tripped me.

A heavy metal door slammed at our backs as we stepped into the dark back alley. The hot night air amplified the stench of rotten food and urine.

Brenton's protective grip loosened as his hand fell to his side. After leaning against the brick wall, he bent forward, resting his palms on the tops of his knees. "Do you want to press charges?"

"What?"

"I'll stick around for the cops if you want to press charges against me. I started the fight. I'm the reason you were hit."

A tight ball of unshed tears lodged in my throat, preventing me from responding immediately.

At my perceived hesitancy, his shoulders drooped, and he stepped toward the door we escaped through.

I wrapped my hand around his wrist. "No, I don't want to press charges. And you didn't start it, B. You were defending me. Getting that drunk ass off me. You had no idea I'd step into the middle of it. Nothing that happened was your fault."

"But still—"

The gravel shifted under my wedges as I moved close enough to grip his face between my hands. Grief and anger swirled behind his eyes as I stared into them. "I know you, B. I trust you. It was an accident. Come on, let's get out of here." When he didn't move, I dropped my hands and shrugged. "Fine, go back in if that'll make you feel better. But I'm not, and I'm too drunk to drive home, so you have to choose. Let me drive home like this alone while you go back inside, or you drive."

There was no doubt which option he'd choose, but I still blew a relieved sigh past my lips when his steady footsteps sounded behind me halfway down the alley.

Not a word was spoken in the truck on the way back. The radio stayed turned off, only the full blast AC blowing and the pinging of gravel kicked up by the tires filling the silence.

We pulled along the circle drive to the main house instead of driving toward the back to Daddy's place.

"Okay, here's where I draw the line. I'm not walking back in these shoes," I said with a smirk, knowing full well what his intentions were but hoping it would invoke a verbal response.

It didn't.

Instead, Brenton shut off the engine and climbed out of the cab.

Damn, wish he would snap out of his mood, because I was fucking happy. The tequila had made everything fuzzy and warm and fun.

My eyes slammed shut to prevent them from being blinded when the bright overhead light snapped on.

"You're staying with me," he stated, leaving no room for negotiation.

Like I would.

"I love you bossy," I responded with a smile.

Not even a smirk or a grunt at my comment before he scooped me from the seat.

I gave a high-pitched squeal. "Brenton, I can walk." I laughed as he shut the door with a boot against it.

"No."

Fine by me.

I snuggled into his arms and took a deep breath of his intoxicating masculine scent. "You smell nice," I said. Focused at his neck, I leaned forward to drag my tongue along his soft skin. "You're tasty too."

"Damn you're drunk," he grumbled, with no anger or frustration in his tone.

His grip tightened to stabilize me in his arms as he climbed the stairs to the main house. I closed my eyes, relishing in the strength, the way he made me feel lighter than I was and protected. Safe. Even after everything that happened tonight, I was safe with him.

That was what Ryder didn't understand. Hell, no one could. Passion. Heat. Jealousy. Possession. All of it described who we were together, what we felt.

Through the front door, he stomped past the living room, down a hall, and turned into his childhood bedroom. Craning my neck, I searched the walls to see what all had changed since the last time I'd been in that same room, but I couldn't see a damn thing in the dark.

Almost like I was his most precious possession, he gently laid me on top of the soft comforter.

"Brenton—"

"Stop it, would you? Just let me do this without a fight. Can't you see what tonight did to me?" he growled. "You're hurt because of me, and I don't give a damn if it was an accident. It happened."

I opened my mouth to respond, but he shoved away from the bed and stormed out before I could formulate a response. Okay, he was taking it hard. Not sure why since he wasn't the one who hit me, but I guess he felt responsible since he started it? Which was crazy. That jackass started it when he wouldn't leave me alone.

Once my vision adjusted to the dimly lit room, I took it all in. A large dresser stood on the opposite wall, and bland pictures like you'd buy at any home goods store accented the walls. Nothing personal, not a single thing that made it look lived in.

I curled my fingers, clenching the soft and probably expensive comfort. Everything looked the same. Boring. No feeling. Hollow.

My heart ached for Brenton's empty life. Even with Daddy being a chauvinistic ass, I still had some happy moments. Most of those were due to Brenton, but I had friends too, good friends.

Tears welled at the thought of Ryder. My best friend who'd had enough of my bullshit. I knew I should call her, but what was there to say? She thought she knew what was best for me, but she didn't. Ryder had gone on ultraprotective mode the moment Brenton stepped across the county line, and it'd only intensified when I told her I wasn't planning on telling him the whole story of our last night.

What did it matter at this point anyway? He didn't remember, and honestly, I didn't want him to. What if he remembered it all and realized he made the right choice to walk away?

"You're crying," Brenton said in a horrified tone. "Does it hurt that bad? Do you need to go to the hospital? Fuck!"

His knees landed with a thump at my feet. Damp cloth in hand, he reached up and pressed it against my injured cheek.

"I'm so sorry, Beks. I didn't know that would happen, didn't think it through." His rapid breaths brushed across my neck. "I would never let anything happen to you. You know that, right? I'd rather kill myself than hurt you." The tremble in his voice sent more tears rolling down my cheeks.

"I'm crying because of Ryder and what she said. And because of you. And because of us. And because—" A sob shook my shoulders, stealing my next words.

"She was right." Warmth enveloped my hand as he wrapped his hand around mine, bringing it up to replace his hold on the cool cloth. I wrenched open my eyes to search his, not understanding what he was saying. The first step he took away from the bed had my stomach dropping with fear. The second step ignited more anger than dread.

"The fuck are you talking about?" I snapped and stood.

"Ryder, what she said—"

"I get that part, you moron. I'm asking what the fuck are you talking about agreeing with her?"

Not a single corner of his lips twitched up as he said, "Good to see that hit didn't stop your smart-ass mouth."

"I know something you can shove down my smart-ass mouth to stop it," I replied with a seductive smile. "How are your balls, by the way?"

"We're not talking about my balls, or me shutting you up with my dick down your throat." Heat flared behind his eyes, showing me he might not 100 percent agree with that statement. "How many times will you let me do this, Beks?"

"Well, I'd like to say as many times as you want, but my jaw might get tired."

"I'm fucking serious," he seethed. At his side, his hands balled into white-knuckled fists. "I hurt you back then, and now, tonight, I'm a selfish bastard asking for your help when I know—"

"Know I agreed to all this after you laid it all out there? You made it clear that you only needed my help to get over your head shit. And by the way," I sighed, then sat back on the bed, "you didn't pass out tonight."

Both his dark brows shot up. "You're right, but here, when I saw you crying, the symptoms came back. I could barely breathe when I was by the bed staring at your injured cheek." His gaze shifted to the door, moving away from me for the first time since he came into the room with the rag. "It was like a replay, but I couldn't see anything. Like a déjà vu feeling without knowing why."

Unease settled in my gut at my guilt. I turned my gaze from him to focus on my clasped hands and prayed he didn't press the topic any further.

Chapter 19

Brenton

I LOOKED AT MY BEAUTY on the bed. Air caught in my throat at the sight of her rounded shoulders, eyes downturned and focused on the hands clasped between her pressed thighs. Apprehension now rolled off her when moments ago, she'd joked about stuffing my dick down her throat.

Shit. I had to stop thinking about that, and mentally replaying what happened in the truck over and over. If I didn't, my stiff cock would pop out of these damn jeans in search of the mouth she willingly offered up.

The night couldn't have gone worse. No doubt whatever happened between the two girls after we got there had to do with me, which sent Beks straight to the bar. Thank fuck she sat by the old man instead of the hundred assholes who were posted up watching her every move. Of course, she didn't notice all the eyes on her, but I did. Fuck, did I.

How in the hell did she go out and not get hit on every two steps? Maybe she did, which made the deepening feelings for her that much worse. Flying for the Night Stalkers required months away from home at a time. How could I leave a woman like her at home? It would drive me insane, wondering who was cozying up to her, only too eager to take my place between her legs.

That was another reason I knew I shouldn't tell her how I felt, or thought I felt, about her. We wouldn't go anywhere with my jealous streak and inability to trust anyone around her. Which was fine. It wasn't like I loved her. There was no way the gnawing in my gut or her always being on my mind was a signal of love. Not that I'd know, I guess. But no way love was the reason I couldn't focus when she was gone, or even when she was close. Or why the only time I smiled or laughed was due to her. Love wasn't the reason I was dreading two days from now when I had to head back to Kentucky.

It was all happening too fast. The feelings, the intensity, the desire for only her—ever. How could that develop after only a couple of days? Love didn't happen that fast. Lust did.

It was lust. She was fucking beautiful, sexy as hell, plus that damn hilarious, crude mouth of hers. That was what attracted me. What I lusted after.

Attraction didn't mean love. It meant sex.

She knew I was leaving and understood it was a short-term thing.

I was fine.

I needed to get a fucking grip. She made me weak, and that was the last thing I needed.

"What do you mean like déjà vu?" she asked with a whooshed breath, like it took all her willpower.

Those soft brown eyes flicked up and found mine in the dark room. I took a single step, then another, needing to shorten the space between us.

"It means you, our past, us, now it's all connected. I can't figure it out. You know how much I need control, and with you, the second you walk into the damn room, all the control I have vanishes."

"What does that tell you, Brenton?" Hope lifted her tone and brightened her damp, sad eyes.

No, I wouldn't lead her on. Not again.

"It means you're sexy as hell and I want to fuck you every time we're in the same room."

Her eyes never left mine. "Is that all?"

"That's me, Beks. I'm a selfish, arrogant bastard."

The disappointed shake of her head hurt worse than her friend's hit to the balls.

"Right, I guess things never change." She wiped her hands down her bare legs, drawing my attention before reaching up to tuck her long hair behind her ears. "This is only about your head thing and sex. Thanks for the reminder."

The small, sad voice stole the air from my lungs.

"Beks...." I paused, not knowing what to say. No way in hell could I tell her the truth.

"It's fine, Brenton." A broad, fake smile was planted across her face when she finally looked up. "So, what can I do to help? Want me to verify if some of the things you're remembering are real or not?"

The relief that seeped in when she didn't press the topic further confirmed I was a selfish prick.

I shrugged and sat on the bed beside her. "I think after everything that happened tonight, I need to know that I never hurt you on purpose. And I'm not just talking about the wreck. I need to know I was a better man than my father. Maybe that I am a better man than my father."

My eyes widened at the brush of her thigh over mine to slide on to my lap. After nestling her knees on either side of my hips, she gripped my face between her clammy hands.

"You were never and will never be your father. You hear me, Brenton Graves? You might share his last name and his DNA, but you are nothing, *nothing* like that awful man. Tonight was a complete accident, and still you felt utter shame. I saw it. I saw how defeated you were at the thought of me hurt because of you. And I know it's not just me. It would be the same with any woman. You're not your father's son."

I weaved my fingers into her hair and pulled her forehead to mine.

A long pause of comfortable silence filled the large bedroom before she spoke again.

"You flew to Dallas to help me. That night. I texted you something, and you came. Never in a million years did I expect you to come that night, but you did. It was a shitstorm in our house when you got there, but it didn't faze you. You marched right past my belligerent father into my room, packed my bags, and grabbed my hand on the way out."

"Then why did—or do—you hate me so much? The wreck was my fault, and your injuries, but if I was there with the right intentions, why be so pissed all these years?"

Her arms and legs tightened like I was her lifeline.

"That night, your dad, your grandfather, my father—everyone found out about us. What we'd been doing behind their backs. I was seventeen, Brenton, and you were almost twenty-one. You were the grandson of an oil tycoon, and I was the help's daughter. No one approved of us, and we knew that, which was why we never told anyone."

"Okay, but—"

"They gave you an ultimatum after the wreck. Your trust fund or me. You chose the money." Hot tears rolled down my neck as her body trembled on top of me.

"No," I bit out. "No, Beks. You had it wrong. I would never have done that. I would never choose money over anyone, especially not you."

"You didn't even have the balls to tell me to my face. You had your damn attorneys write up an agreement, and then they marched into my hospital room, threw it on the bed, and told me... told me you didn't want to see me again. That we were a mistake."

"I didn't. I wouldn't." Tension seized my lower back and crept up my spine. "If you say I'm not my father and believe that, then you know I wouldn't have done that. I know I can't remember, but you have to believe me, Beks, I wouldn't have done that."

"I do," she cried. "A part of me never believed you were the one to make the choice."

Arms wrapped around her back, I rolled us so my weight pushed her against the soft bed. Resting on my elbows, I held her face between my hands and waited for her eyes to open.

Watery, they finally met mine, and I said, "You have every right to hate me."

Wet lashes fluttered, and a small smile pulled at her lips. "You're a moron if you believe that, Brenton. I might've thought I hated you, but no matter what, I always loved you more."

"No," I said, horrified. Anger, hate, resentment—I could handle those feelings, but love wasn't an emotion I'd ever felt or been shown except by the woman beneath me.

"Unfortunately for me, and you too by your response, yeah I do. I did then too. It was why it hurt so bad. Over time, that love grew hard and jagged, which looked like hate, but underneath it all I still loved you. Still love you."

Maybe it was to stop her from saying it again since my heart raced each time the words "I love you" passed her lips, or perhaps it was to show her how I felt since I couldn't voice it. Either way, I closed the gap between us and pressed my lips against hers.

In a desperate request, I slid the tip of my tongue along the seam of her lips, begging for her to open. With a moan, her soft lips parted, giving me full access. Hand in her hair, I urged her harder against me as I angled my lips to deepen the kiss. Every other kiss before was fucking nothing. This right now, devoted to each other and communicating the taut connection neither of us could explain, was the world.

Beneath me, her legs wrapped around my hips and her heels dug into my ass. I groaned into her mouth when her sweet scent floated up from between us. My hips flexed, pushing me harder against her tender spot.

Beks's lips pulled from mine. "Brenton, stop being a damn tease."

"We're taking this slow, baby."

Her loud, frustrated whimper shot a bolt of electricity straight to my throbbing cock. My hands found the hem of her white T-shirt and dragged it over her head. It hadn't hit the floor before her bra was off as well.

Damn, I loved her tits.

Resting my weight on her pelvis, I wrapped both hands around her breasts, savoring the way her eyes shuttered closed with each pass of my thumbs over her peaked nipples.

Her back arched off the bed at the first flick and pinch between my fingers. Unable to hold back a second longer, I sucked a pebbled nipple between my lips. A thick desire-filled chuckle vibrated against her sensitive skin as her hand wove into my hair, pushing me closer.

"So bossy," I murmured against her soft skin, then took a small nip. Her tremble and groan pushed the thought of going slow aside.

The bed squeaked beneath my shifting weight. Elbow on the mattress, I kept my mouth on her while I skimmed the tips of my fingers down her side, sinking lower with each pass. Heat guided me to the spot she urged me toward with the bucking of her hips.

I stifled a groan of my own with my mouth against her neck at the slickness I found waiting for me. At the first dip of my fingers, she shifted in a silent request for more. Each push rewarded me with a lift of her hips and a soft curse from her lips.

"Brenton, I want you," she begged. "Please."

Desire filled every inch of my soul at her splayed out beneath me, her long dark hair strewn across the bed, her eyes soft and fixed on me. With each deep breath, her fantastic tits rose and fell, her perfect nipples hardening further under my focused stare.

"Say it again," I demanded through clenched teeth. Hell, I was hanging on by a thread. I needed to get my shit together or this wouldn't last a full minute once I was inside her.

She repeated her begging plea over and over as her head thrashed against the bed.

Beks stilled when I pushed off the bed, her eyes focusing where my fingers worked the snaps of my shirt. Her upper teeth sank into her bottom lip and her eyes flicked up to meet mine. The soft cotton of my shirt brushed over my shoulders and floated to the floor.

"Hell, you're like a real-life GI Joe action figure."

I chuckled and unbuttoned my jeans, allowing them to pool on the floor, leaving me standing in boxer briefs.

"Do you know how sexy you are?" Her burning gaze licked fire along every inch of me. For the first time, I knew the person in my bed saw all of me. Not just my family name, my trust fund, or the body I spent hours in the gym sculpting. No, this gorgeous woman thought I, just Brenton, was sexy. "If you're ever in trouble on a mission, you better hope the enemy is all women. All you'd have to do is strip to disarm them. Hell, I'm sure they'd drop trou and fight each other over who got your dick in them first."

"Woman," I groaned, gripping my throbbing cock. "The shit you say."

"Sorry," she grumbled. A faint stain of pink flushed across her cheeks.

"I lo—" I squeezed my dick harder at the near slip of the tongue. "It's perfect. Like you."

A shy smile pulled at the corners of her lips. "Enough talking. Take those off." With two fingers, she gestured to my boxer briefs.

"Yes, ma'am." I slipped the underwear down my thighs, relishing in her wide-eyed stare. "Skirt off. Now." While she fumbled with the button and zipper, I pulled open the nightstand drawer. Box of condoms in hand, I turned back to the bed.

"Please tell me those are new and not thirteen years old."

I shot her an incredulous look as I rolled on the thin rubber. Hand still gripping my cock, I stared between her legs. "No way I gave you up for money," I whispered more to myself than her. "I'm a damn fool for forgetting us."

"If you don't crawl on top of me right now, I'll start without you," she groaned with her eyes closed, a grimace crossing her features.

Hell. This woman. Could there ever be anyone more perfect for me?

Smart, honest, straightforward, and just as demanding.

I love her.

The thought jarred through my mind, but acceptance of it sent a soothing wave through my veins. I'd have to figure it out later though, because she wasn't kidding about starting without me.

"Stop," I growled, smacking her hand away from between her legs.

Both her ankles in my grasp, I yanked her ass to the edge of the bed. Every nerve, every sense zeroed in on the heat pouring from between her legs, drawing me closer. Right hand on her hip, I angled her off the bed and slid in an inch.

I palmed her breast with my left hand and teased her nipple between my fingers as I pushed in to the hilt. In unison, we groaned at the perfect fit. I became lost in the way her soft hip molded into my hand, giving me something to hold as I slid in and out. We moved in a slow cadence, giving this moment of two lovers rejoining the reverence it deserved, until the fervor grew unbearable, the urgency pushing me harder and faster.

Curses and versions of my name spilled from her lips in hushed whispers, insisting I go deeper. She was too much; we were too much. I only had seconds before I exploded.

"Beks," I gritted out through clenched teeth.

Shouted unrecognizable words filled the room as she shuddered, clenching tight. With a loud curse of my own, I sank deep once, twice, and collapsed on top of the bed, barely catching my weight on my elbows before I crushed her.

Her soft, muscular arms wrapped around my sweat-slick neck and pulled.

"I don't want to hurt you," I said, eyes closed, still coming down from the most intense orgasm ever.

"I'm not breakable, B. I want to feel you on me. All of you."

Hesitantly I lowered, putting my full weight on her. Those arms tightened, and her nose nuzzled against my slick neck. It felt right, perfect even. Then again, it wasn't surprising, since every moment we were together seemed like it was made just for us. But the clock was ticking until I left.

And I would leave.

The army would never let me out of the contract just because I fell in love with my childhood sweetheart. Even if they did, would I want them to?

The army was my life, one I'd never considered leaving since joining, but what if she was my cure? The one to not only keep me from my addictions but take away the need altogether, to soothe the festering anger and rage boiling in my gut on a minute-by-minute basis?

I shifted to stare down at the beauty beneath me.

She was more than a cure.

This woman was my salvation.

Chapter 20

Rebeka

MY DESERT-DRY MOUTH pulled me from a deep, comfortable sleep in urgent need of water. The bed dipped and sheets tangled around my hips when I rolled over in search of the glass Brenton set aside last night. The thoughtful man was worried that I'd wake up dehydrated due to the cheap tequila, plus the strenuous exercise we put in through the night between the sheets.

I relished every gulped drop of the room-temperature water before setting the empty glass back on the nightstand. Snuggling back under the covers, I tucked my hands beneath the pillow, pulling it tight against my cheek to stare at the still-snoozing man beside me.

Last night was.... I bit back a smile and squeezed my thighs together to relieve some of the building pressure. How in the hell was that even possible? We went round after round; I shouldn't have anything left to get all hot and bothered again. But with my very own naughty, tatted GI Joe snuggled beside me, how could my body not react was the real question.

Yep, I was in deep shit.

Stuck in the emotional muck with no way out.

I loved him, really loved him, and last night only solidified it. I didn't just love him—I was in love with him, and something told me he saw us as more than a diversion until he left. But he wouldn't admit, maybe not even to himself.

"What time is it, and why are you staring at me?" he grumbled before turning his handsome face away from my adoring eyes.

I glanced at my phone and then tucked it back under the pillow. My stomach dipped at the empty screen. Not a single text from Ryder.

"Six," I said, unable to hide my disappointed tone.

His head rolled along to the pillow to face me. "What?"

"Six. The time is six."

"Not that. What's wrong?"

I sighed and tucked a lock of unruly morning hair behind my ear. "It's nothing. I don't have any missed texts from Ryder is all."

Something I couldn't read flashed behind his eyes before flicking to my injured cheek. "It doesn't look bad this morning. Does it hurt?" At the shake of my head, he rested his palm on my cheek and brushed the pad of his thumb along the bruise. "What do you want to do about Ryder?"

The soft sheets rustled when I turned to lie on my back and look up to the ceiling. "I don't know. Give it a few days, I guess? It was just so odd and out of character for her. Something else is going on." I cut my eyes to him. "But she and I can talk after you're gone. It'll be easier without you around to rile her up again."

The hand that was on my cheek slid south and dipped under the expensive sheets to explore lower. At the first brush of his fingers, my eyes shuttered closed and a low moan escaped.

"I'll never have enough of you," he whispered. Slick, soft lips brushed against my neck just as his fingers pushed easily inside me.

A gasp, not my own, snapped my eyes open. To my horror, the lead housekeeper, Mrs. Hathway, stood in the doorway, wide-eyed and flaming red cheeks.

"Can I help you with something?" Brenton asked, utterly unfazed by the interruption. I let out a small squeak when his fingers slid deeper.

"I thought... I wanted...," she stammered, then took a step back.

"While you're here, please make sure there's plenty of coffee and breakfast for Beks and me here. We have a flight to catch and will be leaving shortly."

Mrs. Hathway's accusing glare burned into me. Filled with the shame her stare condemned me with, I pulled the covers over my head in hopes of hiding from the entire encounter. Not sure why. I was a grown-ass woman this time, and I didn't care if she did run off and tell Daddy like last time. Brenton would protect me.

"Now, Mrs. Hathway." The cold command sent a shiver down my spine. I loved Brenton's commands, but when directed to me, they were warm, provocative, not distant and authoritative like the one he just gave. "And if you ever look at Rebeka like that again, you'll find your ass off this property and never allowed back. Do I make myself clear?"

Sweat beaded along my forehead from the heat building beneath the comforter. With my pulse thundering in my ears, I didn't hear her response. A dousing waft of cold air sprouted goose bumps down my arms and chest when the comforter was ripped back.

"You don't ever hide, do you hear me? There is nothing to be ashamed of. Not with me."

Eyes locked with his, I nodded. The harsh lines along his forehead faded, and he fell back to the bed.

"I need clothes," I said to the ceiling.

"Huh?" he said, clearly still ticked, popping his knuckles.

"You told her we were catching a flight. I need clothes and need to know where we're going."

My yelp rattled off the walls as he rolled on top of me to press his naked body against mine.

"I'll take care of it." The happy, boyish smile he wore warmed my heart. I loved seeing him like that. Carefree and happy.

After a deep, leave-me-breathless kiss, he leaped from the bed. One elbow against the mattress, I propped myself up to watch him pull last night's jeans over his bare ass.

With one last confident smirk, he stepped out the door, disappearing down the hall.

In the quiet of the morning, I stretched out along the bed, savoring the soft cotton against my skin. They were way better than the Dollar General ones I bought the previous year.

After wiping the morning out of my eyes, I groaned at the black on my fingers.

Of course tipsy and horny me didn't think about washing my face.

With a sigh, I sat up, flipped the covers back and tiptoed to the en suite bathroom.

After a long hot shower, the sense of someone watching had me shutting off the hair dryer and flipping my dark hair back over to survey the room. Brenton stood expressionless, leaning against the doorframe. The distant look in his eyes ticked up my nerves.

"Everything okay?" I asked, clutching the towel wrapped around me tighter to my chest. His eyes stayed fixed on the wall behind me. "Brenton?"

"Your bag is on the bed. I need to shower too. Then we go," he muttered more to himself than me. After removing his dark denim jeans, he stepped into the shower and turned on the water.

That was odd.

"Hey," he called when I stepped out to rummage through the bag he'd packed. "We need to talk. Do not go anywhere." The harshness of his words and intenseness of his tone left no room for debate.

While he showered, I dug through the clothes, searching for something to wear on the plane. I was still looking for my underwear when the water shut off.

"Seriously?" I shouted. "You didn't pack me any underwear?"

In all his freshly showered, naked glory, he stepped into the bedroom while rubbing his dark hair with a towel. "I didn't want them getting in the way again," he said with a smirk and turned back into the bathroom.

The man had a point.

WOW.

I turned, my mouth gaping, to a grinning Brenton. Inside the small jet, I took the seat he pointed to and immediately fiddled with all the gadgets around me.

"Brenton, this is way over the top." I shifted side to side in the seat, amazed at the comfort of the soft leather. "Is this yours?"

"Technically it's the company's. The board bought it a few years back and let the family use it whenever we want." He took the seat directly across from me but kept his gaze out the window, almost like he was lost in thought.

"Okay, I'm done with this avoiding shit. Spit it out, Graves," I demanded with a sigh. The entire ride here, the tension between us had gnawed at my nerves, and I was done. "What the hell do we have to talk about?"

His green eyes flicked to mine. A nervous pulse of energy passed through his brief glance before he looked to the still-open door. "I need a drink."

"Do I?" I muttered, crossing my arms over my chest while giving him my best annoyed glare.

Instead of responding, he shook his head and moved to the front of the plane. When he returned, he slid a Coke across the table and popped the top of a flavored sparkling water.

"It takes the edge off even if there isn't any alcohol in it. Buckle up," he ordered as he snapped his own seat belt together. "We're about to take off."

The door slammed shut and the plane rolled smoothly toward the runway. I stared out the window, watching the surrounding buildings whiz by as we took off when he said, "I remembered."

My stomach dropped as the plane lifted off the ground. "Remembered what?"

Reaching across the small table between us, he gripped my clammy hand. "Today, I walked into your dad's place, straight to your room, and started packing your bag. Your dad came in yelling about something and I froze."

"You blacked out?"

"No, I froze because instead of seeing what was going on in front of me, I had a whole scene replaying in my mind of what happened that night. I remember. Everything."

My hand trembled as I tried to open my Coke. Giving up, I leaned back in the chair and closed my eyes. "Tell me what you remember."

"I remember walking in to you and your dad screaming at each other and Bradley holding him back. What's crazy is I can almost feel the rage I felt then at seeing your bleeding lip, your eyes red and swollen from crying. I grabbed you, pulled you into your room, and packed your bags. I threw whatever I could find into a small duffel you had, and we left."

"You told me you'd take care of me," I whispered over the roaring engines.

"You know what else I remember feeling?"

"What?" I choked out.

"Fucking happy."

"You were high, Brenton. Of course you were happy."

"It had nothing to do with drugs, Rebeka. Hey, look at me." I tucked a lock of hair behind my ear, took a deep breath in for strength, and opened my eyes. "You were pregnant."

Air stopped filling my lungs and my heart slammed against my chest as I stared wide-eyed into his.

"That's what you texted me. You told me you were pregnant, and that's why I came to you. Last night you said you never imagined I would come to you after you sent that text. Was I that much of an asshole? Did you have that little faith in me that you thought I wouldn't give a shit?"

Fuck it.

We were doing this now or never. It wasn't like I could walk out, which was probably part of his genius plan all along. Get me in this floating tin can with zero exits a sane person would take at this altitude.

I twirled the Coke can between my hands. "Do you have anything stronger?" Brenton nodded and unbuckled his seat belt. "Bring the bottle."

"It's an hour flight."

"Then you might want to bring two."

"So bossy," he grumbled, but a corner of his full lips pulled up in an almost smirk.

After he returned with two travel-size whiskey bottles, I cracked one open and tipped it back. When the burning down my throat subsided, I leaned back in the seat and shrugged.

"Like I said last night, I was seventeen. I was scared, and we never had the whole 'we're doing this forever' talk. Hell, you never even said you loved me. For all I knew at the time, I was just a fun distraction when you were at the ranch."

"That doesn't sound right," he said with enough anger behind it that I looked up through my lashes. "I might not remember everything, but you knew you were more than a distraction. What we had was more than sex."

Again I sighed and leaned against the window. I took another swig from the bottle and grimaced at the bold flavor. "Okay, yeah, that was an asshole thing of me to say. I knew I was more than that, but still, I was seventeen and pregnant with my father's boss's grandson's baby, who happened to be way older. Oh, and to top it off, no one had a damn clue we were even together."

"How did your dad even find out? Did you tell him?"

"Hell no. I went to someone, someone I thought I could trust."

"Who?"

"Mrs. Hathway. She'd been like a mother to me all those years, and I thought she would give me advice, let me cry on her shoulder. But it didn't turn out that way."

"I'll deal with her when I get back," he said with an undercurrent of rage in his tone. "I was happy about the baby. Shocked, but happy."

I didn't hold back my smile. "Yeah you were. The wreck happened about five minutes after we left the ranch. Something darted out into the road. You swerved and then overcorrected us right into a deep drop-off. But in those five minutes, you had our whole lives planned out. You talked so fast, got me excited about our future. You made me believe it." With the back of my hand, I wiped away a rogue tear. "You made me believe in a future with you."

All the color drained from his face. "Then I took it away."

Unable to get another word out without turning into a bumbling mess, I nodded and looked out the window to the white fluffy clouds.

"No, Beks." He wrapped his hands around mine and pulled them close. "I wouldn't have. I swear to you I didn't do that. I didn't make the decision to walk away. Yes, I was high, but my feelings were real. I remember that much. I wouldn't have said all that to you and then walked away. I won't believe it."

"It's the question I've been asking for thirteen years. Why?" I choked out, then downed what was left of the bottle in my hand.

"The fact that I have zero memory, not even a damn hint of what you're talking about when everything else is coming back to me, makes me believe I had nothing to do with it. I'll find out the truth. I'll prove it to you, Beks." Looking down to the table, he took a deep swallow. "I know I have no right to ask, but I have to know. What happened to our baby?"

The world spun. I slammed my eyes shut and leaned back to regain my equilibrium.

Our baby.

Hearing that phrase from his lips, his voice, was too much. My shoulders trembled with every short breath between sobs. A quiet commotion went on in front of me before the pressure from the seat belt disappeared and I was hauled onto his wide, solid lap. Unable to look at him, I buried my face in his hot neck and wrapped my arms around his shoulders, holding him closer.

Even the soothing swipes of his hand down my hair did nothing to ease the pain. My still-raw heart had sliced back open at those two words.

Our baby.

Yeah, our baby.

The chin resting on the crown of my head trembled. Pulling back far enough to look up, I found his eyes sealed shut. A single tear dripped slowly down his tan, scruffy cheek. His pain at the memories, at the raw gash I knew was across his heart like it had once been on me, had me pressing a palm against his cheek, pushing the other against my own.

"You can't even say it, can you?" he choked out. "I killed... it's my fault." His broad shoulders shook in what seemed to be restrained anger or sadness.

"It's not your fault, B." I turned my face to press my lips to his trembling ones. "It was an accident. You didn't make the animal run out into the road. You didn't plan on being in Odessa, saving your underage pregnant girlfriend. Nothing that night was anyone's fault. It was just a tragic event that tore us apart for thirteen years."

Brenton's breaths turned rapid against my skin.

"Brenton, breathe."

"It's my fault. Everything about that night and after was my fault. I ruined your life and took another." He buried his head into my neck and squeezed his arms tighter around me. "Beks, I can't breathe. This hurts worse than when Caleb died. I left you alone with all that. I left you alone to deal with it all."

"Stop," I said soothingly. "It's done."

Internally I was begging him to stop. I couldn't go down that path again. I'd been down it too many times, though less frequently in the last few years, but I couldn't look back now. I was almost whole, mostly due to the man breaking beneath me.

Yes, he might've ruined my life thirteen years ago, but right now he was saving it.

"Nothing we can do about it now. I hurt over this for years, and honestly, I don't want to relive that pain. It still hurts, but never once—not once, Brenton—did I blame you for me losing the baby."

"Our baby."

My bottom lip quivered. "Our baby."

"How old... I mean, how far along were you?"

"Six weeks."

Warm, salt-slick lips pressed against my own, and I moaned at the desperation that leached through the kiss. An unknown urgency had him devouring me, licking and teasing my tongue with his own. He needed this, needed me, needed control, and at that moment I'd allow him to have it if that was what he needed.

"I'm so sorry," he whispered against my lips before sealing them back over mine.

Breathless from pouring all of him into all of me, he pulled back and pressed his forehead against my own. "I don't deserve your forgiveness. I deserve your hate and resentment for what I did to you. Hate me, Beks. Please, please hate me."

"What?" I asked, staring at his dark lashes.

"Hate me. Hit me. Tell me to fuck off and what a hateful, terrible bastard I am. Because that's what I am. Who I am. These past thirteen years, I've lived a damn lie thinking I was better than my father, and look at me. I forgot the woman I loved, nearly killed her, and killed our unborn child. I'm a worthless human being, and that's what I deserve to be seen as by you."

Chapter 21

Rebeka

NOT SURE HOW TO RESPOND to a plea like that, I tugged his head to my chest and hugged him tighter than he held me. Hate him? He couldn't be serious. He didn't understand what love was or how it worked if he thought I could ever hate him or put him in the same category as his father.

Silence encased the cabin the remainder of the flight as we stayed sealed together. Both of us held on to the other as if our lives depended on it. Who knew, maybe they did.

Even after we touched down, his embrace didn't loosen. The pilot and copilot stepped out, their eyes meeting mine before descending the short stairs.

"Hey," I whispered as I stroked through his dark hair and ran my nails down the back of his neck. "It's time to blow this joint. You're leading this adventure, remember? So where are we going? What happens next?"

Cool air brushed the areas where his skin had suctioned against mine. Pure agony swirled behind his dull green eyes while streaks of red lined the whites of his eyes, evidence of his silent tears.

After clearing his throat, he glanced out the window. "I can make them turn around if you don't want to stay."

"Huh?"

"To stay with me."

The uncertainty in his tone squeezed my heart. "Of course I do, B. Maybe I should ask you the same question. I've had thirteen years to process all this, but you've had less than an hour. If you'd prefer we go back and—"

"No." He straightened and rolled his shoulders back. "Here I don't have to share you with anyone or do manual labor to spend some time with you." I bumped my shoulder against his and gave him a shy smile. "Today is about you, remember? I want to stay if you do."

"Well, if you're buying, I'm all in for a 'me' day. Let's go, Sir Fancy Pants. Show me this terrible town of yours."

"Pretty sure Dallas is a city. A metroplex actually."

"You don't deny terrible?"

"I somewhat agree, but I don't think I've seen the good parts."

I turned before taking the first step down the stairs with a questioning look. "What do you mean?"

"The circles my family ran with back then, Caleb and I especially, weren't filled with the best types of people. We were used and leached from for years. Those people didn't give a fuck about us." At the bottom of the stairs, he pressed his hand against my lower back to guide me toward a small side parking lot. "What I mean is I bet there is good in this city, but I've never been fortunate enough to see it."

After tossing our overnight bags into the back of a black Range Rover, Brenton opened the passenger door like a gentleman and helped me in. The inside was as sleek as the outside; the dash looked like you could control the Rover on Mars with a simple flick of the fingers.

I leaned back and rolled my head to look at Brenton, who still stood in the open door.

"How does it work?" I asked.

"What work?"

"Your money? Do you have access to drop millions any time you want?"

He chuckled and leaned against the solid metal of the SUV. "No, it's set up as a trust. Caleb, me, Dad, even Pappy had one from his father. More money goes into the trust each year based on how the company did, but still every month I get a... let's call it a monthly allowance deposited into my bank account."

"Ah," I said like I understood, but I didn't.

"If I went to the firm who manages our trust and asked for a certain amount, let's say for school or something, they would pull the amount I requested from the trust."

"So you have money, but you don't."

"Oh no, I have a lot of it."

"Are you what they consider the 1 percent?"

Again he laughed before leaning in and kissing my forehead. "Sure, baby."

"I like that." I sighed and closed my eyes. "'Beks' makes me feel like we're kids again."

When I opened my eyes, he was staring down at me with an unreadable expression.

"What?" I asked.

"What was said on the plane—"

"I don't want to talk about it anymore. Can we please—" I looked out the windshield, hoping to find my next words. "—table it? I want to enjoy whatever you have planned, and remembering that time, dredging up those awful feelings and memories, isn't something I want dampening it."

The knuckles gripping the door turned white, but he didn't object. "I still have a lot of questions, about that night, about what happened next, so this conversation isn't over. You're not letting me off that easy."

The door slammed shut with a solid thud. I tracked Brenton as he rounded the hood, sliding his sunglass on as he walked. Hot damn, the man was so far out of my league. Back then and now. His tan skin, dark hair, and gorgeous eyes—oh, and that body. It made him the man every woman's erotic fantasy centered around. And I loved all that, loved every physical inch, but what I adored most were the pieces of himself he only showed me. That soft, emotional heart he hid beneath the gruff, arrogant, controlling exterior.

Which I also happened to love.

All the cards were on the table now. He knew everything about that night that I knew, and it was fucking freeing. A weight I'd carried the past few days—hell, the past thirteen years—lifted from my shoulders. Just like Ryder said, I needed closure to let go of that night and the events that followed. Being with him, helping him with his blackouts the past few days, had given me exactly that.

I hated that I was getting closure on an old wound when his agony was beginning. Our conversation on the plane had ripped open an old wound he wasn't even aware he'd had until today.

But he would recover just as I did. Brenton and I, we were survivors. And survivors moved on from the hurt, not allowing their pasts to define who they were and rob them of a happy, fulfilling future.

Sky-high apartment buildings towered overhead as Brenton zipped through the busy downtown city streets. Older homes lined one side of the road while the other had small businesses of varying types. As he drove, I studied the variety of people crowding along the wide sidewalks. I never wanted to live in a big city like Dallas, but visiting, playing the role for a couple of hours, was entertaining for sure.

"You hungry?" Brenton asked, breaking my focus with a heavy, warm hand squeezing my inner upper thigh.

With a broad smile, I turned and said, "Starving. Anywhere around here we can get pancakes?"

"GO AWAY," I MUTTERED into the comforter beneath my cheek.

Brenton responded with a deep, amused chuckle. "You have to get up if you don't want to spoil my plans for you."

"What plans?" I grumbled, opening one eye to see if he was serious. The pancakes, eggs, and never-ending mimosas at brunch had me in a food coma. Napping away the afternoon with him by my side sounded way better than anything he could suggest.

"I made you some spa—"

"Thank you, but no. Nap."

The walls seemed to vibrate with his deep, rolling laugh, which made me smile against the soft duvet.

"There was also some shopping involved," he mused, like he thought that would convince me to leap off the comfortable bed. He didn't know women as well as he thought. Like I'd go try on clothes with my brunch food baby in my belly that already made my comfortable Wranglers snug around the waist.

"No. Bed."

"You're turning down spending my money to lie in bed."

The soft material slid against my cheek as I nodded. "With you. Isn't there a game or something sporty on SportsCenter you can watch while I snuggle you and sleep off this buzz?"

"Now that I can do." The rustling of clothes drew my attention to where he stood on the opposite side of the bed. Green eyes sparkled when he caught me watching. "I like you watching me with that lusty look."

A shiver bolted down my spine at his low, seductive tone.

"Well, I like watching when it's someone as sexy as you, Sir Fancy Pants."

"If you keep looking at me like that, baby, then that nap you hoped for won't happen. Your choice."

Even though I did crave his sexy-as-sin body against mine, the champagne made my eyes heavier with each passing second. After a shake of my head to dislodge all the naughty thoughts he invoked, I rolled to my back and pulled my jeans to my ankles.

When they hit the floor, I glanced to where he stood and smirked at his scorching stare at my naked lower half. "You're the one who didn't pack my underwear." On all fours, I crawled up the bed, bare ass in the air facing him. I reached the top of the comforter, readying to pull it back to snuggle under it when a stinging smack whipped across the right cheek.

Instead of screaming in pain, I buried my face in the mountain of pillows and moaned, keeping my ass in the air, hoping for more.

"Baby," he growled.

"Hmm?"

"You chose nap, not sex, so get that perfect ass of yours under the covers."

"But you're so convincing," I said with a little wiggle, silently begging him for more. "Again, B."

His loud, guttural groan rattled through the room just before a palm smacked the same spot as before. My eyes slammed shut, and an unladylike, garbled moan pushed past my lips into the pillow.

Beneath me, the bed dipped and the mattress shifted. That time, instead of inflicting delicious pain, his callused hands reverently caressed down each cheek. My ass molded in his hands as he squeezed each side with a pleasure-filled moan of his own.

My breath caught at the slide of a hand dipping between my thighs.

"Hell," he muttered, his lips brushing against the small of my back. "You loved it, didn't you." To prove his statement, two fingers slid easily inside.

"Yes," I pleaded into the pillow. A half yelp, half sigh escaped at the twist and curl of his fingers. "Fuck the nap."

At my encouragement, his pace quickened, teasing me to the brink with his two dexterous digits. Soft kisses and not-so-tender nips dotted along each cheek. The pressure built, producing a sheen of sweat that moistened my skin. When I couldn't take any more, he flicked his thumb hard against my swollen clit. On their own, my hips slammed back against his hand and my legs quivered, barely keeping me upright through the force of my release.

Eyes closed, face still buried in the pillow and ass in the air, a slight pressure against my inside knees caught my attention. Obeying, I slid them along the comforter, spreading my legs wide.

"Do you have any idea how gorgeous you are?" he asked while stroking a loving hand down my right ass cheek before seizing a handful of plump flesh. "The sounds you make when you come are almost enough to do me in, baby." The hand not gripping me slid up my back to tangle in my hair, holding my face to the bed. "My turn."

Without warning, he slammed in, sinking deep with the first thrust.

"Fuck me," he gritted out.

Inch by inch he withdrew, only to thrust back in just as deep as before. Again and again he pushed, chasing his release. Echoes of our skin slapping together filled the large room. An open-palmed smack against my ass pulled a startled yet desire-filled yell from my lungs.

"More," I pleaded, shoving back for emphasis.

Everything stilled.

Brenton's heavy, deep pants were the only sound in the room.

"Brenton," I begged. I attempted to wiggle to urge him on but was only rewarded with another stinging smack.

"Say it," he commanded. "Say what you want."

"More. More of you. More of that," I pleaded.

"Of what?" he said in an arrogant tone.

The bastard knew full well what I wanted.

"Spanking, your hand against my ass, all of it. I need more, B," I cried into the pillow. "Please."

Sweat-slick skin pressed against my back, hot breath brushing across my ear. "We're not perfect, baby, but we're fucking perfect for each other."

Both hands dipped to hold my breasts like anchors. He teased and pulled at my tight nipples while he pushed from behind faster and deeper.

"Again, baby," he grunted.

"Please, Brenton," I yelled. Every thought, every sensation focused on him. Each place he touched sparked a fire and added to the building heat between my legs. On the edge, I needed a push to find release. "Again," I whispered, almost like a prayer.

At my request, he leaned back, still pumping hard, and smacked each cheek.

"Holy shit!" I screamed and fell apart beneath him.

Brenton shouted my name along with a few curses before falling onto my back and pushing us down into the soft bed.

My hair tickled over my shoulder as it was swept aside, Brenton pressing light kisses along it and up my neck. He sucked my earlobe between his lips, sending a bolt of lingering arousal through my veins.

"You might be the death of me," he murmured before kissing back down my neck. "How will I ever focus on anything other than you again?"

"Don't," I sighed, eyes still closed, savoring the moment. "I like being your only focus. Don't go back. Then we can do this every day."

A soft laugh brushed over my shoulder. "It doesn't work that way with the military. They call that going AWOL." And just like that, the cherished moment ended, and the reality of our situation washed over me like a bucket of cold water. "But if there were ever a reason to abandon my post and brothers, it'd be you."

"So you are going back."

Cold air replaced where his hot skin had once been. A hand held my shoulder to roll me until I faced him.

"We talked about this. You know I am. You're amazing, we're amazing, but I still have to go back. I have a job to do, people depending on me. I'm good at what I do."

"Tell me more about it. What you do."

"I'm a part of a group called the Night Stalkers. We fly the best of the best our military has to offer into battle or fly into a war zone to pull them out. They need me, and I need them. The order the military life provides, the sense of control flying gives me."

"Sounds dangerous."

"It is, but I can get our men into areas no one else would dare fly. I take those risks because the reward is so great. I can't give that up."

I shifted my stare from his eyes to the soft cream sheets. "I'm not enough to convince you to give it up. That's what you're saying."

"That's not what I'm saying and you know it." He walked to the bathroom, rolling the condom off as he went. Seconds later, he plopped back on the bed, facing the ceiling. For a second he only popped his knuckles before tucking his inked arms behind his head. "I'm saying... hell, I don't even know what I'm saying. I need a second to process it all. Four days ago, you were a figment of my imagination, a distant diluted memory, and now you're here. Plus learning about the baby and what I caused? It's a lot to take in." He turned his head and locked his bright eyes on mine. "Let me work a few things out before we have this conversation, okay? You've had thirteen years. At least give me a day," he said with a slight grin.

He was right. I pushed him to commit when the whole time I knew he was leaving at the end. What did I believe? That amazing sex and conversation would make him do a 180 on his life, make him want to make the ranch his home, giving up the career he'd worked hard for the past thirteen years?

"What would you say if I asked you to come with me?"

I took a shaky breath in and let it out slowly to give myself a second to for-mulate my answer. "I'd say... I'd say let me think about it. Uprooting my life—"

"Which you don't like."

"True," I mused and snuggled under the blankets, pulling them up to my chin to ward off the blasting AC. "But it's all I know."

"Doesn't make it right, or what you want."

"You sound like you're trying to talk me into going with you."

"Maybe I am."

"Are you?"

"I don't know," Brenton said with a sigh, like the weight of the conversation sat on his chest, restricting his breathing. "All I know is the thought of you not being close makes me want to punch something. The idea of you going back to a town that turned on you, near a dad who treats you worse than the ranch dog, makes me want to take you with me, willing or not."

Okay, that was kind of sweet in a kidnapping kind of way. I smirked at the ceiling before looking to him. "But it's not Texas."

"Texas isn't the only state you can live in."

The pillow molded in my grip. I flung it across the bed to smack his chest. "Watch your mouth, sir. Texas is the only state. Don't you remember learning that in Texas history?"

"Right," he laughed. "Kentucky is still considered the south, you know."

The earlier electricity that had pulsed through my body cooled. Exhaustion pulled my lids lower and lower.

"Beks?"

"Sleepy," I somehow muttered before slipping into a deep slumber.

Chapter 22

Brenton

THE RATTLE OF THE PHONE against the wooden side table drew my attention away from the Rangers game I watched while Beks napped. I'd glanced over at least half a dozen times in the past hour, smiling at the naked beauty beside me. Warmth bloomed in my gut each time.

How in the hell could I leave her?

If everyday life was like this, coming home to a woman like her, who accepted me no matter what internal battle I fought, maybe leaving the army wouldn't be such a terrible idea.

She'd already forgiven me for so much; maybe I'd be pressing my luck thinking she'd accept all sides of me. The soldier side of Brenton Graves, the recovering addict side. Beks only saw the stable side of the man she remembered. The rich civilian. Not the man who woke up at night drenched in sweat from near-death experiences, or woke up angry at the world when the ghosts of the men we lost as I flew them toward medical care haunted my dreams. Or the man who would stare at the bottle of bourbon for hours, fighting the persistent urge to take a sip.

Would she still want me if she saw all sides of Brenton Graves? The good and the terrible?

No, she didn't need to know those ugly sides of me.

Because then she'd see how broken I was. Not the strong, cocky, arrogant-as-hell man she believed.

What if telling her everything was the final straw? Could I handle the one woman I wanted more than life itself walking away?

Looking away, I snagged my phone and swiped the screen open.

Kyle: Bradley doesn't want you involved. Said he wouldn't give me the names of his suppliers.

Lips pressed into a thin line, I glanced to the still-sleeping Beks. I told her I'd handle it before I left. No way would that dumbass brother of hers stand in the way of protecting her.

Me: Give me his number.

Seconds later, Bradley's contact information flicked across the screen.

Me: Give me their names and information. Now. I won't allow those fuckers to be anywhere near my property.

Me: Don't give me that shit of you handling it. I saw you yesterday. You can barely fucking walk.

Me: Take the out I'm giving you.

Me: You won't like the alternative. From them. Or me.

Bradley: These fuckers are no joke, rich boy.

Bradley: I'll set up the meet, but I'm not giving you their information.

Me: Fine. Set it up.

An inning later, the Rangers still down by five runs, my phone buzzed on the bed.

Bradley: Tonight. 1 a.m. I'll drop you a pin of the meeting location.

Bradley: Sure as hell hope you know what you're doing.

Me: You're welcome.

Bradley: They want cash.

Me: They'll get cash that I wire them. I'm not a fucking moron.

Me: And your sister stays out of this. I'll do the meet. You keep her busy.

Bradley: If you haven't fucking noticed, asshole, she has a mind of her own and is pretty damn smart. She'll figure out what you're doing behind her back and rip your balls off.

Bradley: I'm not kidding either. I've seen her castrate enough animals. She knows how to do it.

My balls reflexively pulled closer to my body.
Don't worry, boys. She likes you too much to rip you off.
I think.

Me: I'll handle her.
Bradley: Oh hell, man. You have a death wish.
Bradley: You better hope she doesn't ever read that shit.
Bradley: Beka isn't one to be handled.

Almost on cue, Beks gave a soft, happy groan and stretched out beneath the coves.

Me: I'll be there tonight. Confirm it.

I dropped the phone to the floor and shifted across the king-size bed to curl against her warm, naked body. Her honey brown eyes fluttered open, and a small smile spread up her cheeks.

I sucked in a breath. Bedhead, cheeks flushed, and happy, this woman was a dream. I nuzzled her shoulder and bit the back of her neck. No doubt she felt my rock-hard dick pressing into her thigh, eager for another round.

A pounding knock at the door caused both our heads to lift and turn toward the sound.

"Expecting someone?" she asked, still half asleep. "I'm not down with sharing, so you know. None of that ménage shit."

Content with ignoring whoever was at the door, I covered her body with mine, nestling my dick between her ass cheeks. "I'm not sharing you, baby. You're mine and mine only. I'll break the fucker who tries to touch you."

"So possessive," she grumbled with a smirk.

"You love it."

"I—" Another impatient knock from the door cut her off. "Dammit, B, just go see who it is, would you?"

"It's either my dad," I said into her dark hair, taking a deep sniff of the coconut scent, "or...."

With her elbow pressed into the bed, she hauled me off her back. "Who?"

"No one, baby," I groaned, grabbing her waist to keep her on the bed. "It's no one. Just leave it."

At my next tug, she wiggled out of my loose grip with a mischievous smile. "The suspense is killing me," she joked, then slid my T-shirt over her head. On her tiptoes, she sashayed out of the bedroom with a hint of her perfect ass peeking out beneath the black tee.

At least there wasn't a place for her to hide a gun dressed like that.

In the distance, the deadbolt snapped back and the door swooshed open. Low, muffled voices filtered down the hall as I swung my legs over the side of the bed. A familiar deep one shot a surge of rage into my blood.

Dad.

"Fuck." My pants only halfway up, I strode out of the bedroom. By the time I reached where the two faced off in the entryway, the jeans were loose around my hips, though still unbuttoned.

Beks stood a foot from the threshold, arms crossed over her chest, glaring at Dad. He looked amused at the fury behind her eyes. There was also a gleam in his eye that said he'd already mentally undressed my girl in the thirty-second span.

"What do you want?" I barked as I pulled the mostly naked Beks behind my back.

"I called to schedule the jet, but they said it was already here and you were headed back tomorrow too. So here I am." He shrugged and leaned a shoulder against the doorframe. To anyone else, it looked like he wanted to appear casual, but the way his gaze kept bouncing behind me, it was a ploy to get a better visual on her.

I shot him a look of warning and turned to the furious beauty. "Go get some clothes on."

"I'm fine," she said, shifting that glare to me.

"I'm not. Go." Not giving her a chance to argue, I turned back to Dad. "That doesn't explain why you're here."

With an annoyed huff, he pushed off the doorframe and shouldered past into the loft. I slammed the door shut and turned to stalk after him.

He paused in the living room and slowly turned to take in the place. "Haven't changed anything since Caleb, I see."

"Why would I? This isn't my home."

"Right," he mocked. "Forgot you're some government grunt playing soldier. I'll never understand why you left all this." He waved his hands around the cold loft. "Left your brother. Well, we saw how that turned out for him."

"You son of a bitch" came an angry voice at my back. Both of our heads whipped to her. "Fuck you for saying he had anything to do with Caleb's death. If anyone in the room is to blame, it's you."

"I hope for you she's that feisty in bed. More fun to control," Dad said with a chuckle before his attention swung back to me. "We need to talk. Alone."

I widened my stance and crossed my arms over my bare chest with a smirk. "She can hear whatever you have to say."

The hate-filled look he shot Beks drew a warning growl from deep in my gut.

"The attorneys called. Said you were asking about some old legal documents."

I arched a brow in response. With Dad, fewer words were better in case he was attempting to corner you with your own.

"Drop it," he stated with force.

"Why?"

"Fucking do it, son. For once in your damn life, do what I tell you to do and don't give me any shit about it." Dad fell on to the couch and leaned back like he owned the place, stretching his arms out wide across the back.

"No." Now more than ever, it was clear some shady shit went down in those hours after the wreck. Why, I had no idea, but if Dad was involved and nervous about what I'd uncover, it wasn't good.

"It's for your damn good. You and your ranch hand whore."

I didn't think, just acted. Two long strides put me in front of the couch. Instead of beating the shit out of him sitting down, I fisted his shirt in my left hand and hauled him upright. His eyes went wide and wild as realization dawned.

The first punch flung him back so hard that his shirt slipped from between my fingers. Dad stumbled back, his knees buckling when they slammed into the glass coffee table. The piercing shriek of glass shattering resounded through the loft.

Blood streamed from Dad's nose as he pushed up to all fours before falling back into the sharp shards.

"Get the fuck out," I somehow said through my rage-locked jaw.

"She's a gold-digging whore. Can't you see that? Hell, even her father saw it."

A loud gasp sounded in my ears just before my bare foot connected with his rib cage. With a pain-filled moan, he rolled to his back, chest heaving.

Not giving a damn about the glass, I picked up his feet and dragged him across the living room. After depositing his moaning ass in the hall, I slammed the door and turned the deadbolt.

Anger still boiling, I stormed into the empty living room.

"Beks?" I said before scanning the bedroom. "Rebeka."

Turning a corner, I stared down the dark hallway that led to Caleb's side. I hadn't stepped foot in that section of the loft since my return and wasn't planning on it now.

A flicker of movement on the balcony caught my eye. The tight breath I'd held as I searched released slow and controlled.

"Hey." I stepped out onto the balcony and leaned against the railing, mirroring her. "You okay?"

"That?" She huffed and hung her head. A strong gust of wind blew her long hair across her face, keeping me from reading her features. "It's nothing I haven't heard before. After you left and people found out about us, about the baby, the whore name was as common as my actual one."

My knuckles whitened as my grip tightened on the metal railing.

"It's why I had to get out of there. I had to leave it all behind, you know? Leave a father who resented me, leave a town that turned on me, leave a brother who was the town drug middleman. Mostly I had to leave our memories. That ranch, every square inch of the land and star-filled sky, reminded me of us."

"I'm sorry." Even though the words were heartfelt, they fell flat. Being sorry did nothing for her now, nothing to repair the damage I inflicted in the past.

"Some days, simple moments of seeing a mom and her child, or even seeing the natural motherly nature in animals, it still hurts. For years, guilt pulled me under on a daily basis. Then it turned to weekly, then every so often." The wind at her back pushed all her hair toward me, wrapping my face in a coconut-scented blanket. "Never once did I regret us."

"I don't deserve someone like you. Don't deserve your forgiveness."

Her smile pulled at my heart, my breath catching. "That's what's amazing about forgiveness, B. You don't have a say in it. Forgiveness is a gift you have no control over. And honestly, forgiving you is less work than harboring the hate."

"What can I give you? Name it and it's yours." I'd give her every last penny if she asked.

"If you have to ask"—her smile faltered—"then what I want, you're not ready to give."

Me.

Only this beautiful, selfless woman would want me instead of all the things thirty million could buy.

She sighed and turned to lean her back against the rail. Her eyes narrowed as they scanned the living room through the large windows. "What a mess."

"I'll call someone to clean it up."

Her head dropped back with a loud laugh. "Of course you will."

"Hey, something came up and we need to head back tonight. Sorry to cut this short."

She shrugged and closed her eyes. "Everything okay?"

"Yeah, just some things to handle before I leave."

A single nod and Beks shoved off the railing. At the door, she turned back with her brows pulled together in a thoughtful look. "Based off your dad not wanting you to look into the files, I'm willing to bet he had more to do with breaking us apart than you."

I nodded in agreement and followed her inside. "I want to see those documents. Come on, let's go call them."

Chapter 23

Rebeka

BEING A MEMBER OF THE mile-high club wasn't something on my bucket list. I mean, who thought they would ever have the chance? Wonder if I got bonus points for being initiated on a private jet.

"What are you smiling about?" Brenton asked from behind the wheel of my truck. Or was it his truck? Our truck?

"Do I get a badge or something?"

"What?" he laughed.

"You know, the mile-high club, what we just did on the plane—twice. Do I get a badge? Or is there maybe some secret handshake I get to learn?"

Instead of answering, he shook his head and smiled out the windshield.

With a smile of my own, I watched out the window at the diminishing lights of Midland. The day was perfect. Well, minus his dad showing up. And the attorney not having anything new for Brenton. And I guess coming back early was a killjoy too. But besides all that, it was a perfect day.

Because it was just us.

I snuck a side glance his way. One wrist rested on top of the wheel as he leaned back in the driver seat, relaxed. Smiling. Brenton Graves was an enigma. A military-tatted badass with millions in the bank and enough family drama to rival any reality show.

If I had to guess, the man sitting beside me was the true Brenton Graves. The man his dad had shoved so far away with drugs and women when he and Caleb were kids. We were both a little broken in that way. Never been loved un-conditionally. And maybe, based on that slight defect, might not be able to give it.

I was running back to the man who had already hurt me once, and I knew it would happen again. What did that say about me?

"Are you nervous about tomorrow?" I asked, wanting to deflect my deep internal thoughts.

"Honestly?"

The leather groaned as I swirled in the seat to face him. "Always."

"Yeah. I don't know what I'll do if Dad gets the ranch. I want to think Pappy wouldn't leave our family land to him, but it's tradition, what our family's done for generations."

"Would you want it?"

"I wouldn't want anyone else to have it."

"That doesn't answer my question. Would you want it? Could you ever see yourself coming back here and making this place your home?"

"Beks...."

"I'm not saying with me," I said with a sigh. The hesitation on his part sent my stomach rolling. "I'm just asking a question, not trying to hoodwink you."

"The army is my home."

Right. Back to that.

Instead of pushing him, I rested my head against the headrest and shut my eyes.

"It's not you. It's me."

Behind my lids, I rolled my eyes. "Can you not be so cliché? Don't use a line 90 percent of men use as a brush-off. I deserve originality. At least give me that."

No response. Only the hum of the tires rolling along the smooth interstate filled the cab the rest of the drive back.

THE ANNOYANCE AT HIS comment grew to pent-up anger. If he said a single word before I could get out of the truck, I'd probably explode. The engine idled outside Daddy's place, but thankfully Brenton continued to sit silently. I yanked the door handle and shoved it wide open, ready to be alone for a few hours to collect the damn rolling emotions he'd caused.

"I'll walk you in," Brenton muttered at my back.

Oh hell no. No chivalry shit when he just brushed me off. "Fuck you," I gritted out over my shoulder as I slid out of the seat and slammed the door.

"Rebeka," he yelled back. "Stop."

Bag in hand, I shut the tailgate and stormed toward the house. Brenton stepped in, blocking my path.

"Move." I had to get in the house before the damn tears spilled over. No way could I give Brenton the satisfaction of watching me break. Because of him. Again.

"Not until you understand something."

With a loud scoff, I shouldered past him only to be pinned against the truck. With his hands on my shoulders holding me to the hot metal, I shot him my best "fuck off" glare.

"What I meant was... you're perfect. I don't deserve your time, and I sure as hell don't deserve your love or forgiveness after what I've done to you. What I'm saying is... I don't—"

"Spit it out, Graves. I don't have all night."

"It's easier to believe someone loves me for my money than for being me," he whispered. "I'm a broken man who has fucked up more times in this life than any person should be allowed. I'm a recovering addict, a fuckup when it comes to you. What kind of person would I be to allow you to—"

"Allow?" I snapped. "You don't allow me to do anything. If you haven't noticed—"

"Hell, woman, I'm saying if I could love anyone, it would be you. But I can't."

"Yes you can," I said, giving up on holding back the hot tears.

"My mom walked out on us. Dad fed me drugs and women as our bonding time. Most of the women I've been with only want me for my money and nothing else. When in the hell would I have learned how to love in all that? I'm a ruined man who is terrified every second I'm alive that my demons might catch up with me and I'll slip back down that dark hole of addiction. You deserve better than me, and I won't tie you to me and drag you down too."

"You're a damn fool, Brenton." The bag in my hand fell to the dust as I shoved both hands against his shoulders. "Do you think this is easy for me? You know my story, and yet here I am loving you. Loving the man who devastated me once. *Devastated*, Brenton. I don't know how to do this either, but I'd rather figure this love shit out with you than anyone else. No one else makes me feel like you. No one makes me love myself as much as you do."

"You're wrong. You're better—"

"That ruined shit is a lame-ass excuse. You're scared. And you know what? I'm not going to do this to myself again. You were right about something, Brenton Graves. I do deserve better, but not for the reasons you think." Reaching down, I snagged my bag and started toward the house. I paused but didn't turn to him when I said, "For the record, this isn't me walking away from the real Brenton. It's me giving up on the man you believe you are."

A warm, strong hand gently wrapped around my wrist but fell away when I stepped toward the house.

Once inside, the sounds blaring on the TV didn't drown out the rumble of the truck driving off.

"Look at what the cat dragged in," Daddy said from his leather recliner, not looking away from the late-night game show that was on. "Alone. Where's the prick Graves kid?"

"Don't start with me," I gritted out, somehow able to keep new tears from flowing down my cheeks.

"You're a fool if you think this time will be any different. That family won't let him have anything to do with us. You learned that years ago. Stay away from him." He cut his bloodshot eyes over to where I still stood by the door, bag in hand. "I don't want our name dragged through the mud again because of you. The first time was bad enough, being the father of the town whore. Don't want to add being the father of the town idiot to it."

I averted my eyes from his glare to the empty beer cans littering the floor around the recliner. "Right, like I enjoyed being the daughter of the town drunk who killed his wife."

"I didn't touch her," he seethed. The can in his hand crushed in his grip, spraying beer on the wall.

"You didn't force the pills down her throat, but you drove her to it."

"Me? No, that was you and your brother. You two took her from me, drove her damn crazy. Get the fuck out of my house," he snarled. "I don't want someone like you living under my roof."

I'd leave that second to put as much space between me and the life-sucking leech I called my father as I could, but I couldn't. I'd need a truck for that, and mine was now parked at the main house, the keys with the man I loathed one second and loved desperately the next. Too much pride kept me from asking for the keys, so instead I stomped through the living room and down the hall toward the bedrooms.

Bradley tried to grab my attention as I passed by his room, but I ignored it. Only seconds were left before the dam holding back a gush of tears broke. The door shook the room when I slammed it closed. The bag fell to the floor with a thud, and the mattress squeaked under my weight when I fell face-first onto the unmade bed.

Finally alone, I let the tears fall to my pillow with deep, loud, soul-cleansing sobs.

"BEKA?"

Bradley's concerned voice pulled me awake. I rolled to face the door, tucking my hands under the pillow. He stood just over the threshold, leaning against the frame like he needed the support to stay standing. After a glance behind him, he limped the rest of the way into the room to collapse onto the end of the bed.

"What happened?" he asked, staring at the ceiling.

"Nothing," I sighed, then scooted down to lie beside him. When his head lolled to the side and those dark brown eyes locked with mine, I knew he saw right through the lie. "He loves me. I know he does. And what's sad is I think he knows it too, but he's too much of a chickenshit to come out and say it. No idea what he's so scared of."

Bradley said nothing for a minute, letting the silence between us weigh in the room.

"I can see what he's saying. Not all of us are like you, Beka. For some of us who weren't shown love, it doesn't come easy, and it's fucking terrifying when it's in your face. You don't want to accept it, yet the alternative, letting it walk away, is just as terrible." His fingers intertwined with mine along the quilt beneath us. "It's easier to push people away and get lost in an escape than it is to admit you're too broken inside with no way of being fixed."

"Bradley," I whispered and squeezed his hand. "Is that how you feel? That you're broken and beyond repair?"

His nonresponse answered the question for him.

I rolled to my side and leaned up on an elbow. "You and Brenton and all those other people out there who've never been loved, never been shown the basics a mom and dad should give, aren't broken. I'm not broken. Don't give two thoughts to Dad and what he says. You are amazing. You've kept this place going while Dad sat on his ass drinking. You have your demons, we all do, but look at you." I waved a hand to his face, where clear eyes stared back into mine. "You've been through hell this week, and you're clean. You did that, no one else."

"I want a hit so bad it hurts," he said with a slight tremble. It's only then that I noticed his chest rising and falling in rapid, shallows breaths. "I'm trying. I am fucking trying, but it's hard and fucking everything hurts."

"I believe in you," I whispered. "And I love you. You always have me in your corner."

"I know." He focused back on the ceiling with a sigh. "What are you going to do?"

"I don't know." Saying the words out loud stirred fear and loneliness in my gut. "He knows I love him. I've shown him, forgiven him. I can't make him realize he's capable of loving someone. He needs to do that on his own."

"Well, for a guy, actions speak louder than words."

"What do you mean?" Silence met my response, piquing my interest. "Bradley."

"Nothing."

"Tell me."

"No."

"Um, yes?"

"Beka," he said with a frustrated groan.

"Don't 'Beka' me, you jackass."

"You can't call me a jackass. You just told me you loved me and were in my corner!"

"I can. We're siblings, so it's allowed. Tell me, what did you mean by that?"

He sighed and pushed to sit up. "He told me not to tell you."

"Even better reason to tell me."

"He's meeting those guys tonight, the ones I owe money to."

I stared, mouth open. "What? How... when... what?"

"He told me to set it up, Beka. He said he didn't want those guys on his property or anywhere near you."

Anger mixed with fear pushed aside all the sorrow and hurt from earlier. Hands balled into tight fists, I stood and started toward the door. "When?"

"One."

"Who's his backup?"

"I don't know."

"Fuck, Bradley! You sent him out there alone?"

"I had no other choice!" he shouted back. "Not like I could go."

"Where?"

"No. You're not going—"

The warm grip of my SIG pressed against my palm. Keeping it pointed to the floor, I flicked off the safety and engaged the slide. His wide eyes zeroed in on the loaded weapon.

"I won't ask again, Bradley."

"You wouldn't."

"Do you want to find out what I will or won't do to protect that man?"

Defiant brown eyes flicked to mine. "I sent him a pinned location."

Anticipation swirled, making my hands tremble. "Send it to me." I turned to the door, pausing when he pushed off the bed to stand.

"You're not going alone."

With a smirk, I said, "You're right, but you're not the backup I'm taking."

Chapter 24

Rebeka

"WE'RE CLOSE," I SAID to the others as we walked side by side down the old county road.

"Can't believe you talked us into this," Ryder grumbled. "Pulled me out of bed even."

I smirked at the glowing phone screen. Damn, that girl could hold a grudge. We didn't talk about our argument on the call when I asked for her and Kyle's help, or in the truck on the way here. But what made friendships like ours amazing was that we didn't have to. Not right now at least. We could table it until we had the allotted time, and a few bottles of wine, to hash things out and wrap it up with a good romcom movie.

This was not that night.

The weight of the large rifle pressed against my shoulder. I adjusted the shoulder strap to the other side to relieve the growing ache.

"I'm pissed the bastard didn't ask for my help to begin with," Kyle said while tugging the gun from my shoulder. "Beka, calm down. I'll give it back. Don't shoot me that 'I'll cut you' look. Just offering to be your pack mule until we get there and this big guy is needed."

Ryder linked elbows with mine like we were on a Sunday stroll instead of what we were actually doing—heading to a buyout meeting to save the arrogant asshole who held my heart, packing only a rifle, one AR, and four pistols between us. Kyle was a hell of a shot and offered to bring his AR in case things got out of hand, and Ryder being Ryder brought her .40-caliber hand cannon, plus snacks.

It was twenty after one when voices of men talking carried on the gusting wind. I snapped the phone off and tucked it into the back pocket of my jeans to take the rifle from Kyle's extended hand.

On silent feet, we crouched closer toward the lights and voices.

Once the group was in view, we lay along the ground where we had a clear line of sight and waited.

"Can you hear what they're saying?" Ryder whispered between crunching bites. I turned from the group to stare at her incredulously. "What? I eat when I'm nervous. You know that."

I shook my head and turned to look back through the scope. Thank goodness we decided to show up. This could get out of hand quick.

Four men stood across from Brenton, illuminated by two sets of headlights. A couple more of the bad guys leaned against the hood of their two idling trucks.

"I count six baddies and one Sir Fancy Pants," I whispered to Kyle. "You?"

"Same. I don't see any hanging around the edges on patrol, but I want to double-check. Ryder, stay with Beka."

A soft wind brushed through my hair and over my sweaty face. Shit, what would we do if they shot him? Take them all out? We needed a plan. All I could think about was getting out here, and now that we were, I was at a loss.

"Hey," Ryder whispered.

"What?"

"I need to tell you something."

I pulled back from the scope. "Now?"

"Yeah, it's kind of important."

I rested the rifle along the ground and turned to her. "What's going on?"

"I think... I'm calling off the wedding."

I stared unblinkingly at my best friend for what seemed like thirty minutes, trying to figure out if I heard her right. Then approaching steps had me grabbing the rifle and turning to the intruder.

"Just me," Kyle said as he crouched between us. "Just those fuckers we see. No one else. But it looks like it's getting heated down there. Not sure what's being said, but it seems like your boy is toying with them."

"Wouldn't surprise me," I grumbled. "That guy has always loved a fight."

"Except they have guns."

"I'm sure Brenton does too."

I felt more than saw Kyle shake his head. "Look on the ground, by his feet. They made him toss it."

"Shit."

"Yeah, and looks like it's about to get real down there."

I turned to stare through the scope again just in time to see two of the men walk on either side of Brenton to restrain his arms.

"Well hell."

"What do you want to do?" Kyle asked.

I scanned the surrounding area. Plan. We needed a damn plan. But it was difficult to think when half my heart was in the middle of the shitshow.

"Kyle, you go over that way. If things get really bad, ping the sides of the trucks and I'll take out the windows. I don't see anyone inside that we could hit. Maybe they'll think they're surrounded and bolt."

"Or kill Brenton."

"Let's go with *my* version."

"Okay, boss." At that, he patted Ryder's head and slunk off into the dark.

I waited a few seconds after he disappeared before shoving Ryder's shoulder. "What the hell are you talking about?"

"I don't know, okay?"

"What do you mean you don't know? If you're talking about calling off the wedding, you better know what you're doing."

"Remember that one time at Dos Amigos when I got so pissed at you and said a bunch of stuff I regretted?"

"Last night?" I deadpanned.

"Yeah, then. Well, I realized after we left why I said it. I'm damn jealous of you."

"Me?" I squeaked louder than I should've, considering our dangerous surroundings.

"I saw the way Brenton looked at you, the way you love him desperately no matter what he's done or was going to do. The way you talked about him being so possessive and wanting you made me realize what Kyle and I don't have."

"But you get along so well," I said, still in shock. This was not happening. She could not compare the hot fling I had with Brenton to the long-term relationship she had with Kyle. Could she? What they had, people would kill over. The love and respect they had were what I wanted one day.

"We do. We're friends, yeah, but that spark, the desperation for each other, just isn't there. And maybe it never was. We just kind of happened as a couple, and we got along so well that we just kept at it. I want what you and Brenton have. I want that spark. I want the air sucked out of me every time he enters the room. When Brenton looks at you, everyone around can feel it. He loves you, Beka. I know he does. It doesn't mean he'll end up staying, but I want that look from the man I'm going to marry. I want what you have with Brenton."

"He says he can't love. That he's broken," I whispered to the dusty ground.

Not knowing what to say next, I turned back toward the group and brought the scope to my eye.

"The sex is terrible, if you really want to know."

"I didn't," I whisper-yelled back. "How bad are we talking?"

"At least he's good with his tongue."

"See, there's a positive."

"But I'm a 'dick not lick' girl."

My shoulders trembled as I held in a fit of giggles. This was a ridiculous conversation, especially here. But with Ryder, everything was random and fun. One of the reasons I loved her.

"Shit," I whispered.

"I know, right. I mean, I like him down there, but sometimes—"

"Not that," I hissed. "Brenton."

One man sucker punched Brenton in the gut while two others held back his arms. The entire bad guy crew had a good laugh while each got a hit in. Still, Brenton didn't attempt to break free.

"What's going on?" Ryder asked between crunchy bites.

"Shh."

"Wish this reality show came with subtitles."

My heart ratcheted against my chest when one man drew his pistol and pointed it at Brenton's chest.

"Shit's about to get real. Hand me the ammo."

The bullets rattled in the box from her trembling hand as she handed it over. "What can I do?"

"Calm me down. I can't shoot like this." Settling back, I raised the gun to line up the scope. "My hands are fucking shaking."

Ryder rambled about work, her parents, life. With each second, each word, my heartbeat steadied and my nerves quietened. When Kyle's first bullet went through the passenger door of a truck, I was ready.

Taking aim, I focused on the driver-side window and pulled the trigger. Glass shattered less than a second later, echoing through the night. I only paused long enough to make sure our distraction was noticed.

I shot out window after window while Kyle peppered the metal sides with the AR from his vantage point.

The men shouted, and the one holding the gun to Brenton spun around, firing frantically into the dark. Brenton collapsed to the ground when the two men dropped him to run toward a truck and leap in the bed as it disappeared down the road. Within seconds the other truck had roared off in the same direction, leaving only my truck's headlights pouring through the night.

Rifle in hand, I raced through the dust and dirt toward Brenton. At the sound of my approach, he pushed off the ground, only to fall back again. Furious green eyes locked with mine the second I stepped into the bright beams.

"What the fuck are you doing here?" he coughed before spitting a mix of blood and saliva to the dirt.

"It looks like saving your dumb ass is what," I retorted with a smile, which fell when he spit another mouthful of blood to the ground. "Face the beams so I can check your face."

"I'm not one of your damn animals. I'm fine."

"You sure? Because you're acting like a jackass right now." I smirked down at his snarl. "Get it? Jackass? Donkey?"

Stone-faced, he turned into the light. Like I'd done with Bradley just days earlier, I pushed the emotion aside to focus on the task at hand. Not once did he flinch or balk at my prodding fingers along his injuries. Besides a busted lip and swollen cheek, no other wounds were visible on his face, though who knew what was broken or cracked beneath this shirt. He'd be sore for days, that was certain.

"Besides being a dumbass, I think you're fine." I stood and extended a hand to help him up. He groaned in pain as I put my full body weight into yanking him to his feet. A loud thump reverberated through the still night as he fell against the truck for support.

I turned to Kyle and Ryder who'd just walked up staying silent during our spat. "You guys go ahead. I'll drive him back."

"You sure?" Ryder asked.

I nodded. "I still have my rifle and SIG if they come back. Thanks for helping."

"Always, you know that," Kyle said with a wave. "Call us if you need anything."

"Hey," Brenton gritted out with a wince. "Thanks."

"We would've come with you from the beginning," Ryder said with her arms folded across her chest. "Why did you come into this alone?"

His eyes shifted to stare into the darkness. "It's my fight. From what I could gather from Bradley, most of the debt was what Caleb owed before he died. I didn't want to drag anyone else into this mess. Especially not her."

Her.

Me.

"You really are a dumbass." Ryder chuckled. "She"—she pointed to me but kept her glare locked on him—"is the best thing that's happened to you, and you're doing nothing about it."

"I was trying to protect her," he said, then took an unsteady step toward me. "You've been through enough because of me—"

"Oh stop it with that shit," I yelled. "You don't get to decide what I'm protected from or what I'm not involved in. Leaving me out of this wasn't your decision to make."

The distant howl of coyotes filled our stiff silence. Instead of sticking around to hear what other bullshit he would use as an excuse, I waved to Kyle, told Ryder I'd call her later, and climbed into the truck.

Minutes ticked by with the engine idling as the other three stood in the headlights, talking too low for me to understand what they were discussing. With a shake of hands, the small group disbanded and Brenton turned, pinning me with an uncertain gaze through the windshield before shuffling to the truck. He grunted as he hauled himself in and slammed the passenger door.

Turning the AC on full blast, he leaned back and closed his eyes.

Fine. Not talking about it, then.

I shifted the truck into Drive and headed home.

"I'm sorry," he said halfway back. "I really thought I had it handled. And I don't want you anywhere near those bastards. They don't know you exist, and we're going to keep it that way. They'd find some way to use you as leverage if they did."

Ah, so there it was. It wasn't about putting me in danger tonight but the long-term effects that he was concerned about. When he put it that way, it did make sense.

"I get it, I really do. You're a dude, a soldier whose main focus is protecting others. But you don't get to make that decision for me. All you had to do was tell me why you didn't want me out there and we would've figured it out. I let you boss me around in bed, and I love it, but everywhere else, I make my own decisions. I'm not some simpering Dallas socialite."

"Thank fuck."

A small smile tugged at my lips as we pulled up the long drive. "I'll help you inside."

Halfway up the steps, he wobbled and swayed. To prevent him from tumbling back down, I ducked a shoulder under his arm and pulled him close. Inside, we bounced off the hall walls a few times before making it to his room.

"Hope Mrs. Hathway didn't hear us," I said through gritted teeth. Damn, the man was heavy.

"She's gone. I fired her this evening when we got back."

Hell. Was it bad that I wanted to say thank you?

Still processing that bit of information and how I should feel, I guided him toward the bed.

"No, I need a shower." Redirecting, we shuffled as one to the large en suite bathroom. The marble countertops and white tile floors gleamed when I flicked the bright lights on. While I readied the shower, he leaned against the counter and examined his face in the mirror. "Not bad. Not good. But not terrible."

"Could've been worse."

"But it wasn't thanks to you and your posse."

I snorted and tugged the black T-shirt over his head. Those tatted arms fell to his side, then reached back, pulling me flush against his hot skin. With a relieved sigh, I melted against him and pressed my cheek to his back.

"Thank you," he said.

"Thank you for protecting my brother," I whispered. "Is he... I mean, are we good, or will they come back?"

"We're good. I'll wire them the money tomorrow. I made it clear about what I'd do if they stepped foot on my property again."

"Was that before or after they treated you as their personal punching bag?"

He squeezed me closer. "Before. I think they were trying to prove a point."

"Which was?"

"That they would do what I asked, but it wasn't because they were scared of me."

I tensed at the anger in his tone. "Should they be?"

"If they get anywhere near you, yes. I want you to know something." He flipped around, resting his ass on the counter, and pulled me against his chest. "If anyone could make me want to try, want to figure out a real relationship, it'd be you. But I'm not there. I know you've waited, but there's still a lot of shit about me you don't know, that I don't want you to know. What if that's the final straw in you walking away?"

Instead of responding, I kissed his chest above his heart and pulled at his belt. The soft cotton of my T-shirt slid up my back as he tugged it over my head. With a flick of his fingers, the bra's thick band released from around my ribs and the straps slid down my arms. Chest to chest, skin to skin, he angled my chin to capture my lips with his. He kissed me soft and slow, pouring every ounce of emotion that he couldn't verbalize into me.

I toed off one boot and then the other while he did the same.

Face cradled between his hands, I gave up control and savored the way he made me feel small. Powerful but small. An intoxicating combination that only he could brew.

Making quick work of my jeans, he shoved them and my underwear down my thighs until they puddled on the floor.

He flinched when I wrapped my arms around his waist.

"Are you okay?" I pulled back and scanned his chest. "Does something hurt?"

"Get in the shower." For not moving immediately, I was rewarded with a quick smack to my right ass cheek. "Now."

The heat and longing behind his green eyes pushed me back a step, a bolt of excitement and warmth settling between my thighs, building on the heat already there. The shower's rocked floor massaged the sore soles of my feet, and the warm water soothed the tension of the night from my tight shoulders.

At the opening of the glass door, a waft of cold air prickled my already warmed skin. Standing directly across the small enclosure, Brenton lazily perused up and down my naked body. Hand firmly wrapped around himself, he groaned and stepped to meet me under the hot spray.

The water poured over his dark hair, cascading over his broad shoulders and defined chest. Unable to resist, I reached through the steady stream to skim my fingertips down his rippled abs and back up, sliding my hands over his shoulders and down his strong arms.

"You leave tomorrow?" I asked, not much louder than the hiss and patter of the shower.

"Yes, after the meeting with the attorneys. I'm due back on base at 0800 the next day, so I need to get there tomorrow night. The army doesn't do late."

Again I caressed up and down his arms, memorizing every muscle, every curve for future fantasies. "You feel good about the progress we've made with your 'episodes'?" I molded my naked body against his and hugged him tightly.

"I think I have a lot of shit to still sift through, but you've given me the tools to work through it all. You were the key, and now with all these memories... I feel like I have a piece of me back."

A tear slipped down my cheek, disappearing in the streams of water flowing down my face. "Good. Glad I could help."

"You didn't just help, Beks." With two fingers beneath my chin, he tilted my faced up to meet his searching gaze. "You saved me."

My chin trembled at the force required to hold back the tears that wanted to fall. Dropping my head, I pressed my forehead against his chest, my shoulders shaking with a silent sob.

This was goodbye, our last time together, maybe ever.

But he'd given a piece of me back.

And I'd done the same for him.

Even a little broken, I was more whole right then than in the past thirteen years.

He did that, but I still had to protect me. Protect my heart knowing he could shred it beyond repair.

"I love you, Brenton Graves," I choked out. "I don't want to be without you, but I won't beg you to stay either."

Chapter 25

Brenton

I LOVED IT WHEN SHE begged, but not in this case. She was right. Someone like her deserved a man who knew his place was at her side, giving her what she needed on a daily basis.

Not me.

Not with my addictions and fucked-up family.

Someone better, less jaded, able to return the deep, soul-cleaning love she offered.

That person was not me, but still, I couldn't let her go. Which made me a complete asshole since I was leaving. But I was Brenton Graves; it was who I was and what would be listed on my tombstone someday.

Her dark hair slid through my fingers as I pushed it behind her ear.

"I'm sorry I couldn't be the man you deserve," I whispered. Not giving her a chance to respond, I pressed my lips to her neck and peppered kisses along her jaw until I reached her lips.

Fingers tangled in her hair, I pulled her closer. Beks's nails scratched up my back before wrapping around my neck and digging in.

One long, muscular leg hitched around my hip and urged me harder against her with a heel to my ass. There was no holding back my groan of approval from passing through my lips to hers. Guiding her back against the stone wall, I grabbed each cheek and hauled her higher. Instantly the other leg wrapped around my hip, spreading her wide.

"Condom," I mumbled against her collarbone on my descent to her lush breasts.

"Not on me," she groaned.

"I'll go—"

"Don't you fucking dare. I'm good. You?"

I retreated and stared at her, chest heaving from the restraint needed to not push into her that second, and from the twinges of pain radiating from bruises gained during my earlier altercation.

"I'm good, but we don't—"

"Now, Brenton. Now," she pleaded, flexing her hips to push her warm center up and down my cock.

"Fuck," I gritted out before nipping at her hard nipple.

"That's the idea." Weaving her fingers into my hair, she pushed my face harder against her breast. Instead of giving in to her urging, I looked up until her attention was on me, cheeks flushed, eyes hooded. Damn, the woman was gorgeous.

"This isn't fucking," I said. Claiming both wrists in one hand, I pinned them against the stone wall above her head. Each inch I slid into her tightness was torture and fucking incredible. The water washed away the sweat beading along my forehead and temples. "This is me showing you what I can't say."

Brushing my lips against hers, I held her gaze as I pushed in all the way. Tears welled in her lower lids before spilling over the edges and streaming down her cheeks. First the left, then the right, I kissed away each tear. Each drop of salt water against my lips was like pouring it on an open wound. My heart ached to tell her what she wanted, needed to hear. The truth my heart hurt to say.

Taking our time, we moved slow, savoring this last time together. When she squeezed me, finding her release, I devoured her scream, loving the feel of her entire body convulsing as I shuddered into her.

Keeping her legs wrapped around my hips, me still inside her, I pressed my forehead against hers as I calmed my erratic breath.

"Goodbye, Brenton," she whispered.

"Stay with me," I said, nearly pleading. "One more night. Stay with me. Please."

"Yes."

Tucking my head between her neck and shoulder, I pulled her tight, hoping it would somehow chase away the loneliness and devastation that had begun to creep in.

OUTSIDE, THE UNBEARABLE West Texas heat had already warmed the window pane I leaned against. Adjusting my stance to use the wall instead, I held my attention out the window in hopes of a glimpse of Beks. The truck was out front, proving she was there, but where was the question. The thought of her being anywhere near that lousy-ass father of hers made anger pulse through my blood.

I woke up alone that morning, stretching across the cool, soft sheets in search of her warm body but came up empty. At some point in the early morning hours, she snuck out with me passed out from pure exhaustion. Having her once in the shower wasn't enough. Neither was the second or third or fourth. Each time I needed one more touch, one more kiss as much as I needed the air to breathe.

How in the hell would I survive three states over without her? Not knowing if she was okay, safe, happy? Damn, I wanted her happy and taken care of. By me.

But what if I slipped? What if one day I decided to give in to the whiskey's call? Those urges would always be there, so did that mean I was never allowed to be happy? If I did slip, Beks would be there for me, be the one to help me through the struggle of sobriety again.

But was I ready for someone to see me? All of the broken and jagged pieces, not just the good side. If I dug down deep and searched for the truthful answer, it would be a yes. Yes, I was tired of doing this alone and believing I was alone. Having Beks at my side, being the additional strength I needed to continue to fight those demons, was what I wanted, what I needed. Her in my life was a need, not a want.

I needed that woman as much as she needed me.

"Let's get this shit done with," Dad said from the leather couch with a glare. He looked like shit. But I wasn't one to talk—so did I. The lack of sleep and swelling did nothing for my mood or appearance. "I have someone coming by to check out the place this afternoon."

Hell. Of course he did. Money-hungry, gold-digging bastard. Since he couldn't access more than his monthly allowance from the trust, he looked for money any way he could. And selling our family's homestead was it.

The older of the two attorneys stood and looked my direction with a smile. "Before we get started, Mr. Graves left something for his grandson." In shock, I forced all my attention to the man. "He asked me to give it to him, let him read it in private, before we divide the estate."

I took the thick manila envelope from his outstretched hand. The paper crinkled in my grasp.

"We'll be here when you're finished."

I nodded to the older man and turned for the door. Not knowing where to go, I meandered through the house and paused outside Pappy's office. One step inside, the rich smell of leather and Old Spice confirmed I was in the right spot to read Pappy's last words.

The leather chair molded around my back and thighs with a sigh. Using my index finger, I ripped open the sealed envelope and pulled out the stack of papers within. On top was a handwritten note.

Brenton,

There was so much I wanted to say before the end, and I want you to know not coming to find you, settling this in person, is a regret I took to the grave. I'm a coward, and I'm sorry.

I always knew what type of man my son was, what he was molding you and your brother into. All those summers and holidays, I paid your father for that time with you two. I'm not proud of it, but it was all I could do to try and save you boys. Each visit I noticed you two slipping further into your father's lie, and still I did nothing more than keep paying for your time.

And then one night it all changed.

More lives than you can imagine were affected the night of your accident. You deserve to know what happened, what happened behind the scenes. You and that poor girl.

Enclosed you'll find the legal documents we had written up hours after the accident. One is hers, and the other was meant for you. We thought separating you two was the best for both families.

You had no idea the battle that went on behind closed doors.

You didn't just hit an animal. You hit a calf that had gotten out from our fence due to her father's lack of maintenance of the property. Her father wanted to sue us for you driving high and hurting his daughter, plus with the news of the baby, threaten to toss in statutory rape. We had him for gross incompetence, and he had us. It was a stalemate.

Instead of firing him, we agreed to keep him on, pay for her medical care, and give her a small settlement. In exchange, he didn't press charges for the wreck or the relationship between you two and agreed not to sue.

We decided it was best for neither of you to know the truth. It would keep you apart if both of you thought the other had been the one to walk away. It was sheer luck that you didn't remember anything when you woke up in rehab. It could have been from the length of time we kept you sedated to help with the withrawl symptoms or head trama from the wreck. The doctors never gave us a solid reason why your memory from that night and other memories were erased. Then when you went into the military after getting out of rehab. I thought it confirmed the fate story I gave you that we'd made the right decision in splitting you two up. You were walking away from your father, and that girl was going to college with the money we provided.

It wasn't until years later that I found the other document enclosed. It was given to me by my dear friend, who gave you this letter. He found it hidden in the papers from his father.

You have to believe I had no idea what your father and hers did. I had nothing to do with the decision about the baby.

But still, I'm guilty because I held on to the information for years without telling you, because we all agreed that night never to tell you two the truth. And I don't go back on my word. However, it's time you know it all, and she does too.

Take care of her, Brenton. Give her whatever she needs to heal. She deserves that from us. And now that I'm gone, fire that rat bastard father of hers. After I'm gone, the agreement I signed dies with me.

I'm very proud of the man you became, so it's hard to regret the decision to keep you two apart completely. You left, got out of our family's dysfunction and charted your course. The family name means something again because of you, and I thank you for that.

For many reasons, I'm breaking tradition and leaving my full estate and land to you. I know you'll take care of it and keep it in the family as our ancestors wanted. Our family fought and bled on this land, and I'm honored to pass it down to you, Brenton.

Honored.

Take care of it, but more importantly, take care of you. Stay as far away from the evil money brings as you can. Find something stable in your life you can hang on to like a lifeline to reality, or you'll drown. Find someone to remind you of what matters most.

I love you.

Your Pappy

Fear clenched my gut at the words in the letter, but more so I was terrified of what I would learn next. With shaking fingers, I placed the note on the side table and began reading the first legal document.

PICTURES RATTLED AGAINST the hall wall from my storming pace toward the room I'd left Dad and the attorneys in hours ago. There had to be a mistake. My family was fucked-up, yes, but this... no way in hell two men could be so damn evil or self-centered to come up with the agreement written on the papers in my hand.

Please, God, no.

Nausea stirred my stomach, pushing up the coffee I'd sipped that morning, blissfully unaware of the day's future turn of events.

The french doors banged against the wall. Face burning hot with rage, I scanned the room for my piece-of-shit dad, but came up empty.

"Where. Is. He?" I gritted out between clenched teeth.

"Gone," said the older attorney, Pappy's friend. With a concerned look, he shuffled across the room and rested a gentle hand on my shoulder. "Shortly after you left, I explained what was in the documents you were reading and that the entire estate was going to you instead of him. Your grandfather wanted it that way." A small smirk formed on his lips. "He didn't want you charged for your father's murder, which he knew would happen if that man was still around after you read the documents. I had security escort him off the property." The hand on my shoulder squeezed, drawing my gaze to his. "I'm sorry for your loss. Don't be too hard on your grandfather. It ate him up not telling you or her what he found out, but it was done. I'll have some paperwork for you to fill out, but we can do that another time."

With a nod, the men filed out of the room, leaving me alone, still gripping the damning evidence in my right hand.

I turned on the heels of my dress shoes and marched back out the door, knowing full well what I had to do next. Even if I'd rather cut off my dick than shatter her beautiful, loving soul with the truth.

Chapter 26

Rebeka

MOVEMENT OUT THE WINDOW stole my attention from packing to the black SUV halfway down the long drive. It must've been the legal teams leaving.

So, it was done.

Time to step back into reality.

Dread and sadness dropped my stomach, and I fell to the bed.

I was right to leave him before he woke up that morning. Easier for sure. Last night, with our bodies wrapped around the other's, we said our goodbyes. What else was there to say?

Yet there I sat, wanting one more conversation, one more smile, one more kiss.

Who was I kidding? I wanted more than just one more. I wanted it all. All of him. But that wasn't on the table. Nothing was.

I cut my eyes toward the closed bedroom door as a loud commotion sounded in the living room. Bellowing male voices pushed me off the bed and to my feet. I was halfway down the hall when the crashing and shattering filled the house.

My feet turned to lead, preventing me from entering the destroyed living room.

"Brenton?" I called out, utter disbelief in my voice. "What are you doing?"

Brenton turned from where he had Daddy pinned against the far wall, hand wrapped around his neck.

"Doing what I should've done years ago."

Daddy punched at Brenton's face and arms, but Brenton's hold held firm.

"Stop!" I screamed. "You can't kill him."

At my hand on his arm, he dropped Daddy, who fell to a heap on the floor.

"Get off my property and never step foot on it again. The entire staff will have orders to shoot you on sight if you do."

I shot frantic glances between Daddy and Brenton.

What? His property?

"Where's your brother?" Brenton asked, still glaring down to where Daddy crawled across the floor.

"Here," Bradley's voice sounded from the hall I'd just come down.

Not crawling fast enough, Brenton picked Daddy up by the back of his jeans and tossed him out of the house before slamming the door shut.

"You." He whirled around to face a stunned Bradley. "You're going to rehab. I'll set it up, but you go tomorrow. Then when you've finished, you're running this place. Congratulations on the promotion. I'll have a contract written up for you to review on the terms and pay. But first I need your help making sure your piece-of-shit father leaves the property before I change my mind on not committing murder today."

Not putting his back to the fuming Brenton, Bradley inched around the room to the front door. After fumbling with the knob, he darted out, banging the door shut behind him.

"Brenton, what's going on? You got the land?" Nerves on high alert put a slight shake to my voice.

"Yes. How attached to this place are you?"

"The ranch?"

"This house, the one we're standing in."

"I hate it. It's a constant reminder of my mom."

He shot me a questioning look.

"She killed herself here. We were at school, but this is where she did it. Downed a bottle of pills. Bradley and I wanted to move to one of the smaller places on the property, but Daddy said no, that we had to stay here as a reminder of what we did to her."

"What. You. Did."

"Yeah." I chuckled and nervously tucked locks of hair behind my ears. "Not him."

"Fuck, Beks. And you saved his life just now?"

I shook my head. "No, I saved yours."

His face dropped and went ashen. "I'm tearing it down. You're staying in the main house, and so will your brother when he gets back."

"What the fuck is going on?" I yelled. "You're scaring me."

"Good," he yelled back, then slammed his fist into the wall where Daddy's head had been.

I stumbled back a step. "B," I whispered in pure terror.

His fury-filled eyes met mine before storming off into the kitchen. Cabinet doors opened and slammed shut.

Inching toward him, I stopped and watched him scavenge.

"Where's his fucking liquor?"

"No. You're not letting that man break you."

"Where is it?" he roared.

Anger coursed through my veins. "What the hell is going on?" I walked into the kitchen toward him. He moved to step around, but with a soft hand on his shoulder, he paused. "Brenton, talk to me."

His head drooped as his hands found my waist. "I don't want to hurt you."

"You're doing that by not talking to me. What happened? Tell me. Please."

"Beka?" came Ryder's voice from the other room.

Brows raised, I looked from the door to Brenton.

"I called her." That was all he said before tugging me against his trembling chest. "I'm so sorry, Rebeka, but you deserve to know."

"Know what?" I cried and dug my nails into his shoulder, anchoring me to him.

Desperation seeped in at his solid body leaving mine. I wanted his strength back to hear whatever he had to say. Hand in hand, we moved around the small kitchen table and into the living room. Brenton guided me to the couch and gestured for Ryder to join us.

Her tiny hand linked with mine. "What's going on?" she whispered.

"I don't know."

"He called Kyle and said I needed to get over here as soon as possible, that you needed me."

I swallowed against a dry throat. The room spun with each short breath.

Brenton paced, staring at the floor before dropping to a crouch at my feet, putting us at eye level.

"Baby...."

"Just say it, Brenton." Ryder's hand tightened around mine.

"I don't know how," he choked out before leaning his forehead to my knee. "Pappy left me a note that detailed what happened behind the scenes of that night. I'll let you read it so you understand that neither of us knew the forces that pulled us apart."

Hating the pure agony in his tone, I dragged a shaking hand through his dark hair.

"I wish that was the worst of it. Dammit, I wish it was. Beks." His misery-laced eyes met mine with tears rimming the bottom lids. "The wreck didn't cause you to lose our baby."

In shock, I pulled back and shook my head. "No, Brenton, it did. The doctors said—"

"Think, baby. Did the doctors say you lost the baby or did your dad?"

Mind racing, I attempted to remember specifics from those terrible days. "I don't... I don't know. Maybe Daddy?"

"They took it from us."

"I don't—"

"Our fathers decided our baby's fate. Your father told the doctors the baby was conceived under force, and while you lay unconscious, he signed over your rights since you were underage. He gave them consent for termination. And my father paid him to eliminate a future unwanted heir to the Graves estate."

"No, they wouldn't. You're lying," I breathed even though I knew he wasn't.

"Beks, I'm so sorry." Tears dripped down his cheeks to my jeans.

The growing dark spot drew my unfocused gaze.

Brenton spoke.

Ryder wrapped her arms around my shoulders and cried.

But for me?

Not a single tear. No emotion at all. All I could do was focus on breathing and stare at the wet spot on my jeans, at Brenton's tears.

Nothing else mattered. The world slipped. Noises vanished.

And at that moment, I learned what true devastation was.

I was on the verge of a free fall into the darkness I'd somehow kept at bay all these years.

But right now, knowing what they took from me, I dove into the darkness, not caring if I ever came back.

Chapter 27

Brenton

"BABY?" DESPERATION laced the single word. "Please say something."

Hollow eyes shifted to mine, but she didn't see me. My heart shattered at the emptiness where such life and love had bubbled over just hours ago. I hated hurting her, but she had to know, needed to know the truth of what our fathers had done.

Seconds turned to minutes without her responding to either Ryder's or my pleas.

"She's in shock," I said to Ryder, who nodded. Hands under her shoulders and legs, I scooped her off the couch. Clutching the most precious thing in my life close, I stalked to the front door.

"Where are you going?" Ryder asked with pure panic in her voice.

Couldn't blame her.

"Taking her to the main house," I grunted, shifting her in my arms to turn the doorknob. "I want her out of this fucking place."

Halfway out the door, Ryder was at my side.

"I had no idea," I said to her, looking down to the catatonic woman in my eyes. "I don't know what to do."

A tiny hand rested on my back. "I know you didn't know, and you're doing what you can. When you leave, I'll take care of her. She'll be okay."

"How do I leave her like this?" At the words, my heart cracked open, spilling out the feelings I'd been holding back. "How do I leave the woman I love who's fucking breaking apart in my arms?"

Inside the main house, we moved through the expansive halls toward my room. As gentle as possible, I laid her on the unmade bed before pulling the covers over her trembling body. Eyes still open wide, she stared unblinking at the ceiling.

"I'm calling a doctor," I stated and reached for my phone.

"She needs you," Ryder said in a soft voice. "Not me, not some strange doctor. You."

"Give us a few minutes." I toed off my boots.

"I'll be in the kitchen when you need me."

I nodded without looking at her as I crawled up the bed. The thick pillow gave to the weight of my head as I lay down beside Beks. Entirely still, only her soft breaths told me she was alive.

"Beks," I whispered in a plea. "Please talk to me. Anything."

Nothing. Not even a stolen glance.

At a loss, I slung an arm and leg over her and hugged her close.

"I love you. I'm in love with you," I said with my lips against her shoulder. "I've always loved you. Don't leave. Don't give up. Please. Don't give up on us, not now. I need you, baby. Don't you see that? You're the only good in my life, the only one who sees me. Come back to me. Please, please come back to me."

Only her quiet, even breaths responded to my shattering heart.

Me: How is she?
Ryder: Not good.
Me: Seen her father around?
Ryder: Nope. Nobody has.
Me: Take care of her, please. I hate not being there.
Ryder: She's in good hands.
Me: But not mine.

Me: Any progress?

Ryder: A little. She's finally talking to the doctor you hired.

Ryder: I think she misses you.

Me: I miss her, but we've been called out to a mission. Not sure when I'll be back.

Me: Take care of her, okay?

Me: I get email over there, so email with any updates.

Ryder: Be safe. And she'll be fine, just needs time.

Ryder: It's only been three days. Give her a bit to adjust.

Me: I hate not being there. Hate her being in pain. Hate she has to go through this.

Ryder: I don't know how in the hell you ever thought you didn't love her.

Ryder: Are you always so dense?

Ryder: Maybe Beka is better off without you.

Me: You're kidding, right?

Ryder: Maybe. Did I tell you I called off the wedding?

Me: Did I ask?

Ryder: No, but with Beka still not super chatty, I have to tell someone. You're the lucky guy.

Me: I don't feel lucky.

Ryder: Anyhoo, I'm staying with Beka. Moved out of Kyle's place.

Me: Okay.

Ryder: You suck as a chitchat buddy.

Me: Does that surprise you? Email me with updates, and I'll try to fly in when we get back.

Ryder: I'll let her know.

I HELD MY BREATH AS the gate to the ranch swung open.

Four months.

Four long months since I stepped foot on this property. Since I left Beks in the hands of her best friend and the best therapist in Odessa. Somehow the heat had intensified while I was gone, making the short walk from the Tahoe to the main house miserable.

"Hello?" I called out after shutting the front door, but no one answered. "Beks? Ryder?"

Footsteps sounded against the hardwood.

"Welcome back." Bradley smiled when he rounded the corner.

"I should say the same to you. Heard you've been back a couple of weeks." The rehab center had given daily updates on his progress and when he'd completed the program. "How do you feel?"

"Good," he said with a smile. "Great even. I know it's a long road, but to be this clearheaded is fucking fantastic."

"Has your father tried to come by?"

Bradley shifted on his feet. "No. We don't know where he is. No one's seen him since the day I dropped him at the motel. Can't say I'm sad about it."

In full understanding, I gave a quick nod. "Where's your sister?" Why beat around the bush; not like I was there to see him.

His smile widened. "In the barn taking inventory of the supplies. She's come alive since you hired her as the full-time vet for the ranch. Thanks for everything you did, man. Really, thank you."

I nodded and turned for the door.

The familiar scent of hay and manure filled my nose the moment I stepped into the barn. A few horses watched as I stalked toward the supply room in search of the woman I couldn't get off my mind.

The past four months had been torture. Access to email was slim where we were, and even then Ryder wasn't the best at communicating what was going on. All she said in the last email was I needed to get my ass back to Texas as soon as possible.

So here I was.

I wasn't stateside for more than a few hours when I requested emergency leave. That was three hours ago, which meant I had twenty-one hours to figure out what was going on here and get my ass back to Kentucky.

Beks's voice filtered through the otherwise quiet barn. "What are you doing in here? You should be on this other shelf with your friends. See, all the antibiotics go there, and you go here with your vitamin friends."

A shoulder on the doorframe, I watched her work as she talked to herself. A soothing sense of relief calmed my ticking temper at the mere sight of her. Damn, I missed her. For the first time in months, I could breathe.

"I didn't know vitamins had friends," I said.

Her hands stilled midair. Achingly slow, she turned to lock those bright honey brown eyes with mine.

"You're here," she breathed. Wide-eyed, she held the clipboard tight to her chest and smiled.

The distance between us felt like a canyon. "Is that a good thing?"

The clipboard clattered to the ground, her boot heels pounding against the stained concrete floors as she ran full speed and leaped into my outstretched arms.

"It's a great thing. I missed you."

Capturing her lips with mine, I sighed at the intense connection between us. Damn, I missed this.

"I missed you too, baby," I said against her lips. "I'm leaving the army."

The words shocked her, and me. It wasn't until right then that I knew for sure this place was my home. She was my home. Yes, I loved my job, but Beks was my anchor, my life. This was where I belonged.

"What?" Beks pulled back to lay her head against the wall, eyes searching mine. "Why would you do that? You love it."

"I love you more," I whispered. "These past few months have killed me. Every day apart from you, a piece of the man I want to be, the man I am when I'm around you, went dormant. You make me whole in ways I can't describe."

The course pads of my thumbs brushed away her silent tears.

"I love you, Rebeka Harding, and I want to spend the rest of my life loving you. I want to build a family and give our children what we never had. You and me, together, happy, and hopelessly devoted to each other."

"Is that a proposal?" She sniffed with a trembling smile.

"I don't have a ring." Dammit, I should've thought of that on the way here, but I was too damn excited to see her. A ring was the last thing on my mind.

"Sir Fancy Pants, I don't need a ring. All I need is you." Her heart hammered from her chest to mine. A broad smile crept up her cheeks, creasing the edges of her almond-shaped eyes.

"You're killing me. Is that a yes?"

"Yes, Brenton. It's a yes."

Beks's sweet lips molded around mine and parted at the begging request for access. For several minutes we clung to each other, savoring the connection. Soon every day would be with this perfect woman. I'd have the internal peace she offered me, and I wouldn't allow one day to pass from this point forward without telling her what she meant to me.

We were both broken in our own ways, but together we were whole. And hopefully one day we could continue the healing by giving our children the love and unconditional support we were never afforded.

One day.

"Brenton?"

"Yeah, baby?"

"Were you serious about the family part?"

Brows raised, I tilted my head, not understanding.

"Because it's a little late to go back now."

I narrowed my eyes and shook my head. "I don't understand what you're telling me."

"I'm telling you...." Her chest rose and fell in a deep breath. "I'm pregnant."

The world stilled, the noise of the barn falling silent as I gaped down into her uncertain eyes. Fear, excitement, uncertainty, and soul-consuming happiness sank in. The corners of my lips tugged my cheeks up until they couldn't rise any higher.

Pregnant.

"Really?"

"Really. Are you okay with that?"

Pulling her close, I tucked her head to my chest and stroked down her dark curly hair. "Do you hear that?"

Beks's head moved up and down.

"That's the sound of a heart exploding."

Two arms snaked around my waist and squeezed.

Coarse hair tickled my lips as I whispered into her ear, "I can't wait to spend the rest of my life thanking you for saving me."

"I know one way you could start," she said with a flex of her hips against my crotch.

"So bossy," I grumbled with a smile as I stepped into the supply closet and slammed the door closed.

Forever with this woman.

Sounded like a damn perfect life to me.

Epilogue

"BUT I'M NOT DUE FOR two more weeks." My voice broke at the last word giving away my rising fear. "Brenton isn't even here. She can't come today." I was an idiot for not going to Kentucky with B. What was I thinking wanting to stay here just because it was familiar? Going into labor early was always a possibility, but I never thought it would happen. Idiot. Idiot. Idiot. Now here I was going into labor with my husband states away. Husband was still strange to say even in my thoughts. But I guess that was natural considering it had only been a few months since he proposed and later that day stood before the Justice of the Peace.

Bending over my round belly as far as I could toward my crotch I yelled, "You can't come out today. Go back in there."

"It doesn't work that way sweetie," Ryder said with a nervous laugh at the end. "Come on we have to get you to the hospital. I don't want the wrath of your husband if you have this baby in the car."

"No. I'm not going without him."

"Beka...." she groaned. "Stop it with this stupid shit. You know we have to go so stop being difficult. You're not having this baby here."

I crossed both arms across my chest and leaned further into the couch just as another contraction hit making my face contort in pain. "Fuck this hurts," I cried. "I need Brenton."

When I finally peeled my eyes open, Bradley stood over me staring down with concern and determination behind his gaze.

"I'm not going without him," I whispered.

"You don't have a choice sis. Hate to break it to you, but nature doesn't give a shit if your husband is here or not. My niece is coming today and not in this fucking house. Now get your ass off the couch and into the truck. I already have the seat warm for you."

Stupid hormones had tears leaking from my eyes at his thoughtfulness.

"Here," Ryder shoved her cell phone against my ear. "Maybe you'll listen to him."

Knowing who was on the other end of the line, I sat up straighter and cleared my throat. "Where are you?"

"Beks I swear on everything we own I will kick your fine ass if you don't get in the fucking truck right now," Brenton said calmly. But I heard the undercurrent of worry and frustration. He was my husband after all.

"Where are you?" I asked again allowing my voice to shake. I didn't want to do this without Brenton there. I was strong on my own, but I needed his strength to get through this, I needed him here.

"Figuring out a way to get to Midland. Baby, you have to go to the hospital okay. Listen to Ryder and your brother. I love you but get in the damn truck."

In the seconds it took for me to glance between the two staring at me Brenton was already talking again.

"Get your fine ass off the couch." The clear command in his tone, one I loved in the bedroom, struck home.

"Big ass," I grumbled back.

"My ass. Now up."

Reaching out a hand to Bradley I grunted as he pulled me up. An arm wrapped around my waist he held me steady until I had my balance.

"Okay, okay I'm going. So bossy." My smirk dropped as I doubled over with a curse at the sharp cramping around my middle. The phone tumbled to the floor.

"Beka," Ryder yelled. Her small arm wrapped under my shoulders and urged me toward the door. "I hope you packed good snacks in your overnight bag. You're stressing me the fuck out."

Even though the pain I couldn't help but laugh.

From the cowskin rug, Brenton's bellowing voice called out to me.

"Get the phone," I said between deep breaths. "Before B strokes out."

As Ryder ushered me toward the door mumbling a string of curse words I heard Bradley telling Brenton what was going on. Once outside Ryder and I stopped at the top of the stairs knowing full well we should wait for Bradley in case I toppled forward–I was a little top heavy these days.

"He's on his way," Bradley stated and tucked his shoulder beneath mine. "Don't worry, knowing your husband he'll break every law out there to get to you in time."

"And if not you'll have me," Ryder grunted as she shoved me into the truck. "Now let's get the hell out of here."

"THIS SHIT IS LEGIT," I said to the ceiling.

"See aren't you glad we forced you to come to the hospital?" Ryder squeezed her tiny hand around mine. "He'll get here don't worry."

I glanced at the clock. It'd been thirty minutes since the epidural, over an hour since we checked in.

A faint knock at the door drew our attention as my OBGYN walked in.

"How are you feeling?" he asked and gripped the hand, not in Ryder's.

"Better, that drug shit is amazing."

He just chuckled and patted my hand before looking at the monitors. "Doesn't look like you've had any recent contractions. Sometimes the epidural can slow down the process at first, but it will pick back up soon. First ones take the longest dear so be patient."

With that, he scribbled a few of notes on my chart and shuffled out of the room.

I smiled at the ceiling. Baby Grace wanted her daddy here, so she slowed her roll.

"Be patient, little lady, he's on his way," I whispered and closed my eyes.

Deep breaths in and deep breaths out.

Stay calm, and Grace will be calm.

Easy.

Until it wasn't.

"What are you telling me?" I asked my doctor looking between him, Bradley and Ryder. Two hours later and Brenton still wasn't there and, to top off my stress, Grace was sending mixed signals on the monitor.

"I'm telling you to get your head around an emergency C-section Mrs. Graves. Because there is a good chance, it will happen. Your baby's heart rate keeps rising, but you're not far enough along for you to push her out the old-fashioned way. I'll come to check on you in ten."

As he walked out the door, he yelled at a nurse walking by to prepare an operating room.

"This can't be happening." Tears streamed down my face splashing on to my paper thin gown. "Brenton, where are you?"

"I'm here."

All eyes shifted from where I was having a mental breakdown in the hospital bed to the fatigues dressed–sexy as hell–man in the doorway.

In two steps he was at my bedside and his lips pressed against my forehead. "You made it."

Smiling down he wiped away each tear focusing on me like I was the only person in the room. "I wouldn't have missed it. Why are you crying? Are you in pain? Fucking doctors I'll go get them to give you something-"

I gripped his hand before he could storm out. "No, no pain. It's Grace. I might need an emergency C-section because shes stressed, I'm fucking stressed, and I'm not ripe enough down there to push her out."

Brushing a few stray hairs from my face, he pressed his lips to mine. "Ryder, Bradley. Leave. I need a moment with my wife."

Damn, I loved that tone. So strong. So dominant. Even though I was already numb below the waist, just his voice relaxed my muscles and soothed my rising stress.

After the two were gone Brenton dipped his hand beneath the cheap blanket to rub his calloused hand along my belly.

"Our baby," he whispered.

"Our baby."

"You're doing great baby, relax. I'm here, and I won't let anything bad happen to you or her." Leaning down he moved the blanket down and my gown up exposing my belly. "And you little lady calm down in there. I'm here now so no more waiting. Daddy is here."

Long, soothing strokes of his fingertips along my stomach calmed her and me.

"Now I'm going to find the doctors, find out what's going on, and make sure they know who you are."

A twinge of pain shot up my spine. I looked at the monitors showing I had a strong contraction that I couldn't feel – thank you drugs.

"And who am I?" I asked taking a deep breath.

"You're everything Beks. You and this little girl right here. You two are my world, and they need to know that."

"Brenton," I said and gripped his hand tight. "Something is happening."

Brows furrowed he watched me for a second before realization clicked in.

"I'll go get the doc-"

My OBGYN barged through the door cutting him off. "Okay, Mrs. Graves we have OR-" At the sight of Brenton he paused. "Mr. Graves glad you could make it."

"Something is happening," I said. "Can you check me one more time?"

He nodded.

After the quick check, he slid the latex glove off and tossed it in the trash. "Guess you both were waiting on him to get here. Let me grab a nurse; then it's time to push."

Ten minutes, and a lot of sweat and curse words later, the doctor placed a bright red baby girl on my chest. "Congratulations you two."

All around us the doctor continued to work and the nurses scurried around, but Brenton and my attention were on the precious creature we made.

"She's beautiful."

"Just like her mom," Brenton sniffled as he ran a hand over her gloopy head. "Damn you're amazing Beks. She's perfect."

Against my bare chest Grace wiggled with her eyes sealed shut.

"Rebeka."

Hesitantly I took my eyes off my baby girl and looked to B.

"It's not your choice anymore. You and Grace are coming back to Kentucky with me until I finish up my contract with the army. No more of this long distance shit. You, me, and her together from now on."

"Okay," I said with a broad smile.

He eyed me suspiciously. "Okay? No pushback?"

"I don't want to be away from you either. And..." With a hand wrapped around the back of his neck, I pulled him down to press my lips against his ear. "When I'm all healed down there that's when I'll give you push back. Where's the fun in it if my sass isn't returned with your hand across my ass?"

His loud laugh made everyone turn their attention to us.

But we didn't care.

Eyes locked with each other. Hands resting on our new beautiful baby girl.
We didn't care about anything other than us — our little family.

"I love you, Mrs. Graves. Forever."

"And I love you too, Mr. Graves. Forever."

The End

Play List

NIALL HORAN & MAREN Morris – Seeing Blind
 RaeLynn – Queens Don't
 Dierks Bently – Different for Grils
 Beve Rexha & FGL – Meant to Be
 LANCO – Greastest Love Story
 LANCO – Born to Love You
 LANCO – Win You Over
 Danielle Branbery – Sway
 Lady Gaga – Million Reasons
 Cam – Burning House
 Christina Perri – Human
 Lauren Daigle – You Say
 Loren Allred – Never Enough
 Zac Efron & Zendaya – Rewrite the Stars
 Ana endrick and Justing Timberlake – True Colors
 Disturbed – The Sounds of Silence
 B0RNS – The Emotion
 B0RNS – Past Lives
 Miranda Lambert – Tin Man
 Kacey Musgraves – Space Cowboy
 Brett Young – Mercy
 Kiana Grannis – Can't Help Falling in Love
 Alex & Sierra – Little Do You Know
 Heather Masse – Bird Song
 Meghan Trainor – ALL THE WAYS
 Lady Gaga – Shallow

Ackowldegements

I ALWAYS SAVE THIS part to the last and here I am a few hours from publication writing the acknowledgements. So here we go...

I started writign becuase of my two favorite alpha readers – Emily and Christine. You two are everythign in this writing process. It's you who makes me want to write the next book and keep you guessing each morning with new chapters. Thank you for supporting me in all this. All the late night texts, last minutes pages, and anxiety laced calls – you've walked me through them all. Thank you. Thank you. Thank you. With out you two all these stories would be stuck in my head.

And of course my sweet friend Kristin. I love how excited you are about new chapters (and new heros) as much as I am. Thank you for reading even when your four are driving you crazy ☺ I know you don't have the time but you make it for me and I love you for it. Thank you.

There are so many people who support us along the way from editors, to author friends tob loggers. No one is less important. To all of you who've encouraged me, thank you. Allthe random texts or insta messages mean everythign to me. The fact you even read my books is amazing! Thank you for all that you do for me and all the other indie authors out there.

To everyone reading out there, thank you. The fact you're reading somethign I created in my head is... beyond words. I never expected this life but I'm damn glad it found me.

Memories of Us Kennedy L. Mitchell

Don't miss out!

Visit the website below and you can sign up to receive emails whenever Kennedy L. Mitchell publishes a new book. There's no charge and no obligation.

https://books2read.com/r/B-A-UFFF-IORV

BOOKS 2 READ

Connecting independent readers to independent writers.

Also by Kennedy L. Mitchell

A Covert Affair
Finding Fate
Memories of Us

Watch for more at https://kennedylmitchell.wordpress.com.

Made in the USA
Middletown, DE
27 May 2019